Teace Snyder

The Collection: Volume One

The Collection is Teace Snyder's first short story collection and fourth publication. He operates, and can be contacted through, his website www.teace.ca, which he created and launched in 2007. He lives in Scarsdale, New York, where he writes about himself in third person in a futile attempt to make this introduction cool.

Also by Teace Snyder,

www.teace.ca

The Collection: Volume One

Teace Snyder

In association with Original Cliché Entertainment

Copyright © 2008 by Teace Snyder

This book is a work of fiction. All contents herein are either a product of the author's imagination or are used fictitiously. Any resemblance to anything, anyone, anyplace, or any variation of any word starting with 'any' is entirely coincidental.

Book design by Teace Snyder

978-0-557-02952-5

The Collection: Volume One

Tattoo
9

Come and Go
18

Seed Them Men
29

Sun's Blink
39

A Mind in Love
63

Wind's Blessing
74

STAR
84

Lemmings
101

Children of Wrath
117

Ladylike

128

Burgundy Grass

157

Three Little Wolves

169

Deviled Egg

179

When the Silence Comes

194

Morning Routine

199

Burn

214

Pandora

248

Super Nobody

285

Tattoo

Alec: Celebrities have a new war to wage for their privacy. It seems several clips have been placed online of famous actors and musicians using the restroom. We'll have more on that in just a moment, but first: A Syracuse University professor has caused quite a stir for tattooing a racially explicit word on his arm. We'll go now to David Fisher who's reporting live from Syracuse campus. David:

David: Thanks, Alec. The students and faculty here at SU were shocked recently when, Jake Anderson, a respected business professor, came to class with a vulgar, racially explicit word tattooed on his right forearm. Consequently, Mr. Anderson's employment at SU was terminated this morning after the dean received hundreds of complaints regarding the professor.

Alec: Now, David, what was the word that Professor Anderson tattooed on his arm?

David: That would be the N-word, Alec. And I might add, the issue here is not as simple as a professor having a vulgar tattoo but, rather, the placement of that tattoo and Professor Anderson's compulsion to exhibit it.

Alec: And by 'exhibit it' you mean to display it on campus?

David: Yes. The complaints originated immediately after the tattoo was displayed. Apparently, last Thursday, A student noticed the tattoo through Professor Anderson's sleeve and requested to see it. Professor Anderson complied and, for the remainder of the class, kept his sleeves up to continue displaying the tattoo.

Alec: Now obviously there are racial tones to, not only the tattoo, but his conduct regarding its display. Does Professor Anderson have a history of racially-related protest or discrimination?

David: No. In fact, his colleagues went so far as to describe his stance on race as seemingly indifferent. They were as shocked as everyone else was to hear of it.

Alec: Is it known how long Professor Anderson has had this tattoo?

David: The student who had initially requested to see the tattoo gave me an estimate on how long Mr. Anderson has had it. We'll go now to my interview with him…

Student: He just said 'I got it a couple weeks ago.' But like he said, 'he didn't wanna show it until it'd healed' or something.

David: And what was your reaction when you first saw the tattoo?

Student: I couldn't believe it. I didn't think it was real to tell you the truth. Like, who does that?

David: But were you offended by it?

Student: I don't know. I was more shocked than anything. Nobody really said anything in class or to his face or nothing—it was afterwards, when he wasn't around, that everyone started slandering his name.

David: So then the general reaction of the class was to take offence?

Student: Oh, yeah—a couple people got real offended. They went around like rallying their friends to go to the Dean and have him fired. I didn't do nothing like that cause like I said I was just surprised. But you know how people get about race.

David: Do you feel as though his termination was justified?

Student: Personally, I wouldn't a' fired him. I woulda just said 'wear sleeves' or 'cover it up with makeup' or something. I don't really think it's fair to fire the guy just cause of something he put on his body.

Alec: We'll have more of that interview later. But it seems now a statement by Professor Anderson has been released saying, "I am deeply sorry if I've offended anyone by displaying my tattoo. It was not my intention to cause any unrest or harm by doing so." From there he goes on to say that he will be making a public address regarding his motivation for getting the tattoo in the first place, and will be doing so in the next few minutes. Until then, David Fisher has been conducting interviews with the students and Faculty of SU to better understand the reaction to Professor Anderson's actions…

David: Do you believe Jake Anderson is racist?

Professor: Of course not. I've known Professor Anderson for years and have never observed him displaying anything but the utmost respect towards all people, regardless of their ethnicity. I find it absurd that people would jump to the conclusion that he's racist because of a tattoo, albeit a queer one.

David: Do you condone his tattoo?

Professor: It's nothing I'd feel comfortable having myself, and I can't say I understand why he would choose to get such a tattoo, but I do not condemn his decision to get it…

David: Having had Jake Anderson as a professor, would you say he was competent and qualified?

Student: I don't know, man. Like now that everybody's mentioning this racist stuff it's got me thinking like maybe my grades weren't as high as they coulda been cause o' race. Like maybe he was discriminating against me, even if it was only subconscience.

David: Do you advocate his dismissal?

Student: Absolutely. They can't have the KKK teaching classes, lowering my marks just because I'm a different race than him. It's bullshit…

David: Why do you believe Professor Anderson tattooed the N-word onto his arm?

Student: Probably to get on TV.

David: Do you believe he's racist?

Student: What, because he has the word N***** tattooed on his arm? Nah, he must just like N*****'s…

David: Do you condone Professor Anderson's use of the N-word or, for that matter, the use of the word at all?

Student: Shit, I don't know… I mean, I can't use the word N***** because I'm not black. But isn't saying 'only black people can use the word N*****,' a little too much like saying 'only N*****'s can use the word N*****?'

Second Student: Well… I believe the use of the word by the black community nowadays is to signify brotherhood and having overcome adversity—not to demean or insult as is the implication if the word is used by someone outside of the black community. But, at the same time, I understand what he said about its use and how there's implicit anger regardless of connotation.

Student: I didn't say that... I was saying embracing the word to overcome the word is just stupid. And how can you say 'using it signifies having overcome adversity?' If black people had overcome adversity, why would they walk around calling each other N*****s? For fond memories?

Second Student: There's a difference between calling someone a N***** and calling them a N****.

Student: Not if you're not black there isn't.

Second Student: I don't like your tone.

Student: What tone? We're having a discussion...

David: What are your feelings regarding Professor Anderson's decision to have the N-word tattooed on his arm?

Student: I wanna see him go to jail and see what real N*****s have to say about it! I mean, who the hell does he think he is?! You can't just mock generations of African Americans who have suffered at the hands of racist bastards and expect to get away with it! Shit, I'm mad as hell and I'm not gonna take it anymore!...

David: Do you believe it was the right decision to fire Professor Anderson?

Student: Maybe... What color's the guy anyway?

David: As you can see Alec, Professor Anderson's actions have caused a frenzy of debate and anger among the student body here at SU.

Alec: Amazing...We go now to Professor Anderson addressing the camera's and students with the hope that his words will alleviate the tensions felt here at SU.

Jake Anderson: I'd like to make a statement prior to answering questions if I may. I request that during my statement people refrain from calling out, though I understand this is a sensitive subject.

Unidentified Member of the Crowd: Racist!

Jake Anderson: Yeah... that's a good starting point. I am by no means racist. As you can see from the color of my skin, I am granted certain rights to speak about race while deprived of others—this is true for everyone. Race is an overt attribute of all people, though for this address I will speak specifically of African Americans.

    The attribute of race has grown to be regarded, by some, as a stigma. N*(beep) is the word that defines that stigma and concurrently provokes anger simply by using the word. Though, to be fair, that anger is intensified should the word be used by anyone who is not black. This is in large part why I am so surprised by the reaction that people have had to my tattoo.

My motivation to get the tattoo and place it in such a clearly visible location on my body was simple. Misconceptions about an individual's character are drawn from their race and preempt any hope of a prejudice-free evaluation. In the case of black people, they have arguably been subjected to more prejudice than people of other races. The word N*(beep) is seen as the worst word in the English language. Yet, it has been utilized by members of the black community to defy its previous connotation. While this does serve to unify the black community it also isolates them from the world. Every race has its label. Towel head, chink, gook, Jap, redskin, spic, porcelain and N*(beep). But in none of those groups do you see such frequent use of a label as you do within the black community.

My tattoo is intended to transcend racial bounds because of my choice to place an overt stigmatic label on a clearly visible spot. Regardless of whether I were black, white, Asian, Middle-eastern, Native American, or any race, the stigmas label would be the same. While I recognize that the connotation is perceived differently according to my race and that of those around me—my tattoo is intended to serve as a statement that, rather than labeling myself within the arms of a community, I have labeled myself to be perceived equally among everyone. Albeit, the label I chose was one of a specific community, but only because of that labels impact. Once again, I apologize should my actions have offended anyone... You can ask questions now.

(Crowd Erupts With Questions) Journalist: Do you remain confident in your decision about the tattoo?

Jake Anderson: Yes... though I've no doubt that in the days to come my commitment will be tested. But I believe I will remain confident nevertheless.

Journalist: What is Porcelain?

Jake Anderson: Porcelain is a fairly new term that refers to a member of the white community who purposefully oppresses members of the black community. Though, often white people who speak of blacks in any terms that are less than complimentary are misconstrued for being porcelain.

Journalist: Will you seek to be reinstated?

Jake Anderson: No.

Journalist: Why not?

Jake Anderson: I'd planned on retiring this year anyways. But also, I believe too many people would be unable to see past my skin and their anger.

Come and Go

She held my hand and kicked her feet in the air. My stomach felt funny when I looked at her. I kissed her cheek and her face turned red. I smiled and looked at the jungle gym, where my friends were looking for me. She didn't talk a lot and I guess I didn't either. We didn't do anything for a bunch of seconds before she kissed me on my cheek. I rubbed away the spit but kept holding her hand.

"Vanilla pudding is gross," she said, looking through her lunch.

"Yeah. I like chocolate better," I said, thinking about kissing her again.

"What's good is when you dip a banana in chocolate pudding," she continued, looking at me and quickly looking away, like she was scared. "My dad said 'boys are only after one thing.'

"Um... sorry," I said, not understanding her.

"I think they're mean and they only want to make girls cry," she continued, taking a bite of her PB & J.

"I don't want to make you cry," I said, squeezing her hand. Her face turned red again and she swallowed her food.

"I like you, Bobby," she said, smiling big.

"I like you t-," I almost said. My friends were walking to us and I knew they were going to tease me. "I gotta go, Amy," I continued, letting go of her hand and running to my friends.

"Bobby, come on! Joe took a cigarette from his mom," Derek, my best friend, told me. I followed them to the back of the school. I looked at her, eating lunch alone. I missed her.

---------------------------------10 years later --------------------------------

"Oh my God, dude. Like, Amy is so hot," Joe burped, drinking his juice and gin. "You KNOW I'm gonna tap that."

"Joe, shut up. The only pussy you ever got was back when you were a sperm," Derek coughed, over the gurgle of his bong. I laughed while Joe drunkenly tried to think of a comeback.

"Man, whatever. She loves me, she just doesn't know it yet," he concluded, finishing off what was in his glass. "And it's not like you're Don John or anything."

"What the hell are you talking about?"

"Fucking… lover boy, or whatever he was."

"It's Don Juan, Joe," I laughed, taking the bong from Derek. "And I'm sorry, but she's out of your league."

"What? How the hell is she out of MY league?"

"Well, she's attractive for one," Derek exclaimed, filling in for me while I took a hoot. I coughed it out in a fit of laughter from what he'd said.

"Kwww, kwww… plus she's smart enough to know… kwww… the difference between a sock and a package… kwww," I added, passing the bong back to Derek. Joe turned red and stood up, outraged. He reached into his crotch and pulled out the knot of socks he carried under his dick to help pick up girls. Derek started to cry he was laughing so hard.

"Man, fuck you guys!" he screamed, throwing the socks at my face. "I can't help it if all the women in this town are bitches!"

"Oh, so it's their fault?"

"Yeah, it's their fault. Stupid dog-bitches, that's all they are. It's like if you don't give them treats they go for another master."

"Well yeah," Derek wheezed, having just finished laughing. "What do you expect them to do: chase after a guy with pubes in his socks?"

"Man, what-ever."

"Well you could always-" I started to say, my phone ringing mid-sentence and stealing my attention. I checked the call before picking it up. It was Amy, Joe's crush which he'd yet to realize was my girlfriend. I stood up and walked to the far side of the room to talk to her. "Hey, what's up?"

"Hey. Nothing much: just studying and stuff."

"Cool. You need a hand?"

"Totally," she giggled, knowing I was probably getting high with my friends. "Tell the guys 'hey' for me."

"Right... I'll see you in a bit," I replied, hanging up and trying to think of a lie to tell Joe.

"Was that your mom?" Derek coughed, handing the bong back to me.

"No, it was Gary. He said his computer's on the fritz and our science project might have got erased," I lied, surprised how frequently I could use my lab partner as an out for sex. "Anyway, I gotta go. I'll catch up with you guys later."

--------------------------------10 years later----------------------------------

"So how bout I walk you home?" I stated, after a date at the casino.

"Um... no thanks, Bob," she replied, crushing any erection I planned on getting that night. "You're a nice guy and everything but, it's easier to tell you I'm not interested here rather than waiting till you've walked me home."

"Ouch," I laughed, the typical 'bitch' and 'her loss' thoughts flooding to mind. "Nice guys finish last."

"Yeah... it was good meeting you," she said, extending her hand to shake mine. I reached out and lazily returned the favor. I watched her walk away before I made my way to the casino bar. I grumbled to myself over her for a few moments before I began checking around for single women—nothing.

"What can I get for you?" a scantily clad bartender asked, leaning over just enough to increase her tip.

"Just a Bud, please," I replied, contemplating whether or not I wanted to be the guy hitting on the help.

"Sure thing," she replied, smiling—motivated by either her job or genuine-interest... if there's even a line between the two.

I let out an exasperated sigh and rubbed my eyes. This date ended too much like other recent dates to be a coincidence—women were changing. I knew this, quite simply, because I was staying the same—only now they weren't staying with me. Best I could guess, their clocks were running out and they'd finally realized how stupid games are... just my luck. But I lost my concentration when I felt a jitter on my leg. I reached into my pocket and pulled out my vibrating cell phone—Derek, my once-upon-a-time-best-friend, was calling me for the first time in years.

21

"Hello?"

"Bob, buddy. What are you up to tonight?"

"Nothing anymore. How bout you?"

"Nothing. Wife went to a book club thing so I thought maybe we could grab a drink and catch up."

"Way ahead of you," I said, as the bartender slid my beer in front of me. "Why don't you come down to the casino and join me?"

"Sure thing. I'll see you in a few."

-------------------------------10 minutes later-------------------------------

"Long-time-no-see," Derek said, tapping me on the shoulder. I turned around and hugged the guy—old times sake.

"Yeah, we're practically strangers."

"Sorry, man. Between the wife and the kids I can barely find time to sleep."

"If you wanna be sorry that's ok—but you don't owe me an apology."

"Ha… ok," he laughed, looking around for a seat. "So, what were you up to tonight?"

"I was trying to get with this girl but all I got was shot down."

"An all-around-bad-date?" Derek asked, as we moved from the bar to a table.

"No, actually. Just a bad finish," I replied, removing my blazer and putting it on the seat beside me. "Seems to be happening more often than it used to."

"You ever think of settling down?"

"More and more."

"Just waiting till you meet the right girl?"

"Kind of... I've met her many times, she just can't seem to hold my interest."

"Ah... well, marriage isn't all it's cracked up to be. Sometimes I wish I'd spent more time single before I committed myself."

"Nah, you did the right thing locking Amy down," I said, a fleeting recollection of my old girlfriend rushing to mind.

"I guess. Grass is greener and bush is pinker though."

"Yeah, but it still stinks. Even I'm starting to get sick of being single."

"Wow. Never thought I'd see the day."

"Me either. Guess it's just hormones winding down—tired of notches, time for a buckle, you know?"

"Kinda. But, then again, I'm kinda on the other end. Thank god for Viagra—if it weren't for that little blue pill I'd never be able to get it up for my wife."

"That makes one of us."

"Ha ha," he laughed—like old times. The waitress walked up to us and smiled for the new guy.

"What can I get for yah?"

"Scotch on the rocks, please," Derek replied, overtly checking her out in case she cared to reciprocate. She gave a cute little bite to her lip and walked away, swaying her hips—her tip, along with Derek's, was gonna be through the roof. "Holy shit... marriage would be a lot easier if women didn't get ugly so fast."

"Ha... I don't think it's the women, it's probably the marriage. Nothing gets you fat faster than saying 'I do.'"

"Isn't that the truth… you'd think that to keep in love people would do more than take care of each other; they'd take care of themselves."

"Can't say I have much of an opinion on that—doesn't involve me after all," I joked, watching the waitress.

"Well, you don't have to be married to know not to get married."

"I take it the two of you are going through a hard time then?"

"More like a flaccid time. We haven't fucked for months."

"The, uh, 'profound spiritual connection' isn't enough to satisfy you anymore?"

"Yeah, right. If our alleged 'profound spiritual connection' wasn't connected to something nice to look at I never would have married her, let alone, nailed our coffin with kids."

"Jesus, Derek," I muttered, surprised how much he'd changed for the worse.

"You know I don't mean it… I'm just frustrated—gotta vent."

"Well, that's life: a constant battle between who you fuck and who you love."

"Speaking of which… you wouldn't happen to know any girls would you?"

"You're married, Derek. A dry spell doesn't change that."

"I know. I'm not looking for a divorce; that's why I'm looking for a lay."

"Then you rent some porn or go to the strippers," I exclaimed, appalled that Derek was so callously disregarding what I secretly envied. He'd started dating Amy a year after I broke up with her for another girl… two girls actually. Hell of a history to blow for getting blown.

"Bob, I don't need another night with the lights off thinking of a stripper. It's already gotten to the point where I'm surprised to see my wife's face when I fuck her because I'm so damn used to thinking about other girls I'd rather be with."

"Well, don't you think that's something you two should talk about?"

"You ever try telling a woman to lose the weight she gained having your kids?"

"No. But I have cheated on girls enough to know you lose more than a tablespoon of cum," I replied, lowering my voice as our waitress passed and informed Derek his drink would be 'just a moment.'

"Thanks beautiful," he replied, twisting off the ring on his finger so he'd be ready to make his move later. I scowled and quickly finished my beer, fishing around my pocket for whatever bill fit the bill fast enough to have me on my way.

"No, I don't know any girls, Derek," I huffed, tossing some money on the table. "Only people I know anymore are women. And they don't fuck around with married men or losers just looking for a lay."

"What the hell's the matter with you? I'd have thought of all people you'd understand how tedious one partner can be."

"Well she loves you, you stupid asshole. Maybe if you thought with more than your dick you'd see how important that is."

"That's a hell of an irony coming from someone who dumped her for a threesome."

"You're absolutely right, Derek—she deserves better than both of us... Anyway, I gotta go," I stated, turning away as the waitress brought over his drink—it wasn't my place to aid or ruin his plans to ruin himself. Friends come and go, but at the end of the day you have to live with yourself.

--------------------------------10 years later--------------------------------

My eyes lustfully lingered on the high-fat ground beef as I dropped the extra lean into my cart—had to watch the cholesterol and all. A song that was bad twenty years ago came onto the speakers and I remembered hating it when it first came out. Nothing makes you feel old like being old. Except of course, for seeing the people you were young with... Amy, my old girlfriend and perpetual regret, was pushing a shopping cart my way. Her eyes drifted up to see me and a smile spread across her face.

"Hey Bob!"

"Hey Amy," I laughed, giving her a welcome hug.

"Wow... long-time-no-see," she giggled, as amazed as I was that we'd bumped into one another. "So how the heck are you?"

"I'm, uh... I'm doing pretty well thanks. How bout you?"

"I'm good. Kids are almost all grown up. Well, they want to be treated like grown ups but they still depend on me for money."

"Ha ha... too bad we were never like that or we might be sympathetic."

"Exactly," she exclaimed, touching my arm as she said it. "So, what are you up to now? Still working in advertising?"

"No. I got out of that a few years ago. I've been working on starting my own publishing company though."

"Wow. Good for you."

"Thanks, but I've yet to see how good it is."

"I'm sure it'll be great."

"Maybe... So, how's Derek?"

"Oh... we actually divorced a few years ago," she explained, her tone calm, not fragile—I could imagine why they'd broken up and knew why she was better off without him.

"I'm sorry, I didn't know."

"If you want to be sorry that's ok—but you don't owe me an apology," she laughed, the words I'd used with Derek years before making their way back to me. "How bout you, did you ever settle down and have a family?"

"I, um... I came close, but it didn't work out."

"Her loss I'm sure."

"I don't know... I guess. She was too young for me though—still caught up playing games."

"Don't you hate that?"

"Yeah... can't think of why I used to waste so much time... but retrospect's easy to judge," I confessed, our eyes never leaving one another's. "I just wish there was an easier way."

"I know just what you mean: sometimes I wanna be honest; walk up to a guy and say..."

"And, say what?"

"I don't know... there aren't really words. I guess that's what's so hard about it."

"Ha... yeah. One of many things that gets harder with age," I chuckled, looking into her cart to see a few boxes of vanilla pudding. "I thought you liked chocolate?"

"Ha ha... I do, but the kids prefer this so I get it for them."

"Must skip a generation."

"Yeah... wow, that brings back memories," she sighed, her face drifting momentarily from the conversation to recollection. "Remember? How we used to hold hands at lunch until your friends scared you away?"

"Ha ha... sure do," I laughed, my face turning red. We didn't do anything for a bunch of seconds before she swallowed nervously and looked away.

"Well, it was really great running into you, Bob."

"Yeah... you too."

"But... I gotta go," she exclaimed, her eyes telling me otherwise. She started to roll her cart past me and I remembered how much I liked holding her hand. I missed her.

"Hey, Amy?"

"Yeah?"

"You wanna grab a drink sometime?"

Seed Them Men

Casey and Pilib came to a screeching halt as the headmaster burst through the door. They slammed their backs against the back of the cabinet and held their breath, tongues and bladders. Slow, steady, deadly steps came toward them as their eyes frantically searched the wall they were sandwiched against. They'd left the door to their secret chamber open when they'd gone back for feathers out of their pillows. And, if that wasn't bad enough, the hostage they kept secret, in that chamber, wasn't the quiet type.

"Oh jaysus, if yah fuck us now I swear I'll crucify every nun in the place," Pilib muttered under his breath.

"Shut up yah mcfuck mick or yah'll fuck us all," Casey replied, slamming his hand over Pilib's mouth. The two took quick jabs at one another out of frustration until the cabinet door opened. Their every move would be known if they dared continue to squabble and, fortunately, they knew well enough to stop.

"Rotten shite," the headmaster grumbled, sifting through the belly of the next days rations.

But, just then, a squeak came from the chamber. Casey and Pilib clenched their jaws and peeked out the corner of their eyes to see the headmaster turn away from the cabinet.

"Who's there!?" the headmaster growled, drunk and hungry to sink his teeth into something or someone.

"If he finds em now, they're done for," Casey whispered.

"What are we gonna do? He's almost there!" Pilib replied, watching the headmaster stumble blindly through the room, not three paces from the secret-chamber-door.

"I said, Who's there!?"

Casey caught a glimpse of a knife stuck in a butchers block across the room. They could take the headmaster hostage too, and if worse came to worse, stash his body in the chamber. Nobody would miss him. And, if anything, they'd be treated as heroes by every lad in the land.

"Fuck it. Pray for me," Pilib exclaimed, as he jumped out from behind the cabinet and ran screaming past the headmaster. "Yahr cock smells like nun-cunt!"

The headmaster turned deep red and swatted at Pilib, his hands falling just short of the boy. Casey grinned, proud to have such a loyal and stupid friend. Pilib kept screaming, while he was chased down the halls, until fists filled his mouth. Casey ran quickly to the chamber, and closed the door behind him—catching a final glimpse of his friend, bloodied and broken.

"Thank yah, Pilib—this won't be for naught."

Casey made his way down the lengthy corridor, carved over decades by the orphans before him. That it had remained a secret for so long was a testament to strength and dedication—endured for gold enough to live free forever. No one had yet retrieved the treasure—but it was close, and the children knew it.

"Where's Pilib?"

"The headmaster got him," Casey growled, stepping past his friends towards the hostage—strapped to an old wooden chair. His legs dangled over the side, too short to reach the ground, and his head squirmed as Casey pulled a handful of feathers from his pockets.

"Oh Christ... does he know about us? Will Pilib talk?"

"No... he'll keep his mouth shut, and take his beating," Casey exclaimed, gliding a feather along the chin of the hostage—grinning as it forced a laugh from him. "Yah're the reason he was caught—couldn't keep yahr fucking mouth shut, could yah?"

"Yah can do whatever yah want to me lads, but I'll not say a word! The gold is ours, and always will be!" the hostage bellowed, fighting his restraints as best he could. His green suit and furry red beard made the children sick—they had fought too long to let his kind hoard the treasure any longer. He would be an example to the others.

"Aye... I don't believe you will," Casey stated, handing the feathers to his lads. "But, I'd say your friends will have a few choice words for us after we deliver your remains," he continued, as each boy, feather in hand, stepped towards their captive.

All at once, they began tickling him over every inch. His face turned red and he howled with laughter, his stomach throbbing and eyes flooding. Then, after nearly a minute of torture, he let out a final scream as his body exploded into pools of blood and guts—spraying across the walls.

"Fucking leprechauns," Casey muttered, wiping away the remains from his face. "Bag his bits and leave it on their doorstep—it's been too long since they had casualties."

"Our Father which art in Heaven, Hallowed be thy name," chanted the children as they stood at attention— watched by nuns, rulers in hand.

"Stand up," Casey whispered to Pilib, hunched forward from the cracked ribs he'd received as punishment.

"Thy kingdom come. Thy will be done, as in Heaven, so in earth."

"I can't... it hurts to breathe," Pilib wheezed, using a flimsy tree branch to support his weight.

"Give us day by day our daily bread. And forgive us our sins; for we also forgive every one that is indebted to us."

"We're going to draw them out tonight... kill as many as we can, so the ones we interrogate know we mean business," Casey explained, making sure to speak his words in synch with the prayer so as not to alert the nuns.

"And lead us not into temptation; but deliver us from evil."

"I can barely stand, let alone fight," Pilib sputtered, drops of blood escaping his lips.

"Amen."

"It won't be a fight—it'll be a massacre," Casey finished, just in time for the prayer to end.

As the children broke assembly and were directed to their quarters, Pilib's eyes rolled into the back of his head and he fell to the floor—the branch he'd held rattling on the hardwood. The boys turned to look at him, knowing well what his collapse meant—but still the nuns yelled for him to rise. The headmaster crept away, grinning as he caught Casey's eye. The children were told the cause of death was illness, but they all knew the sacrifice that Pilib had made for the war.

"Where the fuck are the twins?" Casey snarled, counting heads before continuing on.

"They… they said they weren't coming," a young lad reported.

"To Christ's asshole with them then," Casey growled, leading the front lines as the children marched off the grounds—they'd found escaping was easy enough if they broke into the liquor cabinet and left wine sitting out for the headmaster to blind himself with. The nuns screamed and hollered at the children for stealing it, but their lashes never proved a thing.

"What's the plan?"

"Did yah bring the clover?" Casey asked, addressing his lower ranking officers—with Pilib dead, he was now the sole command of their forces.

"Aye, a real four-leafer."

"Good, lad… leps can spot fakes from a mile away."

"But what's the plan?"

"We bait their grounds and keep low in the bushes till they come lookin."

"That's it? But we won't get more than one or two that way!"

"Bullshit we won't. Genuine four-leafers like this makes their greedy-stomachs boil for the charm. Next to gold, these are their prized possessions."

"Then why don't we send more men out to find them—search the trees so we can trade for gold?"

"Trade?!" Casey screamed, stopping the children's advance to stomp the suggestion dead. "Yah trust the enemy enough to trade with them then, do yah?!"

"No… I just…"

"Just what!?"

"We ain't seen a spot of reward the whole time we been in this war… I was just thinking…"

"Thinking bout yahrself," Casey interrupted, shoving the boy hard in the chest. He stumbled back and clenched his fist but knew better than to fight his own. "If yah trade with em, they double cross yah. If you trust em, they kill yah—these ain't no fuckin' fairytale-daisies, they'ze the real blood-gargling-cunts o' Mother Nature," Casey hollered, making sure all the lads listened, and listened well. "We ain't just in this war for 'reward'—we're in it to win."

The boys quieted down, and stood proud for their cause. The welts on their arms and the bruises on their backs ached no more when they marched to battle—knowing they could give back what they'd gotten. Pilib knew it, and he sacrificed everything for them; for the war. But this was far more than one boy's life—it was the fight that would seed them men.

"Yah fuckin' nancy's missed it," Casey declared, taking a seat at the table across from the twins—eating their breakfast and avoiding the crowd.

"Shame that… but we kept our lives," the dumb one replied, shoveling a big heap of porridge into his mouth. Casey winced from the words and leaned forward—slamming a fistful of leprechaun teeth into their breakfast.

"Can't say they're so lucky."

"What the fuck," the slow one groaned, picking bits out of his porridge and tossing them aside. "Yah can't blame us that we don't wanna end up like Pilib."

"Yah don't say his name again yah fuckin' traitor."

"Traitor? Just cause we don't aim to be put in the ground we're traitors?"

"No. For that, yah're cowards. Yah're traitors cause yah stayed back to suck each other's dicks when we went after the leps," Casey cried, drawing the attention of Sister Marry—the only one in the place the children feared worse than the headmaster. Her brow slammed down and her gaze burned twice as hot as hellfire. The twins lowered their heads, eating their food faster with the hope that Casey wouldn't get them in trouble. But a rowdy group of giggling children drew the Sister's attention away—giving Casey the room he needed to make an example of the twins. "Yahr options are simple—yah can either kill yahrselves, or murder each other. Cause if yah leave it for me tah decide, I'll give yah to the leps."

"Agh, I'm sick o' this shite," the dumb one groaned, doing his best to keep his voice down. "If yah feel like throwin' your life away over some stupid war, that's your business—but stop leadin' the others by the balls just cause it gets yah hard."

Casey grinned as his brow sunk down—giving a sadistic laugh that ended as a growl. He'd worked too long and too hard to turn his back now, or to let someone take a piss on his efforts. The twins had hidden cause they didn't want a beating, but they couldn't hide now.

"Yah're dead!" Cassey yelled, jumping across the table and emptying his fists and all his rage into the twins. He took six teeth and half a pint of blood before the nuns pulled him off—not the best of times for a general but necessary to keep the troops in line.

Casey didn't cry getting lashes anymore—he'd learned to live with the pain. Every time a stroke came down across his back he'd flinch and then turn it to a smile. 'The leps will get worse this time,' he told himself. 'They can't do this to us without us doing worse back to them,' he thought, feeling his shirt stain with blood—the headmaster would leave it on him after his punishment was done so the other children would know the price of acting out.

Afterwards, Casey wobbled back to the room, sweat pouring down his brow as he struggled to stay on his feet. Even the nuns were shocked as he walked past—but they kept their mouths shut and prayed as they always did. The headmaster drank himself to sleep, tired from a good days beating. And the children stayed in their beds as Casey stumbled into the room. They were scared now—scared enough to do as they were told. And, as Casey hobbled to his bed, no one dared speak, or help him. He collapsed on the floor beside his bed, clenching his fists and teeth with rage. Everything he'd pushed down in himself boiling to the surface—his body shaking from the inside out.

"Those god damn leps," he wheezed, the tears fighting their way out of his eyes. It was too dark for the other children to see him cry, and too quiet for them not to hear. But he couldn't hold it in anymore; he couldn't beat or scream away the pain he felt—he hated this place.

Casey woke in someone's quarters—lying in bed under a crucifix nailed to the wall. He raised his head slowly, looking around him, but could see no one. He reached behind himself to feel his back, covered with damp cloths that soaked up the blood. There was a cup of water beside the bed and he thought briefly of sneaking a sip. But, as the sound of footsteps came towards the door, he quickly placed his head back on the pillow to pretend he was asleep.

The door opened and closed as Casey peeked through his eyelashes, trying to see who had taken him in. He hadn't ruled out the trickery of the leps or the return of the headmaster. But, no matter who had entered, Casey was too weak to stand let alone run.

"Wake up, lad—yah're safe now," he heard a familiar voice say—only the words were too kind to be real. He opened his eyes and looked to his side to see Sister Marry knelt beside him. "Make no mistake boy, yah deserved a scolding for what yah done to the twins. But this…" she sighed, shaking her head.

"It's no matter," Casey whispered, looking away and deadening his face—making sure to keep his words few in the company of the Sister.

"Pilib was yahr friend, wasn't he?"

"Aye."

"There are people who can help yah… help all the children here… but my word's half as good as nothing to the ears of men," she explained, struggling with the truth of what she'd said. Casey coughed lightly, tasted blood, and forced it back down to boil with the pain inside him.

"Thanks anyway," Casey stated, his voice callous and detached.

"Yah need to stop this business with the leprechaun's," she exclaimed, cutting through Casey's resolve. "It's gone far enough."

"I… don't know what yah're talking about."

"Yah're the general aren't yah? That's what all the children say."

"They're lying," Casey replied, his voice sinking as he realized that they had all betrayed him.

"Are they?" Sister Marry sighed, seeing that Casey was too stubborn to admit his fantasy. "When I was a girl, my father did things that he shouldn't a done… And, I imagined a fairy who'd come talk to me to make it better."

"So what?" Casey snapped, flipping to his other side despite the pain it caused him. He faced the wall and tucked his hands under his side to apply pressure to his ribs—feeling them drift apart with every breath.

"A child is a wonderful thing, but a childhood is rarely so lucky. I'd like to say 'growing up makes life better,' and in some ways it does. But it never gets easier."

Casey felt tears pace the short distance from his cheek to the pillow. He'd worked so hard for the treasure and the freedom it would bring. But as Sister Marry spoke he realized that, once again, it's pursuit would fall in the hands of the next generation. The leps had won, not because they put up a better fight, but because Casey couldn't fight any longer. The children were told of his illness, and no one said a word.

Sun's Blink

The water soothed me soul as I lay on the hammock over the tide. The sun was red and the coast was gold. Me legs dangled in the wind and me feet skipped on the sand. I gave a lazy look to the lady on me left and smiled, cause she did too. The wind stopped to whistle for her and I hoped, like I hoped everyday, that one day she would be mine. And, cause right now she was, I was about as happy as I could be.

"How come the birds don't fly tonight?"

"I bet if you asked them to they would," I replied, paddling me steps to sway meself in the hammock.

"Birds! Fly cause I said so!" she bellowed, an echo and me affection the only proof of her words.

"Ah, they probably just gettin' ready. Making sure they have their best feathers for you."

"Stupid birds," she giggled, pushing her leg off the tree to swing her to her feet. "I'm gonna go for a swim and count the fish. You comin?"

"Gimme five more minutes o' rest and I go wherever you want me."

"Aight. But don't chew be takin' too much time or I'ma find me self some other lazy-lay-about to watch me play."

"Now what I tell you bout bein' patient?" I joked, as we always did—she was born in a city. And even though the island raised her, you could see her pulse race any time she had to wait.

"I'ma give you five minutes. But afta that, chew on ya own."

"Don't chew be worryin' bout me, girl. I be witchu in a sun's blink."

"Aight den," she finished, her steps bouncing off the sand as she ran into the water. I watched her like anyone who holds love but is too afraid to speak of it. I didn't say because I didn't want her to say no. Things might change if I did, and then I'd be truly sad. At least as friends we'd have each other, or at least that's what I told meself.

The clouds in the sky soaked in the sun and glowed with thanks to have seen another day done. The moon yawned and stretched out to the stars to bid them their morning, so they might sparkle this night. And all the while I hummed to meself, a slow drum beat from me heart to me head. I looked in me mind and decided five minutes had passed. I rose slowly from the hammock and stretched before stepping in the faded prints of her feet.

"Ain't no fish swimmin' the shores neither!" she cried, pulling her hair from below the shoreline as I came to stand by her side.

"What'chew mean girl?"

"Look!" she exclaimed, taking me arm and pulling me below the water. She was right. No fish, nor shell, nor anything that moved was in the water that day.

"Girl… all me days, I never seen the shore like this," I whispered, worried by the empty water.

"Mother nature needs to keep betta track of her children."

"It's a bad omen this… somethin' not right in the sea."

"Bah… It's no bad omen, it just means there's nothing to do," she huffed, walking out of the water to her towel by the hammock. "I'm a go give me girls a shout. Maybe tomorrow they'll be some fish we can swim with."

"Yes… tomorrow," I sighed, watching me lady walk away. Only… she wasn't me lady. And I scorned meself for continuing to think it every time I thought of her… every time I thought.

I trudged out of the water, forgetting about the barren sea as I was now alone. It's a strange thing to step through life, completely in love, only to stumble every time I tried to say it. For when I looked in her eyes, I could see the depths of her soul cryin' for me. But, once again, I told meself it wasn't worth the risk of losin' her for the chance to make her mine. She wouldn't be interested anyway… "How could she be?" I thought to meself…

But me concentration broke as I left the ocean. A rustlin' came from the palm tree by the hammock and I froze to watch what I didn't understand. The leaves blew against the wind and the moonlight throbbed in the distance. A cool breeze hit the back of me spine and me thoughts returned to the empty beach. Nothing that lived dared step there but me, and I felt sick to remain. Something wasn't right… something was very wrong.

I'd heard stories from me brotha but had never paid them any mind till now. The palm tree started to sway itself, soaking up the moonlight until it lit the shore. Me heart pounded in me chest and the sand blew circles around me ankles. I heard a whisper from inside me head, telling me to run, but I couldn't move. Soon enough that whisper became a scream as I heard a voice echo from the tree.

"A lover's chest and a pirate's breast, a woman who plundered a man possessed…"

The sun fell below the ocean and the night came without stars. The voice grew louder.

"When he was lost, another was found, first love forgotten below the ground…"

The tree morphed to the figure of a man, shining an eerie blue light across the sand.

"He returned for her, but she escaped his grasp, vengeance destined to be became the past…"

And then, before I could scream, before I could run—a ghost stood before me.

"But by moonlit night, the ghost's love will see lovers reunite," spoke the spirit. I trembled in me place as he raised a transparent hand towards me, releasing a locket that fell to me feet.

"Ahhhhhhh!" I screamed, me dread locking me in me place. The ghost shone of an eerie blue light, like the moon poured into a man. He grinned and pushed his chin towards me as I shivered away, falling on me backside. And just as I found the strength to run, the ghost and his darkness disappeared, replaced by the setting sun.

I frantically looked for him, but there was no sign—save for the locket he had dropped at me feet. The waves whispered, gracing the shore, and the sun's golden light blanketed the sky as birds returned to the beach. A crab tip-toed from shell to shell, looking for a good bed. And I wearily plucked the locket from the sand, opening it to see a faded picture of me lady.

"It's no joke, man!" I cried, slapping me brotha on the back of his head. A hiccup of smoke escaped him from the smack and he began to cough.

I'd run home as fast as I could, the whole time gazing at the locket, trying to explain what I saw. A picture of me lady, hundreds of years old, only she was as young as she was today. A golden memento, given by a faded spirit, to prove I wasn't crazy for seeing what I seen.

"Man, how much you had to smoke you going crazy like this?" he grumbled, picking up the roach he had dropped from me slap.

"What you calling me crazy for, man? You the one who told me the stories of the ghost in the first place!"

"Yeah, and I made em up," he coughed, trying one more time to pass me the gunga, even though he knew I didn't smoke. "I just wanted to scare you. I didn't think you'd actually be dumb enough to think em true."

"They is true, man! An the ghost gave me this locket!" I shouted, waving it in front of his face.

"Lemme see that."

"Here, man. It's proof, and that's me lady's picture."

"Your lady? I ain't never heard her say you her man."

"But it's her, though."

"Aye, it is. But that don't make her your lady."

"Man! This pictures as old as the word, but she look just like she do now!"

"An they brought dinosaurs back for movies but that don't make em real!"

"You sayin' it's fake?"

"I ain't sayin' it's fake. I sayin' you crazy an you wastin' me time."

"I wastin' the time you already wastin' smokin' gunga? No, I tellin' you the truth."

"Aight. Maybe you is. Even then, so what? All you got is an old picture, an a locket look like it been swallowed by a whale."

"Man, stop smokin' long enough to start thinkin'! The ghost had to give it to me for a reason!"

"Yeah, so I can't get no peace… this ghost more a menace to me than you."

"Bah… what am I gonna do, man?"

"What you gonna do about what?"

"About the ghost, man!"

"You ain't gotta do nothin'. It already gone ain't it? That is, if it was ever there to begin with."

"But I ain't got no answers, just a locket an a brotha who thinks me crazy for tellin' a story he told me."

"So what you want from me? You need to know more, then go back to the shore an look."

"Yeah, man… you right. We need to go back to the beach."

"We? Why we? I ain't gonna do nothin' but sit an smoke tonight."

"You can't just leave me alone with the ghost. Besides, you need to see this an know I ain't crazy."

"Even if I see it I still gonna think you crazy. Besides, I ain't in the mood for chasin' what's in your head."

"Why? You scared?"

"Scared? No man, I'm lazy. Now leave me be."

"Brotha, you can either come because I asked or because I said so. But either way you gonna meet me at the beach come sundown tomorrow."

A light chatter sizzled under the reggae playin' overhead. The walls of the place had been built around a bundle of palm trees that hammocks now hung from. Their trunks climbed up through the roof so the tops could bask in the sun and save the customers from being knocked by fallin' coconuts. It was the only place in town like it, and the only place in town I liked to go out to. It was busy today an full of too many people to say 'hello' to em all. I waved as I passed the tables, givin' big smiles and quick taps of me hands to theirs.

"Look! A ghost!" me friend cried, pointing out a window. I reared me head to the side, expecting to see the moonlit man glaring at me. But there was nothing in sight as the sound of laughter filled the room.

"Very funny," I grumbled, thinking of how stupid it was to confide in me stupid brother. If everyone knew, likely me lady did too.

I took a seat at an empty table, choosing to be alone rather than have to explain meself to everyone else. I watched as they pointed and laughed at me—drinkin' their drinks till they forgot why they drank. But I quickly forgot about them as me lady came to the table carryin' her tray.

"You aright?" she asked, squintin' like she thought me crazy too.

"Sit with me for a minute if you can."

"I can," she replied, smiling nervously. "What's all this I been hearing about you chasing ghosts? You ain't been smokin' with yah brotha, have you?"

"No, I haven't. And yes, I seen a ghost."

"You sure it ain't just someone playin' a trick on you?"

"I'm sure."

"You sure you ain't just playin' a trick on me?"

"It's no trick."

"Is it anything we can sell tickets to?"

"Girl," I groaned, catching her giggle despite me sincerity. "Yesterday, after you'd gone, a spirit visited me on the shore and gave me this," I explained, holding out the locket to her. She took it in her hand and opened it, trembling from the picture she saw.

"When did you take this picture?"

"I didn't. It was the spirit who gave it to me."

"I ain't in the mood for jokes no more," she exclaimed, her voice cracking while she spoke. "This don't make me feel right."

"What you mean?"

"It... it makes me feel cold. But on the inside."

"That's you though," I stated. She closed the locket and put it on the table before standing up and turning away. "Where are you going?"

"I have to work."

"But..."

"No buts, boy. I don't like this—whatever this is... I'll see you later," she exclaimed, rushing from the table as quick as she could, but never taking her eyes off the locket. I could see she felt as anxious as I did. But it would take us both to be done with this—whatever this is.

I spotted me brotha and sighed, knowing how much I was in for if I plucked him from his gaggle of friends. But as I approached, I no longer thought of how stupid he was for opening his big mouth. Instead, I watched me girl move awkwardly around the room—looking over her shoulder every other moment as though something chased her. I'd never seen her afraid of anything before.

"Can I go now?" me brotha whined, crossin' his arms and frownin'.

"We just got here!" I yelled, standing out in the ocean while he watched me from the shore.

"So? We still been here too long."

"The ghost appeared from that tree as I came out of the water," I explained, trudging out of the sea. I came to stand by me brotha and shook me head in frustration.

"How many times I gonna have to watch you do this before we done?"

"I don't know what's different," I muttered, a pair a gulls flappin' overhead an out to sea. "Turn around this time, maybe he'll show up then."

"Turn around? If I have to turn around then what the hell did you bring me here to witness?"

"Just do it, man!" I cried, rushing back out to the water. I reached the spot I'd been the night before and pulled out the locket, squeezing it hard and thinking of me lady. Then, as I had before, I dunked me head under to look for fish. And, this time, just like the other night, I couldn't see one thing in the water but me.

"The view home looking mighty fine right now," me brotha hollered, his back turned to me as he waited impatiently.

"It's happenin', man!" I yelled, rushing out of the water as I felt a cool breeze come from the ocean.

"Can I turn around then? Or is it a self-conscious ghost?"

The sea started to lose it's light, and everything went dark except for one luminous man.

"What the... what's happenin' to the light?" me brotha stuttered, turning around as he spoke to see the ghost not two steps from him. "Shit, man!" he cried, fainting before the ghost could speak. The spirit then turned his attention to me, his hollow voice echoing across the beach.

"What mockery is this?" he grumbled, floating towards me as I cowered by the water. "I did not rise from the depths to have me patience tested."

"I... I ain't trying to test your patience, man. I just testin' me sanity."

"Your sanity?"

"Yeah... you ain't exactly reassuring that me head's on straight."

"A foolish test it would be. For were I to do what need be done to prove your sanity, surely you would lose it thereafter."

"Ok... I'll take your word for it."

"Why did you bring me this coward?"

"Well... you weren't really clear about what I should be doing, or why I should be doing it."

"Did you not hear me words? Or know of any who know them?"

"Um… me brotha said you roam the shore looking to rape young men."

"What?!"

"Sorry, man… I, uh… just saying what I heard."

"Yah heard wrong! And your brother should consider himself lucky to have been absent for his words."

"Yyyyeah… so, what's the legend?"

"A lover's chest and a pirate's breast, a woman who plundered a man possessed. When he was lost, another was found, first love forgotten below the ground. He returned for her, but she escaped his grasp, vengeance destined to be became the past. But by moonlit night, the ghost's love will see lovers reunite."

"I, uh… what does that mean?"

"It means 'your girl' is the woman I loved in a past life."

"And…"

"I need her to forgive me before I can be at rest."

"Forgive you for what?"

"For murdering her," the spirit sighed as me brotha started to come to. I turned to look at him, rubbing his head and grumbling to himself. But when I turned back to speak to the spirit, he had vanished again.

"What the hell happened?" me brotha groaned.

"The ghost came and you fought him."

"Really?"

"No you moron, you fainted. Why the hell did you have to make up that stupid story an all that garbage about the ghost trolling for booty?"

"I'm sorry... I thought adding that part was funny," he stated, standing up and brushing the sand off his pants. "But I didn't make up the story."

"What?" I exclaimed, grabbing me brotha by the collar. "Then where the hell'd you hear it?!"

The night came darker than those before it—the stars kept from us by the trees overhead. Me brother and I trudged through the forest, hacking at branches with our arms to clear a path.

"How do you know her?" I asked as we made our way to the home of me brotha's longtime friend, Jamila. Strange thing was, I knew every family on the island but had never heard of hers.

"She's me dealer."

"Your dealer? The stuff just grows in the forest! Go pick some!"

"Man... when you smoke everyday, it don't take long before you don't know what you're smoking no more. She let me smoke stuff so good the thought don't even enter me mind."

"So you smoke yourself so stupid, you can't think about how stupid you are?"

"Man... just shut up."

"Fine. But she's the one who told you the story, right?"

He nodded and raised his flashlight towards an old shack, smothered by the forest. The trees seemed to grow closer in this part of the island and every inch of every leaf was covered with birds, bugs and lizards—crawling over each other in the beam of me brothers light.

"Why she allow so many critters round here?"

"She says it keeps them away."

"Them? Who's them?"

"Her family."

"She keeps a zoo at her doorstep just to keep her family at bay?"

"Aye."

"Why?"

"Because they ain't alive no more."

"Oh," I gulped, pausing briefly as me brother's flashlight shone over Jamila's open door. "Is she expecting us?"

"No… this ain't right," me brotha stated, rushing forward and pushing the door in.

The room was black and quiet.

"Jamila?" me brotha cried, scanning his flashlight slowly from left to right. The place was torn apart, everything smashed and thrown about. We stepped awkwardly through the dark, and the rubble on the floor, looking for any sign of her or what had happened to her.

"Look," I exclaimed, the cherry of a joint burning in the corner of the shack — an eerie blue smoke rising from it. Me brotha drew his light across the room until it came to rest on an old woman — her hands clutching her chest while she sat hunched forward, showing us the top of her head.

"Jamila?" me brotha asked again, taking a step towards her and touching her face — pulling quickly away to see blood on his hand. Jamila's head fell back from me brotha's touch to reveal a hundred deep cuts to her face — only bone and blood soaked scrapes of skin remained. "Oh Christ."

"What in hell," I whispered, lifting me hand to me mouth. Me brotha's flashlight shook in his hand as he tucked Jamila's head back down, to be at peace. But, in doing so, he took notice of something she clenched tight to her chest. "What is that?" I asked, turning me head as I heard a rustling come from someplace in the house.

"It's her family diary," he replied, taking it from her hands. But he didn't hear the noise, or see the shadowed corner shake.

Then, as I approached whatever was making the noise, I caught a glimpse out the window to the now barren leaves and ground surrounding the house—illuminated by an eerie blue light. A cold wind filled the house and me hairs stood on end—either the ghost was coming, or Jamila's family had never left.

"Brotha!" I exclaimed, grabbing him by the shoulder and turning him round. "They're here!" I cried, as the front door burst open to reveal near twenty ghosts. They looked upon Jamila's body and growled, before turning their hateful eyes towards me and me brother.

They flew through the walls and the windows, growling and whispering—their hands stretched out to take us to the afterlife with them. Me brotha crept away, pushing me into the corner where the noise had come from. Then, with just inches between us and the ghosts, our feet slipped from under us and I stretched me arm out to grab hold of the wall—catching a black sheet draped over a cage. As the sheet fell to the ground with us, the ghosts attention turned up to a now screaming parrot—thrashing and flapping about in his cage. And then, in a poof and gasp of air, the ghosts were gone.

"Stop hogging the cage!" me brotha whined, as we stepped through the forest, hugging the birdcage, hoping to keep the ghosts at bay.

"Squawk! Family smoke! Family smoke!" the parrot screamed, flailing about in it's cage.

"This is hundreds of years old," I explained, flipping through the pages of the diary. "Each person gave only one entry for their life."

"What was Jamila's entry?"

"It's not here… the page has been torn out."

"Squawk! Gunga ghost! Gunga ghost!"

"Shut up bird!" me brotha hollered, shaking the cage as we entered the border of town, just in time for the sun to start rising. "What about the other entries? What they got to say?"

"From what I read thus far," I muttered, fumbling the flashlight around in me hands. "Jamila's family were pirates… all of them pirates."

"Pirates? Like treasure chest, shiver-me-timbers, Jack Sparrow pirates?"

"Yeah… apparently her family was the most feared on the sea, and every captain was of the same bloodline."

"Does… it say where their treasure's buried?"

"Man, you already scavenged her house for all the gunga you could find, and now you lookin' for treasure too?"

"Ok, it's BLUE-GUNGA, I wouldn't a scavenged no house for no regular gunga."

"What about respect for the dead?"

"Respect for the dead? The dead's the one's who killed Jamila and who was trying to kill us too!"

"Squawk! Captain's escaped! Captain's escaped!"

"Bird, shut up!" me brotha yelled, shaking the cage once more as we approached the police station. "Wait… why we going to the police?"

"What? Why?" I stuttered. "Because there's a dead woman, who's dead because someone killed her!"

"Yeah, the ghosts!"

"Man, it don't matter who it was, she still been murdered."

"Ok… but… I don't want them taking me gunga."

"What they care? They got they own."

"Not like this they don't. I'm gonna go home. I'll meet you there when you're done."

"You were the one who knew her!"

"Gah… fine, then you take it and I'll meet you at home when I'm done."

"Fine. I'll take the bird and your gunga home and finish reading the diary."

"What? No. I need the bird."

"What you need the bird for?"

"For protection, man."

"You're going to the police station!"

"But what if the ghosts come back?"

"Then you can ask em where their treasure's buried."

"Man… just… don't let anything happen to that gunga."

"Man, shut up," I snapped, prying the cage from me brotha's hands. "Don't say anything about the ghosts to the cops—we can't have them locking you up or getting in our way while we get to the bottom of this."

The diary was a legacy of greed and murder spanning near five hundred years. Every member of the family was either a pirate, a thief, or a conman. But it wasn't till I reached the passage telling of one captain Onandi, and his love for two women, that I started to connect the dots.

"Where'd you put the gunga?" me brotha exclaimed, bursting in the house with near twenty birds in cages.

"What the... why all the birds, man?"

"Because birds keep the ghosts away. Look, I even got leashes for them."

"Leashes?"

"Yeah, man. I don't wanna be carrying all these cages all the time," he stated, placing the birds down. "Now, where'd you put me gunga?"

"First, what happened at the police station?"

"They said they'd check the scene but they didn't give me no more to know than that. What the diary say?"

"Listen to this: 'Me love was for them both, though neither would have it so. One sought me gold while the other plundered me heart. But, between the two, me wits were no match. Me fair lady tried to murder the gold-digger, but I was blind to her reason and the justice of her deed. Me actions thereafter pain me a thousand times the pain I caused her... hacking off her arms before sending her down the plank. It was only after this sin that I learned the truth of her love for me and the wretched greed of the whore she had sought to murder and

I was foolish enough to choose. Now I am brokenhearted and weary, finding strength enough only to write this confession before I plunge this vessel to the bottom of the sea.'"

"And... why was that important for me to hear?"

"Because this is just like what the ghost said. I think the ghost on the shore is captain Onandi—a dead relative of Jamilas."

"Oh... can I have me gunga now?"

"Here," I groaned, throwing him his precious blue-gunga.

"Yes! Praise be known," he cried, stuffing the bag of joints in his pocket while removing one to smoke. "Jamila never let me smoke this stuff anywhere but her house. This is a real treat this."

"Uh hu," I muttered, ignoring him. "The pirate murdered one of his wife's but he picked the wrong one. And the passage after his was written by the gold-digger. Says she escaped the ship as it sank and found a new man."

"So?"

"So everything that the ghost said is in this diary, except for one thing," I explained, glancing to me left at the squawking gaggle of birds.

"And what's that?"

"He said something about lovers reuniting"

"So? Sounds like a happy ending," me brotha mumbled, lighting his lighter under the joint in his mouth.

"I'm not sure... he said he needs me lady to forgive him for murdering her," I explained, pulling the locket from me pocket. "That means he thinks me lady is the wife who he made walk the plank."

"So maybe if she forgives him, the ghosts will disappear," me brotha said, puffing away while strapping leashes on disgruntled birds.

"Or maybe she'd end up like Jamila," I stated, as the corner of me eye caught a blue wave of light coming from outside the window—the ghosts from Jamila's house had followed us, and their numbers had grown. They hovered over every inch of everything in sight, swallowing the day into a blue-moon-abyss.

"Oh shit," I groaned, the angry eyes of every ghost bearing down upon us. They could wait longer than we could live and they knew it. But what was truly frightening was the sight of a lone woman surrounded by the crowd—me lady stood terrified, with a knife to her neck and her soul ready to be taken.

"Ok... on three, I'll grab you and then we grab her," me brotha stated, as the ghosts marched us towards the beach.

"They can probably understand you," I replied, watching me lady be led further in front of us in case we tried anything. The ghosts were taking us towards the shore where I'd met Onandi—this must be the night he had spoke of.

"But they haven't touched me," he exclaimed, the birds leashed to his every limb, flapping about frantically.

The ghosts came to a halt—lifting their swords to their sides and pointing to the shore. The waves were black and the white sand sparkled in the moonlight. Me lady walked to the shore and I followed. But as me brother took a step forward, the ghosts surrounded him, blocking his path and shaking their heads.

"How you gonna stop me? I got birds, remember!" me brotha cried, flailing his arms wide—inadvertently tugging the birds leashes. A ghost smiled as he listened, bending down to pick up a rock, before throwing it into me brother's chest. "Ow!" he whined, as the rest of the ghosts bent down to pick up rocks. "Ok, ok… I get it."

The spirits remained on the border of the beach, lingering behind where me brother stood. They looked out to sea, pointing the way until I came to stand by me ladies side. Then, they marched away, taking me brother with them.

"Where are they going?" me lady asked, watching the ghosts leave.

"I don't know."

"What the hell did you do to get me into this?"

"I didn't do nothing. A ghost told me to bring you to the beach, but I didn't cause you said the locket didn't make you feel right."

"A ghost asked you to do something and you didn't do it? What the hell was you thinking?"

"I was thinking that if the locket made you feel cold inside, it probably wasn't a good idea to bring you here."

"So you strapped a flock of birds to your brother and sent hell's army to fetch me?"

"Girl, just try and look at the locket without trembling," I stated, pulling it from me pocket and holding it for her to see.

"Get that away!" she yelled, swatting at the locket and knocking it to the ground. I looked down, ashamed of scaring her, only to see the locket had sprung open in the sand—exposing a piece of paper that lay hidden behind the picture. I bent down and picked it up, unfolding it to see what it was.

"That thing make me feel like... like I'm dying," she whispered, hugging herself and trembling.

I scanned over the piece of paper—reading the lines with a stern brow and an open mouth. It was Jamila's entry, ripped from the family diary, and hidden in the locket. And, as I read it, I understood why this was happening...

'Whomever should read this, pray that it make no sense to you. For if it do, the lady pictured here is in grave danger.

Blue-gunga grew from the graves of me family and proved too tempting for the town fool to resist. As I feared he smoked it, despite me warnings and threats against him. This released the ghost of captain Onandi back into the world and cursed the souls of those he knew.

I enticed the fool to smoke again—to release the ghosts of me family so they might protect me. For, with Onandi back, he will endeavor to take me life and this golden locket, bearing his ladies image, so he may use it to lure someone into his service.

If you read this, do not be fooled by him. If you read this, know that he will try and find his lady, born again, so he may award the locket to someone with the hope that that they will return his lady to him. I pray for her soul and the curse upon Onandi that whomever should read this, will not do his bidding. For if you do, you will be surrendering the ladies life and your own.

Look to the spirits of me family for help and protection—their souls lie in the gunga.'

"What's going on?" me lady asked, shoving me in the shoulder while looking out to sea. A blue light crept from the water as I lifted me head from the page.

"He's coming."

"Who?"

"Captain Onandi," I cried, grabbing me ladies hand and pulling her away from the water.

But, before we could take even a step, the bow of a ghost ship dove out of the water and onto the shore. Its sails stood still against the wind as its captain flew down towards us. In the distance I could hear the squawking of me brother's birds, but Onandi paid no mind to any sign of life now that he gazed upon me lady—frozen with fear at the sight of him.

"Every barren year in the abyss was a privilege in knowing this day would come," he declared, wrapping his arms around me lady and pulling her up to the ship. "Thank you for returning her to me."

I cried out, reaching for me ladies hand, but it was too late. Onandi pulled her aboard and began his journey out to sea.

But, as I shouted her name, waving me hands through the ghost-ship's-hull, the shore flooded with the spirits of Jamila's bloodline—each one screaming, swords in hand, as they rushed towards the ship. Me brother came flailing alongside them as cannons extended from the sides of the ship.

"They're on our side!" me brother cried, tugging me back from the swarm of ghosts ascending the side of the ship as the cannons fired frantically to be rid of them.

"The gunga! Do you have the gunga?!" I shouted, watching the ghosts hit by cannonballs burst into smoke and fade away.

"What? Why?"

"Just give me it!"

"Here," he exclaimed, pulling a bag of joints from his pocket and giving them to me. The ship set out to sea as the spirits attempts to stop it failed. I heard me lady cry me name as I lifted four blue-gunga-sticks to me mouth and lit a fire under them.

"Smoke!" I shouted, handing them to me brother as I lit some more. He made a dumbfounded face but obliged all the same, fighting off the birds strapped to him with one hand while puffing on the joints with the other. I joined him a moment later, puffing as hard as I could to bring the spirits back to save me lady. And as the smoke filled the air, their souls returned to earth.

"What the hell?!" me brother muttered, watching a ghost climb out of his lungs and fly out to sea in pursuit of the ship.

"Just keep smoking!" I replied between coughs, feeling a rush of blood to me head.

The spirits came one after another from the smoke, chasing the captain out to sea. The cannons fired and me lady screamed as the sunlight flickered against the darkness. Me brother and I lay down, wasting no time on air. And the more we smoked, the more the ghosts overwhelmed the ship. Then, suddenly, sunlight exploded into the sky, sucking the moon and the darkness into oblivion. I stared out to sea, dizzy and stoned off me ass—seeing me lady fall from where the ship had been to crash into the ocean.

"Shit!" I cried, running towards the water, tripping over meself, only to get up and run again.

I dove in and swam as hard as I could out to where she had fallen. I prayed her soul remained and that I had not lost her or me chance to be with her. But as I approached where her body had fallen, I could see it sink in the water—down to the depths with Onandi. I took a deep breath and plunged under, wrapping me arms around her to bring her back up for air. I pulled her back to shore, as me brother rushed to help us.

We pulled her body to land and lay her on her back as I screamed her name. I shook her and checked for breath, feeling none. I pressed hard on her chest, trying to catch me breath to breathe it into her. Then, as I pressed me lips to hers I felt her heart beat against mine and her mouth mold to me own.

"Don't make out with her, she's dying!" me brother screamed, falling to one knee before collapsing all together—too stoned to move.

The birds flapped round him as he lay unconscious beside me lady and I as we shared our first kiss. And as I pulled away, feeling relief and joy rush over me, she smiled cause I did too.

A Mind in Love

"**When you live in our shoes, you don't have to walk in anyone else's,**" Amore said to me one night, years before. We danced and made love—I'm not sure which was goodbye.

"I think he's a pig," Diva snorted, plumping her pink lips in a trough of ice water. She wiped her smile and twirled a rose of lipstick to her mouth. "But love shows the animal in all of us."

Her wisdom was not wisdom—and I shuddered that she might be right. Any man would fall to her feet—if not on the dance floor, than for that which they followed her for. But her words were empty and loveless. Spoken for one to hear, not heed. I listened all the same.

"All men love me, and I love them for it," she continued, pinning a bouquet of diamonds to flutter about her ear. "But I have no love for animals," she finished, batting her eyes along the line of her thighs. She turned towards me, already ready, and made her way to the floor—compelling me to follow in the storm of her steps.

I lingered behind, foresight rising of memory, to catch my eyes staring lifelessly from Diva's mirror. My breaths were slow and my thoughts were old—only my heart kept the beat. Amore was here tonight and with him so too was our love—trampled, neglected and forgotten. I would make him beg to remember, as I did to forget; to pray to have my heart his own, once more. And, as I rose, my will a testament to the power of love, I took the first step to win him; to beat him.

The light lay low to silhouette my hips. My dress breathed upon the sweat of my body and I could feel heat brood around me. But I didn't have to look up to know they watched me. Men's eyes swim through crowds of women like sharks on a feeding frenzy. They thirst for blood, pounding in our pores, and squirm to control themselves for the right fish to flaunter—we're the bait; they're the prey. But it's our hearts that get eaten.

He stepped before me—remaining still just long enough to distinguish himself from the other men, clamoring for my hand. His hair was black, flowing along his sandy skin. His expression was as stern as his conviction. But his eyes were what won me, even before our gallop of steps. He reached out for me and I turned into him. His fingertips kissed my hips and I held my breath. It was love; it was fate. It was the music escaping us unto each other. The dance floor swallowed us, and our first night of many began.

The band warmed up, teasing our lust and tickling our feet. I stepped into the room. But my presence went unnoticed as Diva circled the floor, spinning and trotting—passionately, flirtatiously, magnificently. Her dress soared a fleeting leap to every tap of her heal and the audience bathed in her passion. But it was his eyes I sought, not theirs.

The audience was as it always is—awestruck and imprisoned in their seats, while the music played for others to dance. The lights dimmed by watch of the stars and the bulbs that shone with their every whim. The judges shuffled about in their seats, feeding our anticipation for the verdict they would give. But it all melted away when I saw him.

It was a perfect morning to any who woke for it. But for us it was far better in bed. I'd found love: I'd found life. It was something I'd never known men could offer. And, now, something I couldn't imagine with anyone else. It made my friends sick, but I barely saw them long enough to notice. I was in love. Nothing mattered but that. And time melted away within his arms.

I'd read a romantic book once as a girl, thinking it the promise of becoming a woman. But beauty commands an elusive love drowned in lust. For every man sees what he wants, but it is the woman who must see past it—with him I couldn't. He was what I had always dreamed of, and as we lay with one another, I could not help but pinch him to be sure I was awake.

"Ah!" he cried, pulled from the brink of slumber by the clasp of my hands. "What are you doing?" he laughed, pulling me along the bed so I could use him for a pillow.

"I wanted to be sure it wasn't a dream."

"Then why would you pinch me? I know the world when I see it and love when I have it," he sighed, a smirk flashing through the cracks of my hair that covered our faces from the morning sun. Light peeked through the sheets, tented around us, and the warmth of his skin drew me to him. "Should I pinch you to see if you wake?"

"No!" I giggled, trembling from his snapping fingers despite the embrace of his arms. I didn't want to wake up—I knew love like this was too good to be true. He smiled like he always did when I thought I'd done something stupid. And if he didn't kiss me, to calm my nerves and quiet my mind, I would second guess every move until I couldn't move anymore. My stomach growled and I blushed.

"Hungry?"

I nodded a humble admission. He rolled to the side of the bed and flung the sheet that had covered us into the air like a parachute—letting it mold his shoulders as it glided down. I lay naked on the bed. The cool burst of air that held me, after he let go, shivered along my skin until every hair was on end. He extended a hand for me to follow and, in taking it, I was lifted to his side. We walked together to the kitchen, through the beams of afternoon sun.

The view was brilliant as I stepped before the balcony and breathed the new day. The hills climbed to mountains and stole the horizon from the sky. The village was a splash of white, freckled between trees and vineyards. The sun warmed my skin as I felt a pair of hands slide a robe unto my shoulders.

"You want me covered?" I charmed, my eyes aligned with his lips as I slipped my arms into the sleeves. The silky fabric of the robe served the fingers of the wind as I turned to him.

"Never. But, if we do not, soon a crowd will fill all we see. And I want you for myself," he exclaimed, watching as I fastened a bow around my waist.

"Breakfast," I said, smacking him on the butt. He laughed, rolled his eyes, and made his way to the fridge. I bit my bottom lip to stop from telling him 'I love you' again. I smiled smugly instead as he rummaged through the freezer. He emerged a moment later bearing ice cream and olives.

"We need to shop," he muttered, opening the jar of olives and plopping one into his mouth. I took a seat on the counter and opened my mouth. He flicked an olive into the air and I caught it on my tongue.

"We'll shop then," I declared, pushing myself off the counter to try and find clothes that hadn't been ripped off me or cast away. "Get dressed, I need to shower."

"Or," he stated, holding my arm as I took the first step from him. "I could shower with you, and later we dance."

I grinned and kissed him. Never thinking it was the last time we would truly be happy. Soon we left the house and headed to town. We feasted and shared laughter before we danced the night. It was then he saw her. I rushed him home to try and remind him why he was with me. But afterwards, we lay in bed, silent. I saw in his eyes that he had changed. I kissed him goodnight and he kissed me goodbye. I woke up the next morning and he was gone.

The room exploded into applause when the announcer said Diva's name. People stood and whistled, pounding their hands together and feet on the ground. She blew kisses to the crowd, posing in the first moment of her routine. I slunk to my seat, my eyes locked on him looking at her. It was as though nothing had changed since that night except for time to pass and my heart to wither. The music began and the crowd grew silent.

Time together was a gift and time apart a curse. Every moment without him was a shattered beat of my heart, bleeding through my eyes till they would fall upon him again. And like the mirage of water in the desert, he would appear long enough to give me hope to be with him, only to fade and walk where I could not follow. Endless days died in the abyss of my night and still I waited for him.

I knew he would never return to me or so much as see me on the nights I spied and watched him with her. I knew he didn't love me and I told myself he felt the same about her. I wondered if he had ever truly cared for me and if I truly cared for him. If not, why did I hurt so? Why did my eyes see him no matter which way I turned? These questions and more led my mind where he once stood. I had to know, if only for him to deliver the final blow.

I followed them one night, watching from afar as he took her everywhere we had gone, as he showered her with affection, praise and love. I wanted to kill her and take him back. To scream to the heavens and demand God answer me for the pain he had given. But tears were my only relief from what made me cry. Life without love is unbearable; life with love is suicide.

I watched them part—a long kiss and lingering gaze. He walked away, hands in his pockets, and I foolishly approached—fragile and alone. His eyes were dead when they fell upon me, as though my presence was a burden to him. He walked past me. But I followed, speaking empty words from my broken heart.

"Did you not love me?" I demanded, pushing against him to ignite the passion I knew burned dormant.

"Not anymore," he replied, a callous indignation the only print of our past.

"But why? We had so much together," I explained, stepping behind him as he led us through the empty streets.

"No, we had nothing," he grunted, hurrying his pace no matter how I tried to block him.

"Why do you do this? Why do you hide from me?"

"I didn't hide, I relocated. And why not?"

"Because I love you more than her, more than she ever could. Because I know you love me too, no matter what you say," I cried out, my ribs a brittle cage that quivered with every beat of my heart.

"No, you are blinded by a mind in love. You see only what you feel, not what's real."

"Why do you deny how you feel? Why do you run from me?"

"Why, why, why?" he groaned, exasperated by the bellows of my soul.

"Yes! Why!?" I howled, grabbing his arm and pulling him to a stop. He turned angrily towards me and flung my hand from him.

"Because I am too good a man to be with you," he hissed, leaning in close so I could see hell burn below his brow.

"Too good to be with, but not to have been with?" I whispered, his words ringing in my ears. "No… you keep the truth so you do not hurt, but because of that you hurt me. Please, Amore—why do you not stay? I am good enough, I know I am."

"Not to me… I find women sexy for what I see, not what they show me."

"And because you saw her you no longer see me, no longer love me?"

"Love is a moment, not a lifetime."

"No. Love is a lifetime that seems like a moment," I replied, my tears having dried in the cold of his words. "But you do not admit it because it would make your life wrong," I continued, now realizing how he had used me, how he had lied, cheated, and disserted me. "You keep yourself from women because the only love you know is what you hold for yourself."

"Leave me alone," he huffed, turning his back to me and walking away. I followed, closer than before.

"But that's not love. Love is when you feel another person become a part of you. It's giving yourself, forever, to what you desire more than what you have," I exclaimed, my hurt turning to anger—the words already ready. "You can only find love like that with another person, and you can only find another person if you love more than yourself."

"You'll want to diet. They don't let pigs on the dance floor," he snapped, turning to insults to eclipse my insight.

"You are too weak to love," I explained, speaking my pain become vendetta. "Instead, you charm women into loving you, only to leave them before you're found out. Does it make you feel powerful to hurt others? Does it make you love yourself more?" I demanded, the bubbling mess of emotion trapped inside me cannibalizing itself in the moment. He turned quickly back towards me and whipped his arm out to the side, a hard palm and loud slap crossing my face. I stood a moment, stunned.

"You think I haven't heard this before? You think you're the first bitch to try and tell me how terrible I am after I've said I'm not interested?" he screamed, his mood the proof of my words, even without his admission. "We danced well, but we were no lovers. Now leave me alone," he finished, his sudden shift from anger leading me to believe he felt sorry for his actions. He walked away and turned a corner. I cried that I had fallen for someone as cruel as him—someone who could never allow himself the air of love for fear he might breathe.

A tear echoed from the grave and my mind returned amidst a parade of applause. Diva had finished her routine, and stood in a victorious pose, panting and flaunting her smile for the crowd. Amore rose to his feet for her but stood only to her knees. I did not clap for I had not seen Diva. Instead, I looked only at him looking only at her. I let a flicker of a grin grow under intention as I took to my feet and walked the stage. The announcer named me, the spotlight traced me, and Amore's eyes befell me. I posed, took a deep breath and thought of every waking minute spent dreaming of this moment. The music began.

Each step was a beat of my heart and that of a drum. I kept his eyes to mine and watched them grow hungry as I moved. He saw me now as he did before. I danced from the pain he had left me to the floor he had led me. I screamed passion with every breath and more than words with every move. For words say nothing of dancing. Those feelings are too visceral to speak, too powerful to ignore or squander with thought. The song played as if from me, as if about me. I broke my eyes from his, knowing he watched me still—that I had already won. Music tells a story but dancing makes it true.

The final moment was a shivering calm that haunted the air, as I stood still—the only person in the room. Diva's face turned sour and she crossed her arms. But the crowd didn't look to her now that they saw me. Applause and cheers erupted from all around and the weight on my shoulders melted away. He stood for me, smiling with the perfect teeth I'd so generously left intact. I flicked my hair as I twirled from the spotlight, showered in praise and pride. The next performer took the stage but the audience was mine. I swelled in relief till I felt a hand brush the air from my arm. I turned to see Amore standing before me, extending a hand for me. And like the fool I was, the fool I am followed.

The street was torn from the bulls and muddied by the rain. The bars were satiated with men, full of brew, spewing tales of bravery. But the fight was not my concern nor what concerned me that night. It was a crescent moon that might as well have been blue. My lips relaxed to gasp and I tore a poster from a wall. I looked upon it, stunned. Amore was to dance at the very same competition I was now determined to win. Not for glory, money, or fame, but for the look on his face and the taste of his shame.

But the hurt that held me was born of love and in that I wondered if I would ever allow myself to be his again? If he could see me, and his wrong doing, perhaps we could be happy together. Perhaps we could be in love as we were. I wondered if he had grown and learned the truth of my words to him. I dreamed that he thought of me and shook his fists in rage that he had ever laid a hand on me, or another woman. If I was everything he'd ever wanted, he'd never need anyone else. But, then again, if I was everything he'd ever wanted, I'd have no need to prove it to him.

"I missed you," he whispered, taking the few minutes of time before his routine to address me, not the crowd. "I feel terrible for leaving you."

"Terrible?" I asked timidly, playing the sheep.

"Yes. I've laid awake nights thinking about you; about how foolish I was to leave you," he confessed. When men say everything you want to hear, something has to be wrong.

"And you've changed?" I asked, a glimmer of hope pumping through my veins.

"Yes. A thousand times, yes," he explained, taking my hand in his and holding it to his pounding heart. I looked in his eyes, past the beauty of his face and the promise of his words. I saw there what I had seen before—what he would have me believe so he could believe it too. But the heart that beat for me was dead, as were the words he promised.

He spoke out of a pitiful regret he expected annulled by his return. But he had ruined me. He had taken my heart, given in full, and thrown it aside for a woman who would do the same to him. Whether he understood that—whether he understood me—was irrelevant. Any sign of change would only revisit who he had convinced me he was. In the world I'd lived, that he had shown me, he would say everything right and I would fall captive to his claims. But I was stronger than him for having lost him. And because of that I could see his intent. I cleared my throat, and pushed aside any notion of forgiveness—happily ever after is too much work if you pick an asshole.

"A mind in love," I stated, feeling the shattered love I had carried now fill me with pride. I walked away from him and returned to the floor.

Wind's Blessing

Father always said 'wind brings blessings for garden.' But for me, wind was not a blessing—wind was my escape.

"Take me with you!" I begged, my kite jumping in the wind while I remained planted on the ground. I wanted freedom, like the kite—freedom so I could fly away and see the mountain tops. But father's garden was as near as I had seen mountains—only my dreams were content.

A noise came from the gate, and I quickly pulled on the kite, bringing it down towards me—hoping that father had not seen it. He told me 'the garden is sacred;' he told me 'kites are not.' He had caught me flying my kite in the garden before and become very upset. He warned me against such foolishness. But it made me feel happy and alive—not because I had disobeyed father, but because I was doing what pleased me.

I quickly plucked the kite from the sky and hid it in the laundry basket—safe inside mother's yukata. The basket was full and, for me, lifting it was clumsy. Father looked at me and smiled—picking the basket up and me along with it.

"Emi! How strong you are!" father joked, tickling a laugh from me while carrying me towards the house. "The monster should be scared of you!" he teased, not believing what I had said about monster—but it was real; it visited me.

Father set me down beside the house and patted my back—he had not seen the kite and I was lucky. I stood at his side, reaching for the laundry basket, but he kept it—looking inside for a change of clothes. I bit my lip and trembled. If father found the kite he would be upset with me and I would lose my favorite possession. He pulled out a robe, accidentally knocking mother's yukata on the ground. I gasped and covered my mouth with both hands—surely I had been caught.

"Don't worry, it's still clean," father whispered, winking at me as he placed the garment back inside the basket—fortune had found me, for father did not find the kite. "Where is mother?" he asked, removing his shoes and stepping inside.

"Resting," I replied, looking up at father as he walked towards his bedroom where mother rested. "Should I put away the laundry?" I cried, fearful as father walked away, still carrying the basket.

"No. You may help your mother with dinner," he answered, smiling again as he entered his room. I sulked and gave out a sigh. I could only hope that my kite would not be discovered before I was given a chance at retrieving it. But first, I would be needed for preparing dinner with mother. She would usually have it made already. But, lately, she rested often and left her work for me—it was not like her; she was a strong worker and a good wife.

I scuttled around the kitchen, readying ingredients and preparing the plates. Tonight we would enjoy one soup, three sides—tonjiru, sashimi, gyoza and unagi. Father insisted on plentiful meals, and provided mother and me many things for preparing them. We were a prosperous family, while few in number. Mother had not given more children as father had wanted. But he did not become upset—he was contented with what life had given him.

"Emi!" father screamed, throwing open his bedroom door—clutching my kite in his hand. I trembled and lowered my eyes. "What was this doing with the laundry?"

"Sorry, father."

"Answer me!" he cried, suspecting that I had disobeyed him. "Were you flying your kite in the garden?"

"Yes, father," I whispered, cowering below his bellows.

"The garden is sacred! If you disrespect it, you disrespect me!" he shouted, throwing my kite on the ground. I gasped, seeing it's frame crack. "Finish preparing dinner and then go to your room!" he demanded, storming away. I remained behind, ashamed and afraid.

There was no other place than the garden that I could fly my kite regularly. And it was the only thing that made my days special. I picked up my kite and held it close—sobbing as tears filled my eyes. I would do as father said and finish dinner.

"Emi," the monster groaned, locked in my cabinet. I lay in bed, with the covers pulled over my ears. I peeked out so I could see that I was safe, but still the monster called for me. "Emi, let me out."

"Go away," I exclaimed, hoping that he would leave and let me rest.

"Why is your kite broken?" he asked, fascinated with my kite as always. I called him Fūjin because he only visited me on windy days. He was large, but still fit in small places. He looked like a leopard, but he was fat and walked on two feet. He carried a sack of wind with him and always beckoned that I get my kite and play.

"Father broke it," I replied, telling him what had happened earlier.

"Why?"

"Because I flew it in the garden," I continued, thinking how foolish I had been by disobeying father. "And now it's broken. So I cannot play with you. Now go away," I finished, kicking the cabinet from where I lay in bed. He grumbled as his container shook and stopped talking for a moment.

"I fixed your kite, Emi," he declared, no doubt telling lies so that I would play. But, still, I was curious that he may actually have fixed the kite as he said. I crawled across my bed until I sat beside the cabinet.

"Show me."

"I cannot, unless you let me out," he explained, giving another reason that I should set him free. I frowned and pushed up my chin. I did not know if he was telling the truth, but the idea of having my kite back was tempting enough that I believed him. I reached forward with my shaking hand and unlocked the cabinet. The room was quiet and still.

Suddenly, Fūjin exploded out of his hiding place and flew around the room. I cried out but was silenced by the roar of his wind. It was as though the entire house shook from his mischief, but father did not come and investigate the noise. I crawled back under my covers and pulled them over my head.

"Stop, Fūjin!" I hollered, cowering under my blanket.

"Don't worry little one. I was just showing you that your kite still works," he replied, stopping his commotion and presenting me with my kite—as though it had never been broken at all. I smiled and jumped out of bed, overjoyed that Fūjin had been so kind.

"Thank you Fūjin!" I cried, wrapping my arms around his belly and squeezing. He laughed and patted my back.

"Can we play now?"

"Yes," I replied, realizing that I owed him for fixing my kite. The garden was dark at night, but the stone lantern gave enough light so that we could play. Fūjin took my hand as we walked towards the garden. I was worried about disobeying father again—if he caught me, I don't know what he'd do. But, then again, if he caught me, he would finally believe me about Fūjin.

"Fūjin, what are the mountains like?" I asked, watching the dark figure of my kite glide across the sky—the snow topped mountains appeared blue in the night. I sat on the stone lantern, with my feet dangling over it's side. Fūjin lay on the grass, blowing at the sky so my kite would soar.

"Big."

"But, how do they make you feel?"

"Small."

"I already feel small," I sighed, a flicker of light catching my eye—a lamp was lit in my parent's room.

"Are we caught?" Fūjin asked, rolling away and hiding behind a rock.

"No… it's my mother," I replied, watching the shadow of my father against the wall. He held my mother while she became sick and he whispered good words in her ear. Her medicine was not helping her recover—I worried that she would never get better.

"What's wrong with her?" Fūjin questioned, crawling out from his hiding place so that he could hear me better. He watched my mother as I did, wondering what could be done.

"She's ill."

"What is her sickness?"

"I don't know. Father told me to play when the medicine man visited," I answered, wishing that I had been told the truth. Father said I was young and should not concern myself with kampō. Instead, I should care for mother and smile when she is better. But I could see from the medicine man's face that it was not so simple. I was a child but I did not like being treated as one.

"May I help?"

"No," I whispered, wishing that Fūjin could help her feel better as he did me. "All we may do is pray and hope."

"Then that's what I'll do."

"Me too," I declared, as I watched my kite fall out of the sky and land on my lap. It was late and I needed rest for the day ahead. Even Fūjin appeared tired. But as we crept back inside and passed my parent's room, I heard my father say something that kept me awake all night.

"You have to hold on… for Emi, for me. Life is in you still, no matter what the medicine man said."

"Itadakimasu," father exclaimed, bowing his head at the meal before us.

I remained silent and looked at my noodles without eating. I had not slept at all because I was worried about mother. But father still spoke with me as though she were alright—still lied as though she would get better.

"Why do you not eat?"

"I'm not hungry."

"You need to eat," father said, tapping his chopsticks on the rim of my bowl. I glanced up, keeping my head low. I could not look at him for long without feeling sad. Mother remained in her room—silent and hidden.

"No."

"What?"

"I want to see mother," I stated, my eyes wandering the door my mother was kept behind.

"She's resting," he explained, saying the same thing he had for days. My mother rested all the time—and soon would be at rest. I'd heard father say so himself. I had been awake all night dreading his words—'there is life in you still, no matter what the medicine man said.' And now… I could not face him— I could not face it.

"Does she not want to see me?" I asked, feeling my eyes water, though I fought against them. I had not seen mother for a whole day, and had not been comforted by her company for much longer. But, before I could weep or speak further, mother emerged from her room.

"Emi, I'm ok," she exclaimed, walking slowly over towards us. She sat down and put her arm around me. I opened my mouth wide with surprise. She smiled and I smiled also. Her and father exchanged glances, and I could see that there was more than they would say. He put his hand atop her stomach and whispered in her ear—concerned that she might damage herself by leaving bed.

I decided at that moment what I would do. If they would not give me their knowledge, I could not offer my aid. But, if I solved the trouble on my own, there would be no need for keeping secrets from me. I would wait until dark before flying my kite. And then, when I had drawn Fūjin from his slumber, I would save my family.

"Father says 'wind brings blessings for garden,'" I told Fūjin, as we climbed atop the roof of my house.

"Wind?"

"Yes… that is why he does not want my kite to interfere," I explained, removing a bed sheet from my back and unraveling it. "But, I believe the kite does not interfere — I believe it keeps the wind, and traps it's blessings."

"Then, why have you not brought your kite?" he asked, wondering why I had brought a sheet and rope instead.

"Because, my kite has not been able to capture enough blessings," I exclaimed, fastening the rope on the sheet. Fūjin was confused at first, but quickly understood — I intended on capturing the wind's blessings in my bed sheet. The kite had not been enough on it's own. And, with Fūjin's breath, surely a larger kite could soar.

"Oh. I understand!" Fūjin declared, picking me up and placing me on his back. The sheet fell over my shoulders as I sat upon Fūjin's — staring up at the night sky. The garden seemed small from where we stood — as though we were the mountains. And, as I flapped the sheet, Fūjin blew with all his might.

"Blow more!" I cried, watching the wind fill the fabric as it ballooned and spread. Fūjin's cheeks grew also as he puffed wind into the air. I laughed and cheered, telling Fūjin where he should blow next. "More blessings over there!"

"Yes!"

"And over there! My parents will need them most!" I announced, pointing at my parent's room as the kite lifted us from the rooftop. We flew above the house and the garden, looking down and giggling as the blessings fell. The stone lantern trembled in the breeze and the mountains crumbled by the wind's howl—my plan was working.

"And what of your blessings, Emi?" Fūjin asked, flapping his arms in the sky as we glided through the clouds.

"My family is my blessing," I replied, my arms wrapped safely around Fūjin's neck and shoulders.

"Yes. But you still desire more," he exclaimed, swooping down towards the mountains. The wind whistled past my ears as we descended. Soon, my feet rested on snow atop the mountains I had always dreamed of visiting. A great smile filled my heart as I looked down at my tiny house.

"I don't feel small," I announced, knowing now that the mountains size did not make me small. "I feel happy," I continued, holding Fūjin's hand as we lifted up in the air and returned home. Our flight had been successful, and I could see the blessings soar around the house. My mother would be well again, and our family would be happy—just like father said.

The sun rose after a short sleep. I jumped from bed, overjoyed by the light of the day. But, as my ears awoke, I could hear talking from outside my room. I quickly dressed myself and gave a final prayer at Fūjin's hiding place. "Blessings and thanks for you Fūjin," I whispered, praying that I had been successful and father's warning of flying my kite in the garden was not correct.

"Emi," father stated as I emerged from my room.

"Yes, father," I replied, walking quickly over towards him and mother—sitting beside each other, waiting for me before they would begin breakfast. They frowned at each other, though they gave their best attempt at hiding it from me.

Perhaps I had been wrong by interfering with the blessings—perhaps I had trapped evil spirits and brought a curse upon our house. I trembled where I stood, hoping for words that would put smiles on our faces. But nothing was said for some time. Father and mother ate their breakfast, whispering in secret so that I would not be concerned. I could not eat—I could only sit and wait.

"Eat your food, Emi," mother said, tapping her chopsticks on the rim of my bowl. I frowned and hid my eyes. "What's wrong?"

"I don't want you to die," I exclaimed, expressing my deepest concerns for mother. Father sighed and gave me a stern look. But mother did not. Instead, she laughed and placed her arm around my side.

"Die? Why would I die?" she chuckled, wondering how I had gained such thoughts.

"Because of your illness! Because the medicine man said there was not life in you!" I cried, admitting that I had heard father speak of the medicine man.

"When did you hear that? You were told to do your chores!" father scolded, demanding that I answer for my stolen knowledge.

"Husband," mother exclaimed, placing her arm on father's shoulder so that he would be calm. "She is scared and worried for her mother. Do not add to her problem," she explained, turning her attention away from father. She smiled and pressed her hands on my cheeks. "Emi, I have been ill lately. But I am not dying."

"Then it worked!" I cried, standing up quickly and jumping with joy. "The blessings healed you!"

"Blessings? What are you talking about?"

"The blessings that wind brings to garden! Last night, I trapped them in a kite with Fūjin so that you would be well again!" I explained, telling how Fūjin and I had saved the family; how we had collected blessings at night so that mother would feel better.

Father frowned at my confession for it meant I had disobeyed him once more. But he did not shout. Mother smiled and covered her mouth. She hugged me and I could tell she was very happy that I cared so much for her.

"There is life in you still," I stated, kissing mother on her cheek.

"Yes, there is," she replied, touching her hand to her stomach. She looked at father who was struggling with what he should do. "I was worried too, Emi. But everything's going to be alright—the baby is going to be all right."

"Baby?"

"Soon, you will have a brother or sister," father announced, deciding against anger even though I had disrespected his wishes. I covered my mouth from the surprise and wondered if the blessings had brought with them the good news—a new brother or sister was more than even I had hoped for. And one appearing in mother's stomach overnight was a great blessing indeed.

"I did not know the blessings could do so much," I exclaimed, shaken by the power of the blessings.

"Your mother has been pregnant for some time, Emi. We did not tell you because," father began, until mother shushed him. She opened her eyes wide as though she wished the news of her baby kept secret still—just as the news of her illness had been kept from me.

"But thank you for ridding me of my morning sickness!" mother said, finally admitting the 'morning sickness' that had plagued her. I hugged mother and thanked Fūjin for all he had done. I felt as though I were on the mountain again—smiling from the wind's visit.

STAR

10 years prior

"Even now we can't explain what we see when we look at the sky," I announced, my hands tucked under my head as I lay on my back, looking up.

"Colors have different wavelengths. When light comes in contact with the earth's atmosphere..." my brother, Brian, started to say—missing my point.

"That's not what I meant," I interrupted, stirring my Slurpee to keep the syrup and ice from separating. "It used to be celestially revered, but now... it's just space."

"There's a lot more to space than space. Stuff we can't even see like dark matter or..." Brian explained, taking every opportunity to recite his favorite textbooks.

"Again, not what I meant. And, by the way, we have the same major, remember?"

"Ok... So... are you talking about God?"

"No, I'm talking about stars."

"Why?"

"Because they're the closest thing to an explanation we have. And they're the only thing we see in space."

"Uh... moons, planets, comets, asteroids..."

"Brian... never mind," I sighed, giving up on discussing something outside of what we knew—something that I felt.

We're not alone. And, when I looked up, that was the feeling I couldn't explain.

Day 1

The room was quiet just long enough for me to hear myself think. Brian sat hunched over his screen, watching the coordinates update every few seconds. Everyone else fidgeted or paced—too anxious to keep their bodies from racing along side their minds. But, despite the blistering unrest I'd caused, it was comforting to think I'd actually discovered something.

"Shouldn't this be classified?"

"If we let the people who are able to classify it know about it… then, yeah, it'll be classified," I replied, blowing into Brian's ear to try and pull him away from the screen.

"It's probably a manmade probe or satellite that's malfunctioned, and we witnessed it by chance—there's nothing to worry about," Dennis suggested, flipping through the data printout. He kept a stern expression and a skeptical tone. He was the only member of a SETI organization that didn't want to find anything—too much paperwork.

"I'm not worried about being worried… and it isn't a satellite."

"It's not a satellite according to 'a snapshot from a few hundred million miles away, and your personal opinion,' that is."

"Satellites don't do what this thing's doing. So, like I said, it's not a satellite."

"This thing, and kites wrapped in aluminum foil, are how conspiracy theories start."

"Only if we tell someone," Jan interrupted, raising her voice to an audible level for the first time in weeks.

"We don't have a choice."

"We have a choice."

"Not if we want answers we don't," I muttered, the bureaucracy of discovery resonating in my skull. "Bottom line is that we don't know what it is, and we lack the resources to find out. All we have are theories based on assumptions. And unless we tell someone who can tell us otherwise, those theories are all we'll ever have... right now, that thing is a dot in the sky and nothing more."

"It's a UFO," Jan exclaimed, acting as the angel to contradict Dennis over my shoulder.

"If I **sneeze** hard enough it's a UFO," Dennis grumbled, triple checking the data.

"Look... we don't know what it is and that alone should be enough for us to clue into the possibilities outside of the norm."

"You're right. Now that I think about it, it's probably the mother-ship towing the monolith, balancing on the tip of E.T.'s glowing cock."

"If we keep its existence in this room, then it becomes a conspiracy. But, if we hold onto our balls and go out swinging, we may get the answers we want."

"Or, more likely, the lies we don't."

"That's a risk we're gonna have to take," I insisted, making my decision with or without his consent.

"And why's that?"

"Because it's a risk I'm going to take and you can't stop me."

"I don't see the point of doing anything... It's getting closer to earth, and our telescopes will let us know what it is before any expedition can. So why bother asking anyone if it's just a matter of waiting?" Jan mumbled, close enough to me that I could actually understand what she said.

"Because, someone else may already know about it."

"And you think they'll just welcome us into their club? Not likely," Dennis complained, adjusting his glasses to rub his eyes. "I've seen stats like this in the past. But when I called them in they either disappeared or were accounted for by computer error."

"You've seen stats exactly like this?"

"Not exactly," he replied, as Brian stood up slowly from his chair—breaking his silence with a loud gasp.

"Holy shit!" he screamed, plunging his face so close to the monitor that he bumped his nose. We all crowded around him to look at the screen as the coordinates refreshed. Only, this time, they didn't change.

"What is it?" Jan yelped, jumping behind us to see over our shoulders. Dennis and I stood with our mouths open as Brian started to laugh, grabbing the back of his head with both hands as he paced around the room. "What is it?" Jan asked again, squinting to try and see what all the fuss was about.

"It stopped," I exclaimed, barely believing it myself. "It stopped moving."

Day 3

"I really don't like public speaking," Brian said, bobbing back and forth as we stood to the side of the stage—waiting for our cue.

"You'll be fine," I replied, glancing out over the waves of reporters and camera crews.

"Noooo… I don't think so. Cause if I'll be fine, that means I'll be ok, and I am not ok. No, definitely not ok."

"Ok… Remember when we were in college?"

"No, I've repressed most of it."

"But do you remember taking the telescope to the top of the dorm?"

"I remember the telescope getting thrown off the top of the dorm."

"Block that part of the memory. Or even better, think about those assholes watching us now."

"Yeah… uh… that just… made it worse," he babbled, wiping away a bead of sweat rolling down his forehead.

"Ok, then just let me do the talking," I replied, as the final seconds of our anonymity faded away.

"So, here they are—the two men responsible for discovering STAR," the speaker announced, as everyone's focus came to rest on Brian and myself. I swallowed hard and smiled big. Brian waved anxiously as he followed my lead towards the bushel of microphones at center stage.

"Hi," I exclaimed, emulating every game show host I'd ever seen. "My name is William Stewart and this is my brother Bri…"

"Hi," Brian interrupted, cutting off his own introduction.

"And we were the first people to see STAR," I finished, saying exactly what I'd been instructed to say before answering any questions. I let the photographers get a few preliminary shots of us before we fainted from the pressure—Brian looked like he was gonna hurl. "So yeah... we'll take questions now."

"What led to STAR's discovery?" the reporter, who had been delegated first in line, asked.

"It's trajectory changed as it passed by Jupiter. We speculate that this was to avoid Jupiter's magnetic field," I explained, keeping it as laymen's as I could in accordance with the networks instructions—less science meant more funding for the sciences. "In addition to its varying trajectory, we noticed it 'blinking' at consistent intervals."

"What do you mean 'blinking?'"

"It emits high levels of light and radiation that pulse, decline, and repeat every ten seconds."

"What does the STAR acronym stand for? And why did you name it that?"

"Sidereal Transient Anomalous Radiant. And we named it that because we had initially mistaken it for a star, until we calculated it's location relative to other stars."

"What is it?"

"We don't know."

"Is it a UFO?"

"Well, it's in space, so it's not really flying... but it's defiantly a UO."

"Has it made any attempt to contact earth? Or have its emissions or presence had any effects here on earth?"

"There has been no attempt at contact—we don't even know if it knows we're here. Or for that matter, whether or not it's capable of affecting us beyond our simply being aware of its presence."

"You reported that, shortly after discovering STAR it came to a stop and has since remained motionless, is that correct?"

"Yes. It came to a complete, unprovoked stop and has not moved whatsoever since."

"Immediately after that took place, you disregarded your established protocols and contacted a small network of 'UFO enthusiast websites,' is that correct?"

"Yes."

"Why?"

"Because at that point we were positive this was more than a computing error or explainable phenomena… we leaked its existence, so that nothing could be done to conceal its existence."

"Are you saying you anticipated it would be kept secret?"

"I don't know. But it wasn't a chance I was willing to take."

"What gave you the right to decide whether or not the public was made aware?"

"Freedom of speech."

"There have been mass reports of hysteria in numerous parts of the world in conjunction with widespread religious outcry against the validity of STAR. Do you feel unsubstantiated claims warrant genuine human suffering?"

"We haven't claimed anything more than its existence. However, its existence suggests it to be extra terrestrial or a creation thereof. If someone suffers as a result of that knowledge, it is their compulsion to do so."

"Based on what's known about STAR, what's the most likely explanation for 'what it is' and 'why it's here?'"

"There isn't a 'most likely explanation' for either one of those questions—there's only conjecture. It could be completely coincidental or completely intentional—we simply don't know."

"Could it be hostile?"

"It's possible."

"Does its behavior suggest hostility?"

"We haven't observed any behavior… it just is," I explained, getting the impression that telling the truth came second to calming people's nerves. "I can't tell you 'why it's here,' 'what it is,' 'what it will do next,' or anything beyond the fact that my brother and I looked up and saw something that wasn't like anything else in the sky."

Brian swallowed hard, having retreated a few steps behind me—letting the reporters and journalists address me alone. As I glanced over, I could see the same apprehensive confusion in him that there was in the crowd. I gave an exasperated sigh away from the microphone, realizing the simple truth—we knew more about STAR than anyone.

Day 6

"'Take your bogus bullshit claims and shove them up your godless nerd ass,'" Brian said, reading one of many hate-emails we'd received. It was just like us to stay on our computers despite the hotel we were in having one of the largest indoor pools in the world.

"What a troubled young man," I replied, instant messaging with Jan, still trapped at work—her and Dennis having managed to dodge the recent barrage of media attention.

"He then goes on to tell me that things stop moving all the time, like my 'ability to get laid' for example," Brian continued. "How do you think he knows that?"

"Dude, he's just ripping on you cause he's confused—don't' worry about it," I exclaimed, sipping my free latte—from just one of many organizations generous enough to donate to our existence.

"How are you staying so calm through all of this?"

"I don't know… I just feel good," I said, scanning over Jan's message. "Apparently, Dennis has been bragging about knowing us."

"Think he'll give us a raise?"

"I think anyone who contributes to figuring out what's going on will get a raise," I stated, turning up the TV.

"The man was selling the DVD's on eBay that he claimed were 'burnt by STAR from outer space.' His is just one of many scams trying to capitalize on the still unexplained phenomena of STAR," a reporter explained, showing footage of every kind of fanatic running amuck.

"I wonder if he was telling the truth," Brian stated, closing his laptop to look at the TV.

"Are you kidding?"

"I don't know… I mean, it hasn't tried to contact us or anything—no transmissions, no signals, not even a wave 'hello'… it's just sitting there."

"It's still pulsating."

"Yeah, and so do un-programmed-clocks."

"I want something to happen as much as everyone else, but we don't know whether or not 'nothing happening' means 'something's happening.'"

"Thanks for the paradox, Fermi."

"Well, just think about it… It could be observing us or our reactions to it. It could be communicating with wherever it came from or maybe a ship that launched it. Hell, maybe it's just taking a nap."

"Yeah, I know… it could be a Von Neumann Probe, or an interstellar creature, or a rift in the fabric of time, or, you know, maybe it's just a global glitch in Windows. But, frankly, I think sitting around trying to guess what it is, is just a waste of time."

"Yeah, but what else are we gonna do?"

"Until it does something we can detect, I think it's more important to examine what's changing on earth. I'd say it's entirely possible that this thing is doing something right now — regardless of whether or not we have any idea of what that is."

Day 14

"Ladies and Gentlemen, please give a big round of applause for William and Brian Stewart," the late night show host announced, pointing to the side of the stage as we were cued to walk on. The audience clapped loudly and cheered enthusiastically — perhaps expecting some news, or anything except more of the same — 14 days and counting, and STAR had yet to change, or do, anything. "Welcome to the show."

"Thanks, it's great to be here," I stated, my brother and I taking a seat next to the host, Ray.

"So, you two are brothers, right?"

"Yeah, came out of the same mother and everything."

"And you've been into astronomy your whole lives?"

"Yep. As kids we wanted to manufacture kaleidoscopes until we realized that the universe was way ahead of us."

"Did you ever expect to find anything like this?"

"No, never. It's been really amazing."

"Now what does Sidereal Transient Anomalous Radiant mean exactly?"

"Ha, yeah… that means that we determined it's position relative to other stars; that it's only been here for a short time; it's an anomaly; and it's emitting a great deal of light. But, hopefully, we'll have some sort of contact with it and be able to rename it accordingly when, or if, that happens."

"Do you think it will try to contact us?"

"I really can't say… I hope so, but… there's no way to know."

"Now, NASA recently announced the 'Frontier' which is a manned voyage that will launch in one week and, eventually, rendezvous with STAR. What do you think about that?"

"I think… it's zealous, but that's not necessarily a bad thing. It could be exactly what STAR is waiting for—you know, for us to try and contact it. Or, it could be perceived negatively."

"What do you mean negatively?"

"Well… we don't know what STAR is yet, why it's here, or really anything about it. And from it's perspective, it may look at us with equal ignorance and confusion. So, just as we may have initially perceived it to be hostile, so too could it make that assumption of us."

"Hmm… very interesting stuff. We'll be back with more about STAR after the break," Ray exclaimed, as they cut to a commercial break. He leaned in towards us as Brian took this opportunity to squeegee the nervous sweat pouring down his forehead. "So, honestly guys, should I be building a bomb shelter, or what?" Ray whispered.

"Well… if it did come all this way to kill us, it'll succeed. But, frankly, I'm more concerned about us than I am about it."

Day 21

"What's it doing now?"

"It's blinking," Brian replied, watching the 24-hour STAR broadcast on his cell phone.

We sat at a hotel bar in Chofu Japan—completely awake at three in the morning. We were scheduled to give a brief speech at the JAXA headquarters, no doubt to receive more questions about why STAR hasn't done anything but blink.

"What about now," I asked, taking a long sip of beer and swishing it around in my mouth.

"It's still blinking," Brian muttered, as the server dropped off his margarita, with extra mini-swords and umbrellas.

"What do you think's going through their minds?"

"Who? The astronauts?"

"Yeah… they've certainly got a while to think about what to say when they get there," I continued, watching the video of the Frontier's launch from earlier this morning. Six people had been selected to travel further from the earth's surface than any man has dared.

"Well, they're still refueling right now, so they're probably worried about not blowing themselves up."

"Yeah... I'm worried about that too."

"You think they will?"

"No... I meant us... on earth."

"Huh?"

"I read yesterday that 27 members of a radical cult died in a fire started by their attempts to manufacture a rocket that would take them to STAR. When questioned about it, one of the surviving, severely burned members, said: 'We must stop it—it will steal the light away.'"

"Weirdo."

"Earlier this morning, seven kids were gunned down by a student who claimed to be 'acting out STAR's will.'"

"Well, I prefer to get my fill of senseless killing playing videogames not watching the news," Brian stated, laughing nervously.

"Yeah... me too."

"Well... what's your point? I mean, we didn't make those things happen."

"No, I know," I sighed, finishing my beer. "But it got me thinking."

"About?"

"Maybe there's a reason STAR stopped."

Day 27

"Why would people send flowers?" Brian asked, moving bouquet after bouquet away from his workspace.

"Just be happy you didn't get any underwear like I did," I exclaimed, throwing the envelope containing some woman's panties into the garbage can—Jan eyed me, happy to see me dispose of them. "So... did we miss anything?"

"No. While you two were out having a good time, we've been doing your jobs," Dennis bitched.

"It's no trouble, we haven't really had much to do lately," Jan stated, tapping a mound of Nerds into her palm. "What have you guys been doing?"

"Bullshit mostly," I laughed, happy to be home and away from the fake smiles and simple answers. "Apparently, curiosity and impatience are something all cultures share."

"Did... you meet any girls?" Jan asked, too nervous to look at me while she said it.

"No," I laughed, as Dennis answered a call on the central line. His face turning from disgruntled to distraught. "What is it?"

"Turn on the TV," he cried, pointing to the remote beside me. I picked it up and hit the power button—watching a news broadcast slowly fade onto the screen.

"We do not know why, or whether or not the Frontier will be called back," the newscaster explained, the title below her reading 'STAR leaves.'

"Oh shit," Brian groaned, letting his mouth hang open as we all stared in disbelief at the screen.

"As of thirty minutes ago, STAR's location changed, and it's trajectory became one heading away from earth. This comes some 27 days and 7 hours after its initial discovery by William and Brian Stewart."

An image flashed on the screen of the blinking dot in the sky, moving from its once fixed position. Everyone stayed silent, and I could sympathize with the disappointment the world would feel. We knew now there was something out there. But knowing wasn't enough—we were still alone.

Lemmings

The horizon was slung across the ocean. The cliff side above us blocked out the sky, letting the artificial lighting take its place. A brigade of photographers, activists, socialites and protesters all squabbled around me as I used the stem of my sunglasses to stir my thermos full of apple cider. Allie had started giggling uncontrollably while my worst enemy, Peter, tried to set up a net to catch the soon to be dead rodents.

"It's like an existential moment. Only it's surreal," Allie laughed, appreciating the moment a little more than she was supposed to—particularly since it was at my expense.

"How can people be this," I muttered, searching my mind for something to justify their… "Preposterous," I finished, turning back to the loving embrace of my thermos.

"Like, I'll wake up tomorrow and it'll be like this never happened. And the only proof I'll have is the face you make when I bring it up," she chuckled, coming in and out of laughter with each buffoon that passed us by. The activists managed to set up the net but the protesters were using their signs to hack it back down—the photographers were shitting themselves.

"This will be the urban myth about my life that people will plunder me for answers about. I will spend the rest of my days, justifying this moment," I explained, speaking as though hearing it, and thus completely destroying myself, could help the situation. "Can I use your last name from now on?"

"Dona, you'll be fine. This will let everyone know about you and how great you are," she stated, as reassuringly as the stampede's siren would allow. It was official—any second, hundreds of four-legged-kamikaze-rats were going to plunge to their deaths and the animals below, debating their lives. "After all, things could be worse."

"How?"

"We could be like them," she wheezed, just before collapsing in a full belly laugh from the sight of lemmings pouring over the side of the cliff—show time. I dropped my head into my hand and my mouth to the thermos. It was best I got drunk before any more memory landmarks could hit.

The event I had invented, supported and whole-heartedly-backed was, as of now—fucked. The lemmings fell off the cliff, taking their lives and stacking their bodies on my name. I'd had time to cry over them; trust me, they're better off dead. I looked on apathetically, hoping nobody was filming me yet. The protesters cheered, the activists cried, the photographers feasted and everybody else watched, humbled by the magnificent display of… preposterousness.

Three weeks earlier…

"I should host a banquet on the beach," I exclaimed, lowering the paper from my eyes to see Allie eyeing me. "What?"

"A banquet?" she questioned, raising a brow which caused her eye under the other brow to squint. "Why would you wanna do that?"

"Because, the paper said that because of the shark attacks, people have stopped going to the beach and the town's tourism is suffering because of it," I explained, trying to take time between words to examine the idea before she'd ask me to explain it.

"Uh... so?"

"So tourism can be a big deal for small towns. It's been bad enough with so many people getting hurt without it negatively affecting the economy too," I finished, double dipping my biscotti as Allie watched me, giving the look she gave when she didn't know whether to laugh or cry.

"And a banquet would diversify the shark's diet?"

"Shut up," I mumbled, a few crumbs shooting out of my mouth as I chewed my cookie. "I know I'd get good press for it too. A big, glamorous bash in a quaint little town—it's perfect."

"Quaint? Just because it's small doesn't make it quaint."

"It's old too, so it's probably quaint," I replied, defending my idea of two minutes as though it were my life's work.

"Whatever. Just look before you leap this time," she muttered, flipping through the paper.

"What's that supposed to mean?"

"You know exactly what that means. You just don't like that I said it," she announced, referring to an event I'd hosted a year earlier to try and raise money for a country that no longer existed.

"It was a typo!" I cried, now slamming my biscotti into my coffee. "And it's not like the fact that it didn't exist affected how much money I earned on it's behalf," I huffed, saying so not so much to prove a point as to pat my ego on the back.

"You're right. Maybe Peter Pan could use a sponsor too," she laughed, somehow able to read an article while carrying on a conversation with me—I hated it when she did that. I picked up the paper again and angrily fluffed it flat. She'd see—this was a great idea.

"I love it," Jonathan stated, as I walked with him to get a new coffee before the one he had ran dry. "What better way to defy nature than by throwing a party on it's doorstep? And it's for the community too!"

"I know. I figure that the press for the event will help negate the diminishing tourism rate and potentially increase it too," I explained, having made the necessary phone calls on my way to Jonathan's office to see if the idea were plausible. "I mean that poor village. What the hell are so many sharks doing there anyway?"

"Global warming, honey—the whole world's trying to find a new home," he exclaimed, as we turned the corner, past the line leading around it. We walked halfway to the front of the line before Jonathan recognized someone. "Jeffrey!" he shrieked, not only Jeffrey turning to look at him but everyone else as well. Jonathan raised his cup and shook it lightly back and forth. Jeffrey nodded and sighed with relief that today was not his turn on the guillotine. "But if it were me, I would have picked someplace warmer—I mean don't get me wrong, Canada has great pot and everything but... I mean how do you accessorize a snow suit?"

"Maybe you'd like to come along and start the trend?" I teased, knowing well that Jonathan never left the office, let alone New York. "What kind of press could you coax?" I asked as we walked to a table while waiting for Jonathan's coffee.

"Well... it's not for me to say. But, you can likely hope for highlights across the board. It all depends on how you want to spin it," he continued, glancing at Jeffrey who was approaching with his coffee. "Were you thinking fun-killer or gaudy-party?" he asked, drawing the line between fundraiser and fun. Jeffrey walked up to us and placed Jonathan's coffee on the table. He then backed away without saying a word.

"Nobody's gonna spend the money to fly there just to spend money," I declared, thoughts of elegance and pertinence flooding to mind.

"Since when have people cared about the price of a good party? I say bleed em dry and make them thank you for it," he exclaimed, taking a long, lustful gulp of his coffee.

"But who would I be raising money for?" I wondered as I asked the question aloud.

"Any of those shark attack victims survive?"

"I think so... oh my god!" I shrieked, an idea's-spark sparking my yelp. "I could stay with one of the victims and add meat to the story!"

"Ooooo... city girl, small town, big heart. Are you really that bored?" he joked, completely serious.

"At least I'm thinking about other people for my pet-projects... I wonder if Allie will go for it?"

"You wanna take your girlfriend to a middle-of-nowhere hole to live with the commoners? Haven't enough people been killed in those types of situations?" Jonathan gasped, a glimmer in his eye telling me that that was the best way of getting press.

"If this were ten years ago I'd be worried; if it were twenty years ago I'd be afraid. But, as it stands, I'm excited," I declared, already tasting the salty sea air.

"What the hell is that smell?" Allie coughed, covering her mouth as we stood along the rocky sea wall staring out to the ocean.

"Where's the damn beach?" I growled, triple wrapping my scarf around my neck.

"Dona, wake up—this is the beach," Allie replied, picking up a stick to poke a nearby stack of rotting rodent carcasses. "Are these hamsters?"

"This can not be the beach. A beach is… it's not ugly and it doesn't smell like whatever the hell those things are!" I whined, a bubble of stress ballooning in my head, giving me a migraine.

"A beach is where a body of water meets land. Are you telling me you didn't even bother to check what kind of shoreline they had?"

"The paper said they had a beach!" I yelled, my knee-high-boots and three inch heels keeping me at a snails pace as I walked over the rocks. "What kind of psycho tourist would want to come here to vacation anyway?"

"We could totally die right now and no one would know," Allie laughed, skewering one of the hamsterish corpses and flinging it out so sea.

"I feel like a fucking mummy the way I'm walking," I bitched, my hands fully extended to try and keep my balance as we made our way back to the car. "Shit!" I cried, frantically flinging my arms in circles as my heel snapped out from under me. I was going down so I grabbed onto for Allie for support, inadvertently taking her along with me.

"Bitch!" Allie snapped, rubbing her ass before slapping my arm.

"I'm sorry!" I hissed, pushing myself up from the rocky, muddy, seaweed-swallowed ground—I was beginning to think asking stupid questions was a better idea than being stupid. I hadn't thought this through.

"Hi, is this the McLaughlin residence?" I asked, out of breath from heaving my luggage from the car. The woman who had answered the door glared at me a moment before nodding. Allie was trudging up to the house with a suitcase slung over her shoulder—showing off her rugged nature for the small-town folks.

"Are you Dona Chatterton?" a young woman exclaimed, poking her head in the doorway. She was the kind of small town beautiful that could bring a city to it's knees—I stared at her, stunned for a moment. I suppose living in the city had made me forget there are things worth seeing elsewhere.

"Yes. Are you Anise?" I replied, grinning largely with the hope that it would break the ice-cold-stare of the woman who had answered the door—likely Anise's mother, and from the looks of it, her guard dog too. "And this is Allie," I continued, giving a slight gesture to my side as Allie came to a stand still.

"How's it going?" she cheerily remarked, extending her hand to give a nice firm handshake to Anise and her mother. "You guys have got some wicked cool scenery around here," she stated, diving right into her uncouth manner of introduction. The mother released the door and sunk back into the house, leaving Anise to address her guests.

"Thanks. Come on in," she said, pushing aside a few stacks of boots and shoes obscuring the entranceway. "I don't know if you've eaten already but dinner will be ready soon."

"Yeah, that'd be awesome," Allie chirped, lightly kicking my foot with hers to remind me that people remove their shoes when entering a house in Canada. I cooperated, and popped off the dirty old pair of sneakers I'd slapped on to replace my recently ruined boots. "How's the bite doing?"

"Doesn't hurt anymore; just hurts to look at," Anise laughed, leading us behind a stairway. The house wasn't decorated as much as it had pictures and heirlooms strewn about—I was right, this town was quaint. "This is where you'll be staying—there's only one bed so I'll leave it up to you two to decide who gets it. But there's a good air-mattress for whoever gets shafted," Anise explained, seemingly ignorant of my relationship with Allie. But I saw no need to complicate our accommodations or the time spent here by informing her.

"This is great. Thanks again," I stated, as Allie and I simultaneously dropped our bags onto the bed. She gave me a half-glare to signify that she was entitled to the bed for having come along.

"Don't mention it. I'm glad to have you—I've read every article you've written," she gleamed, her small town devotion to what I considered a city staple, leaving me momentarily speechless.

"Wow… I didn't know they distributed the magazine up here," I exclaimed, being honest enough to make myself sound as stupid as what I'd said was.

"Ha ha… we're not as secluded as you might think," she laughed, clearly accustomed to outsider misconceptions.

"Don't mind her. We've seen everything except how out of place we can be outside of the city," Allie said, speaking not only of my worldly-ineptitude but hers as well. I blushed, realizing my big mouth wasn't around the big apple anymore.

"Ah-nease!" her mother bellowed, breaking our discussion. "Din-her!"

"And don't mind her," Anise, whispered. "She doesn't hate you, she just doesn't like strangers," she finished, doing her best to reassure Allie and me that her mother had no plans to murder us in our sleep. I remained skeptical.

"How many days is it now without a Starbuck's?" Jonathan joked, being sure to sip extra loud to make me jealous.

"Shut up," I grumbled, doing my best to stay calm for the few moments I had him on the phone. *"Ok, first of all—I'm fucked."*

"That doesn't affect me, right?"

"There's no beach. It's just a bunch of rocks and seaweed."

"Didn't the paper say there was a beach?"

"Don't even get me started on that," I groaned, double checking the address of the lemming hunter I was tracking, as I blindly stumbled the town. *"The dropping tourism rate is because of the danger the sharks pose to people who come here to fish—not sunbathe."*

"O... k..."

"Also, the town is apparently suffering from some sort of lemming pandemic."

"Like, the videogame?"

"No... like the wannabe-hamster-sons-a-bitches that have set out to destroy my life," I exclaimed, becoming increasingly aggravated that I'd gotten myself lost in such a small town.

"Dona, start from the start."

"Lemmings are not supposed to live around these parts. But, for whatever reason, it's swarming with them. Some people think the reason the sharks have been hanging around the shore is to eat the lemmings who fall into the water."

"Any chance they'll just run off a cliff before the banquet?"

"As it turns out, that's a myth. Lemmings don't commit suicide. That's something Disney made up," I explained, rubbing my head as the stuff I was saying was actually true. *"But, ironically, the guy in town who's been hired to control the lemming population disposes of them by dumping them off the rocks and into the ocean."*

"And you're upset about the way he's killing them?"

"No, I'm upset because the one place I managed to secure, that looks even half decent to host the banquet, also happens to be under the cliff that the lemming killer uses to dispose of his prey," I muttered, doing my best to juggle my cell phone with the crudely drawn map Anise had given me. "I'm on my way to meet him now and try to convince him to move the killing field over. But, even if he does, I'm still gonna have drones of rodent corpses washing up all evening!"

"This is why I don't leave the city."

"Jonathan, what do I do? Should I cancel the banquet?"

"It's less than a week away. If you cancel it now it had better be because you're dying not because some rats are," he said, doing his best to keep from laughing. "If it's any consolation, I got you the press you wanted."

"Great, more people to photograph what an idiot I am," I exclaimed, as I double checked the address in my hand with the one tacked against a run down shack. "Start believing in God so you can pray for me."

"I'll try to schedule it in."

"And I'll call you after it hits," I muttered, hanging up and clearing my throat to start kissing some major ass. But, just as I extended my hand to knock on the door, it burst open and a rather angry man threw someone out onto the street beside me.

"Yew can shuv et up yer arse!" the lemming killer screamed, pointing angrily down at the man he'd thrown, who I came to realize, I recognized—Peter, my (and many people's) worst enemy. "Chatterton?" the lemming killer inquired, turning his attention and mood towards me.

"Y... yes," I stuttered, looking away from Peter as he slowly stood up.

"Ey'm knot chengin' enyting!" he yelled, slamming the door in my now terrified face. I winced, feeling my head explode as I turned slowly away from the door.

"Murderer!" Peter cried, wiping some of the mud from his coat.

"What the fuck Peter!?" I exploded, using my purse to bludgeon him. "What the hell are you doing here?"

"I'm here to stop that asshole from killing any more lemmings. What are you doing here?" he replied, fending off my barrage of purse swinging.

"The same thing until you fucked it up!"

"Since when do you give a shit about any animal you can't wear?" he smugly exclaimed, after I'd stopped hitting him for fear of damaging my bag.

"It doesn't matter. How are you going to stop him?" I demanded, deciding to forgo murdering him as long as we were on the same track.

"Well, he won't listen to anything I have to say about animal rights," he explained, watching my eyes carefully in case his landslide of bullshit sent them rolling. "So it looks like I'm going to have to set up a net to catch the lemmings when he throws them off the cliff."

"What!?" I shrieked, the very thought of Peter catching lemmings under a cliff proving enough to push me over the edge. "That's a joke, right?"

"What's it to you?"

"I... I," I tried to say, in limbo between recognizable emotions. It was just like Peter to do this. He was one of those psychopath activists who, rather than presenting his opinion and acting on its behalf, chose to push his opinion on others and act like a child. I never forgave him for organizing a protest at a fundraiser I'd thrown, or for throwing paint at the guests he presumed immoral. Who fucking cares *if some of the rations distributed to third world countries were packaged in containers that could potentially harm the wildlife? Sorry laughter, tears win this time.*

"And now he wants to try and net them where the banquets set to be!" I blubbered, using Allies shoulder as a hanky—I bought her the shirt, she should have known to expect this.

"It's not that bad," she replied reassuringly. "It's free entertainment for the guests. Plus the sharks seem to like eating rodents, so maybe they'll get Peter too."

"All I wanted to do was help and now everything's fucked!" I whined, thrashing my hands about in between sessions of shoulder time. "And don't give me that 'parties are to change as good-intentions are to war' crap," I whimpered, pre-empting Allie's disdain of how I tried to be charitable.

"Just because you know what I'm going to say, doesn't mean that I said it," she replied, doing her best to disregard my emotional crap, stinking up my thoughts.

"No. But just because you didn't say it doesn't mean you didn't want to," I bitched, being a bitch. "Why don't you just do what you usually do and shit on me when work isn't working out?"

"That's as good a last straw as any," she exclaimed, pushing me off her shoulder. "Dona, when it comes to helping people, you have a big heart and a tiny brain. It's wonderful that you wanted to help this town when you heard it was going through a rough time. But how in the hell would a banquet help the town other than to have it paraded as a charity case in front of a bunch of snooty socialites?"

"Because those snooty socialites are people who can afford to make a difference," I stated defensively. "Do you resent everything I've done to try and make a difference?"

"No, I respect and love you so much for trying to make a difference," she exclaimed, lingering in sincerity for a moment before the but. "But... money won't make a difference here and neither will bringing people with money. All they're gonna do is enjoy the party, get drunk, look down on the town and toss a handful of change to feel like they've done some good."

"And how haven't they done some good?"

"They did what was expected of them—what all people expect of the rich: to give back, not necessarily get involved," she continued, able to keep her voice calm through and through. "It's the status quo of doing good. And I just hate to see you throw so much into a cause that'll result in little more than satisfying the upper classes conscience."

"That's an overstatement and way too simplisti..."

"I'm not talking about every fundraiser you've thrown, Dona. I'm talking about this one."

"So what? You think I should just cancel the banquet?"

"No. I think it was a nice thought. One that, unfortunately, you followed through with and are now obligated to follow through with," she concluded, able to work me out of a bad mood without breaking a sweat—I think she did it just to say she could. "But I do think you need to give the money earned to a cause other than advertising for tourism."

"Yeah..." I sighed, feeling the 'guilty tears' billow where the 'feeling sorry for myself tears' left off. When you're wrong a lot you get pretty good at admitting when you're wrong—otherwise you end up without any friends. "I'm such an asshole."

"Yeah, you are. But you're my asshole, so I kind of have to put up with your shit," she joked, kissing me on the nose.

"Not all people who give money are..."

"I know, and you know I know. Now, are we gonna have make-up sex or what?"

"I brought you something," Anise chirped, removing a thermos from her bag. "I know you have drinks here but this'll give you something more than a hangover," she chuckled, as the heat lamps and artificial lighting kicked in... such a sweet girl.

"Thank you," I exclaimed, tucking the thermos under my arm and giving her a hug. "Your mother gonna make an appearance?"

"She doesn't feel comfortable in crowded places," Anise replied, either telling the truth or politely phrasing a lie.

"Well, I'll have them pack her a plate anyways," I stated, a crowd bearing picketed signs and pissed-off looks approaching the site. "Oh shit... if you'll excuse me," I grumbled, leaving Anise with Allie as I went to deal with the riffraff. "Ok, here's the deal. You may not step onto dry land—this area has been reserved for a private party. Your failure to comply with what I've just said will result in your removal from the premises. Do I make myself clear?"

"Are you Dona Chatterton?" one of the protesters asked.

"Yeah... where's Peter, I want to make sure he's clear on the rules."

"I assume he'll be here soon but... we're not with him."

"Say what?"

"We're here to protest his attempt to save the lemmings. They're not native to this part of the world and because of that they pose a threat to the ecosystem—perpetuating their lives endangers the environmental equilibrium and puts other species at risk," he informed me, every word spreading the grin on my face. Jonathan must have found God.

"In that case, can I get you anything to drink?"

"Come on sharks, where are you?" Allie groaned, swirling her wine while watching Peter fumble a lemming like a football—the environmental protesters acting as the opposing fans who cheered every time he made a mistake.

"This cider was worth the trip alone," I exclaimed, my mood picking up even faster than my buzz.

"Anise seems to be having a good time," Allie laughed, looking back at Anise showing off her scar to the photographers and socialites.

"You know... the environmentalists said that the lemmings are posing a threat to the ecosystem," I explained, thinking aloud.

"Because they attract idiots like Peter?"

"Touché," I said, pulling out my cell phone to call Jonathan—I'd told him I'd call after it hit. "I figured out who to give the money to."

"Who?"

"The lemming killer," I stated, raising the phone to my ear along side my sweet words of revenge against Peter **and** for the better good. "That way he can slaughter every last one of the little fuckers."

"Ha ha... when you put it that way I can almost see where Peter's coming from."

"Tell me you love me," Jonathan exclaimed, answering the phone the way he always did when he thought I was calling with bad news.

"Not this time."

"Oh? How goes the banquet?"

"Great"

"My God… do my ears deceive me?"

"No, I do," I laughed, taking a large gulp of my cider. "It's a shit show, but it turns out that it's better than what I'd planned."

"I assume your soon-to-be-written article will make what you just said sensible?"

"About that… what's the magazine's stance on short stories?"

"We're… not against them."

"Glad to hear it."

"What's all the noise about?"

"Oh, you need to see this to believe it," I chuckled, my eyes fixated on the war between the animal activists and the environmentalists. "Don't worry, there'll be plenty of pictures," I finished, hanging up and turning my attention back to Allie as I came to realize Peter was an alright guy after all. But, like me, he had thrown himself off a cliff trying to make a difference.

Children of Wrath

Samantha threw another piece of wood onto the fire and returned to her daughter's side. She pulled her close and made sure the blanket covered every inch of her. The cold was worse this year than that before.

"Mommy?" Adrian said, her voice a note above the wind.

"Yes, darling?"

"Will I go to school this year?"

"Of course you will," she lied. "You'll see all your friends again and have a great time."

"Will Daddy be there?"

"No, sweetie... Daddy went away."

"When will he be home?"

"I don't know... I don't know," Samantha muttered, her mind drifting from her daughter's side to the unknown fate of her husband. So many died she could not imagine him alive. But she stopped herself from thinking of him and stayed strong for her daughter. The night echoed a distant crash and Adrian clasped her mother, afraid.

"What was that?"

"Don't worry. We're safe here," she stated reassuringly. The broken home around them provided little shelter or hope. But they were more fortunate than most as the rest were dead.

Samantha felt a chill having nothing to do with the cold—their supply of wood was dwindling and they could not afford to break the walls around them. "Mommy has to gather supplies," she told her daughter. "You remember what to do, don't you?"

"Yes."

"Tell me so I know you know."

"Stay hidden and don't come out unless you say so," Adrian said, not fully understanding her mother's rules but obeying them all the same.

"Very good," Samantha stated, bundling herself up for what she hoped to be a short journey. She made sure Adrian was well hidden before she stepped outside the shelter.

The sun was buried by eternal clouds—created on the last day. The streets were cluttered with rusted cars and broken homes. Snowflakes and ash lingered in the tender, brooding hands of the wind—falling one by one to join the dead on earth. Samantha hobbled on her bad leg that had broken, and healed, fighting to survive. Now it served as a hard reminder of better days that would never return. She tossed through rubble, saving bits of wood and paper to take back with her. On occasion she would find remnants of storage providing food enough to get by but not count on. However, this day, there was no such luck.

She thought to herself about their supplies, about how everyday she had to travel further and further from the shelter to get them. Her eyes fell on the black shaded ruins of skyscrapers scrapped by the sky. She had not been to the city since it happened, but she could hear the war continue to wage. Even after tomorrow was ruined, people still fought each other today… her husband… when she was not with her daughter, he came to her side and filled her heart. But he was dead. He had to be. She could not live with the hope of seeing him again if she hoped to see her daughter grow—it was their life now; nothing mattered but that.

She heaved a torn backpack onto her shoulder and looked through what she'd collected—it wasn't enough. Her stomach growled and she tucked her hands into her pockets to warm them again. She would have to stay into the night to gather more wood. Her lip trembled and her chin shook—she had learned to be strong; she had to, for her daughter. But it wasn't long ago that every care in her life was of the utmost irrelevance. It wasn't long ago that food was plentiful, shelter was assumed and life was assured… value is measured by need, not desire. And, now, man's desire was no more than shattered remnants to be picked through by the needy. Samantha collapsed to the ground and sobbed—releasing the pain that tore at her soul no matter what face she wore or what lie she told. Her tears cooled her face as her echoes died into the barren abyss.

She wanted nothing more than for her daughter to grow up and enjoy what every child deserves—a childhood: if not one of laughter and delight than at least one free of torment and misery. Instead, Adrian was left to cower in a desolate wasteland with no understanding of reality but for the lies her mother told her. Samantha felt her heart plunder a beat and remind her that she lived; reminding her that as long as she lived, her life, needs, and desires, were to see her daughter given as much a childhood as the world would allow. It was hopeless… but if she died trying at least she would live dying.

They ran as fast as they could—the crash came from a building collapsing. It would inevitably release more and more desperate people into the surrounding area. The city was no longer safe nor the haven people had hoped it would become. No phones, no electricity, communication or reason to stay. The numbers were more there, than anywhere, simply because if one died three could live to see the next fall — soon no one would be left to eat or be eaten.

"Where are we going?" Susie cried, her tears dried to salt on her cheeks. "Mother!"

"Quiet!" Carrie snapped, pausing her steps to listen and decide on a direction. The howls of people echoed from the wreckage of metropolis — she had to get as far from them as she could before the night set in. The roads were paved with the dead, leading nowhere but to share their fate. Carrie looked into the rolling clouds to see a speck in the distance — what was once a town. "Hurry!" she yelled, pulling on her daughter's hand. They were right behind them... a mother and daughter would provide a week of rape and a feast to follow. They ran as fast as they could.

Samantha watched the last smudge of grey fade from the sky as the sun set — only black remained. She carried with her a flashlight she used only when absolutely necessary. She pulled it out of her bag, along side a dull hunting knife, and began her journey back to the shelter. She breathed low, under cover of a scarf, listening intently to the sounds around her.

A commotion came from the city — more than she'd heard for months. Something had happened there and she worried that her secluded patch of property would soon be invaded by outsiders. The feeling drew shivers along her skin and the fear sped her steps — that she had made it so long without seeing another person was luck more than she had hoped. No one could be trusted — she had learned her lesson well and suffered for her charity.

Many months before Samantha had discovered a wounded man, near death, on the outskirts of her home. He cried for her help and begged for her aide. She could not find it in herself to leave him, though she knew he would prove a burden to her and her daughter's survival. But, she thought, perhaps he could heal and help them; perhaps he knew something of the outside world and carried with him hope to pass on to others. His eyes bled desperate tears, and she could see within him nothing remained—foolishly, she brought him back to the shelter.

For weeks he was unable to move, or even remain conscious for more than a few hours. But, slowly he healed and regained his strength. Slowly he grew from nothing to demand and expectation. Samantha could feel his eyes upon her at all times and soon enough his hands followed. She said no but there was no one to hear her. Her daughter slept, safe for the time, but Samantha knew if she were to give into him, his demands would soon grow. It was not long before he stopped asking.

He knocked her from the walls of the shelter and she fell hard onto the rubble bellow—her leg breaking. He pounced on her and pushed her to the ground, but she did not scream for fear her daughter would wake. His hands clawed her clothes from her, leaving her exposed to the cold. He pushed her head to the ground with one hand and forced himself into her with the other. She slammed her eyes shut from the pain and bit into her lip, clawing at the dirt to feel something cut into her hand. He thrust violently and she scrambled to unearth the sharp object from the ground—a rusty old hunting knife. He breathed heavily until she turned and slid the knife into his throat. His body twitched as his blood emptied onto her. He swatted with quickly diminishing vigor to try and remove the blade but could not. Within a few moments he was dead—still erect in her. She removed the blade and pushed his body to the side, doing her best to gather her torn and bloodied clothes. She wept and clenched her jaw, the rage exploding within her. She stabbed him over and over again until the pain from her leg became too much and she lost consciousness. She woke up, some time later—her daughter having found and cared for her. Adrian never asked her mother what happened or spoke of the man. They survived—just barely.

Samantha rose horrified from remembering the nightmare to see her flashlight flicker and begin to die. She was still too far from the shelter to find her way in the dark. She banged on the case and cursed its name but the light continued to die. Soon it was out and she could see nothing—her daughter would be alone for the night. She prayed Adrian would not come looking for her. But life had taught Samantha that God made us to die—she would live in hell till she could see her daughter safe.

Night fell as they arrived on the boarder of rubble—once a town. An eerie silence lingered in the air as Carrie carried Susie on her shoulder—she had grown tired and collapsed an hour before. The cries from the city had silenced and so too had the footsteps of their pursuers. Now, all they needed was to find shelter for the night. When morning came they could look for food and supplies but until then the night was too black to maneuver.

Carrie caught a glimpse of a flickering light not far from her— terrified, she stopped. Perhaps others were here; perhaps they wouldn't take kindly to her intruding on their domain. But she could not leave for there was nowhere else to go. Susie adjusted herself on her mother's shoulder but remained asleep. The light Carrie had seen flickered once more and then died—a flashlight. Had they seen her? Could they offer food and shelter? She contemplated crying out but kept her mouth shut. She stepped blindly through the night, creeping slowly so as not to make a sound. No matter who it was holding the flashlight, it wasn't anyone she cared to meet.

Adrian shivered, clenching herself for warmth—her mother had not returned after hours and she had begun to worry. Faint echoes of screams whispered through the night and Adrian tormented herself with fear for her mother. Without her she was lost—without her she had nothing. She dreamt of her father's return and how happy she would be to see him... of how he would make all the bad days go away and replace them with hope... that she would see life in her mother's eyes again.

A rustling came from the side of the shelter and Adrian rose her head from under the covers. But, as she had been instructed, she did not reveal herself, and rightly so. Two figures emerged into her home and stepped blindly towards her. Had her mother brought another back with her? Had her father returned at long last? She kept quite, hopeful but afraid. She remembered the man they had tried to save—she remembered finding him dead beside her mother. She hated him. And she feared everyone because of him—she didn't make a sound.

"Will we be safe here?" Susie asked, clasping her mothers hand as they climbed down the wall of rubble they would use for shelter.

"Yes," Carrie replied, speaking nothing of the future. Her eyes squinted in the darkness to find a clear patch of ground to sleep on. Her feet throbbed and her body ached—they had gotten away. But she knew they would not be safe for long. "Are you warm enough?" she questioned, tugging at the clothes bundled around her daughter. Susie nodded and mumbled 'mmhmm.' Carrie smiled, so happy to have her daughter with her; to have escaped the hell of the world with an angel on her shoulder.

The city was a pit of agony filled with those desperate to survive. The skyscrapers that still stood provided a landmark to entice people from all around. Supplies were once plentiful but as they dwindled so too did people's spirits and patience. Murder became survival—either by the need to defend or compulsion to eat. Carrie and her daughter had lived under the most fearsome men in the city—those who would do anything to reign. She was their whore and servant. And in return she and her daughter were given food and shelter. It was her job to clean the bodies... to disembowel and butcher them along with the other women who chose servitude before murder. But in the end, it made no difference—they ate at the sides of those who had murdered for them. Once satiated, the men would retreat to their rooms and the women would embrace them with their bodies to keep them contented.

Carrie lay Susie down and pulled her close, acting as her blanket. The nights were becoming colder and the days shorter. The air had taken on the taste of soot though it no longer fell from the sky. Who knew what had come of the world beyond the border of hell... she had long since lost any hope of returning to what was—to a life worth leading. But she continued and persevered solely for the sake of her daughter, for the hope of her future. She closed her eyes and told herself they wouldn't find them—that they had escaped and weren't worth chasing. She couldn't sleep.

Samantha awoke shaking—she had done her best to find the warmth of shelter but had not been able to keep it through the night. The sun was beginning to rise and with it she would make a final effort to reach her daughter or collapse trying. Now that light crept through the clouds she could see where she was and how far she had to go. She had to make it, for Adrian. She prayed she was safe. It had only been one night but all it takes is a night to take.

She pulled herself from the ground, holding a broken door of a rusty car. Her fingers were nearly frozen and curled making a claw of her hand. Her bad leg exploded pain through her as she forced it forward. She could feel the bone and cartilage scrape with each footstep but would not dare remain still. The cold of the air burned her lungs as she brought herself to a near run. Love triumphs over all for a time but pain wins in the end. The pain was... she had to think of Adrian—she had to know if she was safe.

Carrie hadn't slept—something wouldn't let her. Not the fear of her former captors, or the worry for her daughter's safety but... the release of hope—finally accepting the end, though it had yet to come. In the city, those who lived had done so by murdering the last who could stand and make a new world. But even with the evil they'd harnessed to survive, there could be hope for a better future. Now that their horrors had vanished—that she and Susie had escaped to the barren world—it was a matter of waiting for the end.

"Mommy?" Susie whispered, raising her head slightly from the ground. "Look," she finished, pointing to a crevice within the shelter, revealed by the morning's light—a little girl hugging herself for warmth as tears descended her cheeks. Carrie froze, frightened for a moment—not of the girl but of seeing her daughter in her.

"Are you alright?" Carrie asked, the little girl shaking and trying to push herself further into the crevice upon hearing the

strangers words—but there was no place to run. Her mother had not come back and she was left with no one to protect her. "It's ok, I'm not going to hurt you," *she said softly, reaching out her arm towards the girl.*

Samantha heard voices coming from the shelter and frantically scrambled to see inside. Her body had begun to shake and a cold sweat had sunk in. Something was wrong. Her head cleared the outer layer of rubble that surrounded the shelter and she could see two figures, one reaching for the crevice her daughter lay hidden in.

"No!" she screamed, using the last of her strength to thrust herself over the rubble and into the air. She fell hard upon the person who had tried to take her daughter and knocked them to the ground. Her frozen, claw like, hand clenched the hunting knife and slashed over and over again. The second person who had intruded the shelter screamed and pounded on her back but Samantha ignored her. Her breaths became coughs of blood as tears of rage exploded from her eyes. She released the knife, no longer strong enough to hold it and fell off the person she'd killed.

The grey sky rolled with brooding storm clouds, weeping rogue snowflakes that whispered of more to come. A young girl screamed beside her, clenching the body of what Samantha could now see was a woman—the little girls mother... what had she done... Adrian emerged from the crevice and scrambled to her mother's side—erupting snot and tears as her hands clasped Samantha's stomach, gushing blood. Samantha looked down to see that the woman she had murdered had not died without a fight. She felt as though her mouth was dry, though she sputtered drops of blood into the air with every breath. The world burned bright with an intensifying light as she tried to speak to her daughter, but could not. Her head fell to the side and she lay dead. Susie and Adrian wept beside one another, clutching their mother's bodies—a crash came from the city.

Ladylike

"Why are women not permitted to join the clergy?" Ellis asked the father as they refastened their trousers.

"Because jobs are done by those who can do them. And I've never known a woman to know God so well as men do," he replied, plucking a coarse hair from between his teeth.

"Is it women's distance from God then that stifles them?"

"No, it is God's distance from women."

"But… why would God make the lesser sex so privileged?"

"Privileged?" the father gasped, pulling his robe over his shoulders and furrowing his brow. "It is no privilege to be a woman, and it is certainly no privilege to be kept from God!"

"Of course not. But women are not charged with the hard truths of life as men are. They are coddled, not only by God, but their husbands as well," Ellis explained, wiping a speck of semen from his shirt collar. "Awarded every luxury in life without having to work the least bit for it… seems to me, women have quite cleverly secured themselves at the expense of their male superiors."

"Perhaps… but if we did not care for them, they would be too overcome by the brutality of life to continue to live. So, in fact, they are not privileged—they are imbecilic pets, cared for out of necessity."

Ellis bit his tongue and swallowed his point. He suspected women were not as helpless as they seemed. For he had heard of a lady so fair that she could bring any man to his knees. And, as Ellis's present occupation was no more than the duties of a wife, the notion of being a woman fascinated him. After all, his delicate features and boyish voice often saw him mistaken for a woman. Yet, he still struggled and toiled in life simply to scrape by. It was unfair that the fairer sex should receive, for nothing, all that Ellis's endeavors could not produce—feasts, riches and wealth the likes of nobility and kings. And, as Ellis finished dressing himself, his curiosity on the matter got the better of him.

"Father... what do you know of madam Bailie?"

It had been a merry afternoon on the hills above town—the first day of summer. Gay children and frolicking lovers took to the grass with a lustful exuberance not felt since the plague lifted. Kites danced in the wind, tickling the clouds in such a delightful manner it might have made God himself chuckle. And while the townsfolk went blissfully out to play, the young, beautiful, Elisabet Bailie took to investigating a private estate—one treasure at a time.

Gold-trimmed-wallpaper and crystal-ivory-chandeliers were unwanted distractions to Elisabet as she did not have the time to peel the paper or the strength to carry the chandeliers. Instead, she found the currency of her meals sandwiched in jewelry boxes or sprinkled on countertops. If caught she'd spend the rest of her days in jail, or, be hung and awarded to the local mortician for his personal preference. But she would never allow it to come to that—after all, it was her errand in these explorations to find a husband and bring an end to her pilfering. For though, Elisabet was a fine and respected lady, she was now too poor to sustain her reputation, and was thus obliged to rob out of necessity or ease.

Elisabet tapped her fingers along the jewelry box as though she were petting a poodle; licking her lips to taste the tart residue of the strawberry she'd plucked from the pantry. She had managed to limit herself to no more than a few bites of fruit, a wedge of bree, half a baguette, and a set of china wrapped in bed sheets. But, before she could satisfy her appetites further, a noise drew her attention—a man stumbling from room to room, drunk and disorderly.

The man appeared lost and confused until he spotted the bar. Then, with long, uncertain strides he toppled himself forward into a chair, repositioning himself until he was seated upright. Elisabet crept slowly down the hall so that she could have a better look at him, and see, whether or not, he was in fact the owner of the estate she was presently intruding in—a widower who had locked himself away to be eaten by his grief

His wife had been murdered with his little one not three weeks before, and though Elisabet did hesitate to rob from him, she did so only to observe. The man had a sullen tender face and ragged posture—slouched in his chair like the drunkard he'd become. He clung loosely to a decanter, open at his side. His vest had been stained either by consuming or expelling his bodily fluids along with those at the bar before him. He was a complete mess, and exactly what Elisabet had been looking for—so far as the man would know, it would be love at first sight.

The guard dogs were easily distracted by a slab of meat. And, the servants, according to the accounts of the townsfolk, never entered within ten rooms of their master. Ellis, rushed from bush to bush of the expansive garden surrounding the mansion. It appeared meticulously tended to, yet deserted all the same. He looked upon the house contemplating the best entry, eventually deciding on a wall of vines, which he climbed up towards a tiny window.

The mansion was very large. So large, the footsteps and words of it's occupant would echo themselves ten fold before finding her other ear. It was a home often spoken of by the people; one rumored equally for it's walls as it was for it's owner—madam Elisabet Bailie—as fine a lady, and profound a beauty, as there had ever been. But, it was not long ago that a fire ravaged her figure and dignity, forever confining her within the walls of her late husband's mansion. Accompanied now only by silent servants and the haunting memories of all she had lost.

Ellis, however, was far from a lady. And though he did everything in his power to be regarded well by others, it was simply out of his hands—for he was too fair a lad to be treated as a man. And, though, his feminine features did play their part in finding him beds to sleep in, and clients to sleep with, the reward of more than a night's sin was beyond Ellis.

Thus, unable to entrance the wealthy, Ellis found his riches in others keepings—burglarizing households for every scrap of extravagant-wear that would otherwise have eluded him. Though, on this day, he crept through the halls of the Bailie estate not for it's spoils, but for his desire to stumble upon the madam herself; to see what had become of who Ellis would give anything to be.

"I can hear a mouse's heart quicken when it enters the pantry," a voice whispered, as Ellis crept through the halls—frozen in his place by the sound of someone approaching. But though he ducked and twitched his head every which way, there was no one to be seen. "I can hear the bells of the cathedral before they sound and the song of the birds deep in the forest," the voice continued.

Ellis, now afraid that he had been discovered, turned quickly to try and retrace his steps. He no longer desired his curiosity over his life, nor any treasure that would see it forfeit—the voice was getting closer.

"And I most certainly can hear you... whoever you are."

"Sorry, I must have the wrong house," he tried to explain, his voice high and shrill.

"Oh child... I heard your lie slither from your teeth even before you spoke," the voice exclaimed, closer and closer with every breath. "Why did you intrude here today? For some foolish jest, or wager placed upon you by someone lacking the nerve to come themselves?... or, perhaps... for me?"

"A mistake is all... one remedied best by my immediate departure."

"A mistake indeed," the voice whispered, a dollop of breath warming Ellis's shoulder. He turned quickly to and away from the figure at his side—a melted woman, the likeness of a prune left under the sun. Her eyes were white and her features barren: an ancient witch so hideous even death would not take her. "All this way and you cannot look upon me?" madam Bailie hissed, taking Ellis by the shoulders and shaking his eyes open. "Isn't this what you came for child? Isn't it!?"

"No!" he cried, thrashing about to break free, but he could not.

"Then, what?! What has brought you here?!"

"I... I..."

"Do you think I wait for guests to sneer at me?!" madam Bailie shouted, bringing her hand down hard on Ellis. "To mock and wound me!" she continued, her voice sinking to despair.

Though stripped of it's features, madam Bailie's face still showed signs of human emotion. She was crying—rigid lines of her tears falling from one scarred crevice to the next. And though Ellis suffered blow after blow from her hand, he felt worse for the expression she showed.

"Please, miss!" he begged, now curled into a protective ball on the marble floor. "I was only curios!"

"And I will skin you for it!" madam Bailie shrieked, a tear falling with every agonizing swing of her arm—over and over again. She breathed heavily, gasping for air in between sobs. She had not had a visitor for some time and was now too filled with rage to regard anyone any better than she did herself.

"I only wanted to see the greatest lady there ever was!" Ellis explained, announcing his curiosity in an attempt to end his beating.

His words struck a flicker of life into the pale dead eyes of madam Bailie. She stumbled a step back, as though all the air in her lungs had been stolen. She could in fact hear as well as she claimed to, and had only stopped her assault for the sincerity of Ellis' tone.

"W-what did you say?" she whispered, her lip trembling as she gripped the wall for support.

Stunned, Ellis clutched his bruises and rose to his feet. He looked upon the blind old woman with both pity and admiration. He would not return her blows nor toy with her dignity—it was her council, after all, that he had come for.

"They say 'royalty would kneel to you,'" Ellis exclaimed, recalling the father's words that had led him to her estate. "They say 'men would leave their wives incase they should happen upon you; they say," he declared, stopped short by madam Bailie's hand upon his mouth.

"And what do they say of me now?"

"That you are locked away… and no one has seen you."

"And if I allow you to leave... what will your words be?"

"I do not wish to leave," Ellis declared, raising his arms in defense in case she attempted to remove him. "I have come for you; not for the sight of you, or the story of it, but for your council."

"Council? What council could I give?"

"I... I wish to be a lady," Ellis whispered, with barely nerve enough to say his true desire. He had known she was blind, and hoped it enough for him to fool her. But, as he watched the scars on her brow twitch in reaction to his words, he was weary of his own ruse.

"A lady?"

"Yes. I wish to be a lady; to woo a man of wealth so that I need not struggle in life any longer. But... I'm afraid I don't quite know how."

Madam Bailie turned her eyes up toward Ellis's face as though she could truly see him. Her lips parted and sealed three times before she uttered another sound. "In striking you, have I drawn blood or damaged your features?"

"No, madam."

"Come here then," she said, raising her hands to Ellis' face. Her fingers smoothly caressed and tickled every inch of Ellis' head. His hair, long, thick and lustrous had been washed for the occasion. His lips, plump and ripe, had been polished with diluted-poison so they would blossom to their fullest. And his skin had been soaked, replenished, and, finally, shaved so closely Ellis feared the wind could now pierce him.

"Please be honest."

"A man is a simple creature," she replied, closing her eyes and smelling the air. "They are persuaded by beauty, overcome by lust and maddened by desire. It is not your features alone that will win a man, but the manner in which you feature them," she explained, returning her hands to her side and exhaling a grumbling sigh. A smile cracked along her face as she coughed a giggle. "You are right… you don't know how to be a lady. But, I suppose, these things happen."

Since the widower, Arthur, refused to leave his home, Elisabet had devised a scheme to lure him out. Though, not the most clever, original or dignified, it was quite suiting to captivate a man. She waited until the sun had nearly fallen before making her way to his mansion. She wore one of her finest gowns that she had decided to sacrifice for the occasion—torn as though ravaged by wolves, concealing just enough to keep her warm, and revealing more than enough to catch a man's eye. She could only hope that Arthur had not yet drunk himself asleep.

Elisabet pinched herself to draw tears before beginning her charade—taking deep breaths in preparation for her performance. For years she had sought this moment, and now that it was upon her, she could barely contain her delight. For too long she had suffered the hardships of poverty and the meager reward of a hard days work. But now, she undertook winning herself a man, and with him, freedom from life's worries and toils. She would give everything for that, and planned do to no less.

"Help me please!" she cried, crashing her bare hand upon the door, rather than using the knocker. She paused a moment and readjusted the stuffing against her breast. "Oh, please, I beg you!" she continued, shaking her voice and knocking again. She heard a rustling in the house followed by a cautious call to her.

"What do you want?"

"Sir, I have been attacked and barely escaped with my life! Please, let me in! I am not sure it is safe!"

There was a moments pause before Arthur emerged, his scowl wiped clean by the sight of Elisabet. His eyes gazed down upon her exposed skin with a hunger his solitude could not quench. His mouth fell open in awe and it was some time before he could utter another word.

"C... come in," he exclaimed, placing his hand upon her arm and leading her inside.

"Thank you so much!" Elisabet stated, lunging into his arms and sobbing upon his shoulder.

"It's no trouble... please, follow me to the fire and we'll warm you up," Arthur said, taking her cold hand and raising a candle to light the hall.

"Are you injured?"

"No, sir... thankfully not."

"Who is it that attacked you?"

"I don't know, sir—beastly men without souls to restrain them."

"How did you escape?"

"I broke free and ran, finding your home and, thankfully, you inside it."

"You're quite brave to fair as you have," Arthur exclaimed, showing her to a chair before throwing another log onto the fire. He was determined and sober now, for his grief had melted away at the sight of Elisabet. He looked upon her with a fluttering heart and soul shaking desire—it was love at first sight.

"You are too kind... I hope I have not disturbed you much by my intrusion," Elisabet said, crossing her bare legs and rubbing them for warmth. "Or that I have disturbed your family."

"No... no trouble," Arthur whispered, taking the seat across from Elisabet. "I am the only one at home."

"Oh? No family, or servants?"

"No... I've sent my servants away so that I may be alone."

"Well... I am thankful that you were here to save me."

"Your dress is... I'll fetch you another," Arthur exclaimed, leaping from his chair and out of the room. Elisabet heard a rustling upstairs followed by the sound of someone quickly descending them. "Here you are," Arthur announced, presenting a fine golden gown draped over his arm.

"My word!" Elisabet gasped, placing a hand before her open mouth. "I couldn't possibly!"

"Nonsense, it's just your size."

"But... surely it's owner would not..."

"I am it's owner, and I dare not see you without it... Come, I'll show you to a room you may dress in."

Elisabet rose to her feet and glided forward. She locked her eyes with his and leaned in to place a puckish kiss upon his lips. He stood stunned, without breath or speech—motionless, refusing to surrender the moment.

"How may I ever repay you, sir?"

"Stay the night... so I am sure you're safe," Arthur said, smiling for the first time since his wife and child's death. Elisabet nodded and followed him up the stairs, lowering her chin to conceal her surprise—she had him, in no time or toil, she had him. And though she had worked and struggled for years, none had been so fruitful as this day. Yet... she did not feel relief as she had expected. Instead, pity simmered in her stomach and worry consumed her mood. It was not uncommon that she should win a heart without giving her own—for it was, as she had been taught, the place of a lady. Elisabet now had what she desired, but she was lost because of it. She took Arthur's hand and squeezed it for direction—her first mistake of many.

For years, madam Bailie had been awoken every morning by the bell of her servants, rung at the crack of dawn far from where she slept. She refused to be near them, or to allow anyone to look upon her mangled frame. In fact, save for the late doctor who had tended her wounds, no one could attest to her condition. And no one could rival her legacy with the truth. Thus, permitting her adoring intruder to leave, after having seen the madam's deformed state, was unthinkable. And as she transcribed her instructions for her servants to read come morning, she made sure to inform them that: her rations were to be doubled; that her finest gowns were to be fetched, and that no one should be allowed to leave.

"Your kindness exceeds even the most grand words of you," Ellis exclaimed, seated in a leather upholstered arm chair.

"For such an experienced intruder, you speak quite well," the madam replied, making her way to the center of the empty room she had chosen to give her lesson in.

"I've kept dignified company in my life," Ellis replied, thinking just the opposite of those he referred to and the deeds he had done with them.

"Oh? Then why did your mother not teach you to be a lady?"

"She… she died when I was young, and my father abandoned me soon after," Ellis explained, having never allowed himself to remember, or love, the wretched duo that birthed him.

"How did you survive?"

"As you said madam, I am an experienced intruder."

"I see," madam Bailie sighed, her voice lacking the scorn that Ellis had expected given his confession. Instead, she seemed entranced by what he'd said—as though she knew more of him than his words could tell. "Before I became a legend, I was young—much like yourself. And, as chance would have it, I too experienced similar things."

"Oh... did you?"

"Yes... I was wealthy as a child. But, after my parents fell ill, our servants seized all they could to purchase elixirs vendors assured them were cures," the madam explained, closing her eyes and lowering her head as the memories flowed through her mind. "But of course, there was no cure... and they left me behind to fend for myself," she whispered, drifting from the room to her youth.

She had awoken to the sound of distant screaming—a fog hung in the air that clung to the corpses on the streets. Her family had not fled to the countryside as had so many of the rich. Her father's wealth, after all, depended upon the heads of those who now perished before they could settle their debts. And with each life that withered away, so too did the Bailie family fortune.

Madam Bailie remembered calling for someone, for anyone, but heard no reply. She pulled herself from her bed and walked the dark halls of their pillaged estate towards her parent's bedroom. There she found them, cold and limp. They had refused to see Elisabet after falling ill, for fear that she too would suffer their fate—relying on their servant's loyalty to abide their will. But they were wrong. And, though Elisabet was not ill, she suffered as though she were—alone for the first time.

"Madam Bailie?" Ellis exclaimed, following a silence so long he feared she had passed away. The madam gasped and raised her head again, returning her ears and mind to the moment.

"Yes… I'm… I'm sorry… Sometimes being blind isn't enough," she chuckled, her laugh delicate and deceitful. "You have said, you wish to be a lady."

"Yes, madam, more than anything, I do."

"And yet, you are masculine."

"Yes… as such I have had to fair in life."

"But no longer," madam Bailie stated, drawing a long, slow, breath that lifted her chest into the air. "Under men, and their husbands, women stand on their knees. Groveling, begging—helpless by their own choosing. Abiding every demand for fear that, if they do not, they will be cast aside—replaced by someone younger, more beautiful, more slavish. A lady, however, does not fear men, nor her husband; does not kneel to him, or for his every desire. A lady is a bridled puppeteer—able to control men by their desires… There are some who are regarded as though they are ladies—fair and beautiful, married for children and the orifice that bears them. But, beyond their feminine tools, they are empty shells—no more ladylike than the contents of their bowels. And, as age tears at their skin and pulls it to the ground, the world loses all love for them, and they are, for the first time, truly exposed… truly pathetic… But what I will teach you is beauty everlasting—to be more than a doll, more than a trinket, or a married whore. I will teach you of the power women hold; of our strength that men fear, and of the world for our taking."

Following a brief courtship, Arthur And Elisabet were engaged to be married in one month's time. Yet, already it seemed all the world knew of the occasion. Their days were filled with tea and nobility—introductions and conversations with every person of significance and worth. And, though, the sort of people Elisabet were exposed to were known to her, the manner in which she was now regarded was not.

"What gifts has Arthur given you?" heiress Aldora Kingston the Second asked, after the men retreated to speak of things not meant for the ears of women; thus, leaving their women together, to stroll through the orchard.

"Gifts?" Elisabet replied, fully aware of what Aldora had said and why she had said it.

"Yes… **gifts**," she sneered, never allowing more than a tickle of expression to adorn her face.

Aldora spoke with a pretentious exasperation that she should have to endure the company of others. Just one of many reasons that Elisabet hated her. But, Elisabet had not voiced her contempt, and instead made sure to smile often. For, unfortunately, since Aldora's husband and Arthur were the best of friends, the same would be expected of their wives.

"He has given me many fine things… gowns, jewels… the promise of a wonderful future with a wonderful man," Elisabet explained, her corset preventing her from taking a full breath.

"When my husband and I were engaged, he lavished gifts upon me every time he laid eyes on me," Aldora exclaimed, pacing her steps to the slow beat of her callous heart. "Emeralds, diamonds, gold and silver… everything that's anything, over and over again."

"How lovely," Elisabet grimaced, trying to focus on the flowers around her rather than the shrew beside her. "How long have you been married?"

"Six years."

"And, do you not wish to have children?" Elisabet asked, taking a mild joy from the unrest her question caused Aldora.

"No... we simply haven't the time," she replied, her tone falling from insincere to insidious. "I suppose the prospect of children is why Arthur has taken such a fondness to you... among other things, of course."

"Of course."

"Tell me, do you feel that, as thin as you are, you'd be able to bear children?" Aldora inquired, beginning to smile just as Elisabet did.

"I suppose. But, even with a full figure, such as your own, children are not promised."

"No, but they are delivered safely."

"Yes, but only if they are conceived."

"There you are!" Arthur announced, his voice bringing a temporary halt to the lady's duel. "Come Elisabet—we'd best be off to get ready for the ball," he continued, tying his arm to hers.

"So soon?"

"I'm afraid so."

"Oh well... I'm sure Aldora and I will have other opportunities to indulge each other's company," Elisabet exclaimed, raising her chin higher than Aldora's head. "That is, if our children don't occupy all our time," she finished, bating a future rivalry for a petty victory. But, Elisabet had never been any good at controlling herself, or any good at recognizing a formidable foe.

Aldora watched them walk away, holding a stern expression and a seething contempt. After all, she had been the one to remove Arthur's wife before Elisabet, and would not hesitate to do so again. She did feel some guilt that the apple she had poisoned was shared by the mother with their little one. But found it an acceptable inconvenience for being rid of a woman she had whole heartedly despised. And, as Elisabet turned to wave 'a friendly goodbye,' Aldora *decided not to wait until Arthur had children to get in the way this time.*

    Ellis, and the person he had been, were no more—the beggar, the thief, the prostitute. No longer was he lost or confused in the world; no longer did he question his desire or himself. For now he was not only the pupil of his idle, but a lady as well.

    He slept and ate at the madam's side; he learned and practiced every minute of everyday—repeating every word, gesture and detail according to madam Bailie's instruction. It was a long and tedious endeavor to become a lady, and one that Ellis had not fully anticipated. For, his attention, though determined and ambitious, continued to stray from his lessons to his teacher—madam Bailie wore her secrets on her face and Ellis' curiosity ate at him constantly. She did not speak of the fire, or who had started it. She did not even speak of her husband—the man whose past wealth continued to feed her to this day. And, though, Ellis did try his best to hold his tongue on the matter, his best was not good enough.

    One night, after the madam had fallen asleep, Ellis crept from his chambers to investigate the mansion. The dark halls glimmered with blue moonlight, trickling in through window cracks. Ellis held a flickering candle before him to navigate the labyrinth—pausing a moment to look upon a framed portrait of a young madam Bailie and her husband. She was even more lovely than the finest words spoken of her—dressed in an elegant gown and complimented with jewels more plentiful than the whole of England. But while her beauty burst from the canvas, the pain in her eyes was all Ellis could see. A grim, solemn man stood at her side, his hand firmly pressed atop her shoulder as though mimicking a loving gesture for the portrait's sake. But, as Ellis drew his candle along the canvas to see it in it's entirety, a noise from a nearby window caught his attention.

A man walked leisurely around the house—a sword at his hip and a whistle on his lips. But he did not look for a point of entry or for something to steal—instead he looked away from the mansion as though guarding it. Ellis quickly extinguished his candle and made his way back to the madam's quarters to avoid being seen. But he could not help but wonder about the man he had seen. For, there were dogs, not guards, when Ellis first came to the Bailie estate. He thought, perhaps his presence alerted the madam to the vulnerability of her home. But what Ellis did not realize, was that the man was not there to keep people out, but rather to keep Ellis in.

"Balancing a book on one's head is only impressive if one is giving fellatio," madam Bailie exclaimed, in response to Ellis' suggestion on proper posture. "Now sit up."

"Yes, madam," Ellis replied, exhausted and restless.

"Hold your chin up at a twelve degree angle, while keeping your jaw firm and lips puckered. You must never smile or frown, unless you aspire to earn your fortune from your wrinkles," madam Bailie explained, as they entered into their fifth continuous hour of study. Ellis repeated her words in his head and tried his best to conceal a yawn, knowing she would hear it anyway. "Have **your** words been so many today that you cannot listen to mine?"

"No, madam," he replied, correcting his posture and adjusting his gown yet again—he could now appreciate how uncomfortable it was to be beautiful.

"Then why have you been so rude as to yawn?"

"I… it's just… have I not been taught this lesson already?"

"You have been taught, yes. But you have yet to learn."

"Yes, madam," Ellis sighed, looking to the window, smeared with fading sunlight that marked another day done.

"Speak then," the madam growled, plucking Ellis' desire from his tone.

"Madam?"

"Your mind… I assume you have one, do you not?"

"Yes, madam."

"Then speak it."

"Very well… I am very grateful for all that you have taught me and the kindness you have shown, but… I wish to find a husband to care for me… might we have a lesson on that?" Ellis exclaimed, suggesting heavily where he wished for the conversation to go.

"A husband?" madam Bailie whispered, distressed by even the word.

"Yes. Was your husband not a joy in your life? Come to think of it, I don't believe you've ever mentioned your husband… what was he like?"

"He's dead and buried. And so too are my memories of him."

"Come now, surely you hold some recollection of the man you loved."

Ellis' words stabbed a harsh image of madam Bailie's late husband into her mind. But no matter how she shook or trembled she could not be rid of it. He was the man she had chosen to usher her into a life of luxury—to save her from the toils of common people. But he was also the one to ruin her—the one to make every day more terrible than the last.

They had been married after a brief courtship—she was a young, beautiful, bride, and he was a rich and powerful man: At the time, madam Bailie could not imagine a more perfect life or a more promising future. But the truth of things came quickly to her the more he drank. And so it was that her reputation became her only escape from a cursed life. But, even that was not enough, even that was just another cage in which she remained a slave.

Thus, one night after an extravagant ball; after a beating, and a reminder of just what she was—madam Bailie decided to end her torment. She plucked a lamp from the cupboard and doused a rag in ether. She crept slowly into her husbands quarter's where he lay asleep—so drunk he had incapacitated himself. Her heart pounded as she lifted his head, fastening the rag under his nose so that his breaths would be full of ether. Then, after removing her jewels and prized possessions she had sold her soul for, she pulled him from his bed. He did not wake as she dragged him, or stir as she lifted him. It was as though he was dead already—just what madam Bailie had in mind.

After nearly fifteen minutes of labor, she had managed to hoist him out of his home and into a horse drawn carriage. She snuck to the barn and brought two fine horses, bridles, and three armfuls of hay. She then harnessed the horses to the carriage and removed the rag of ether from her husband's face. He stirred awake a few moments later to find himself submerged in hay—his wife standing before him, bearing a flickering lamp.

"What in all hell is going on?" he grumbled, attempting to lift himself and regain his focus. But the ether clouded his mind and he could not move more than his tongue.

"Goodbye, dearest master," madam Bailie growled as she lowered the lamp to the hay and set it ablaze—slamming the carriage door shut and whipping the horse's backsides.

The night was soon illuminated as the fire engulfed the carriage, cargo and all. But as madam Bailie watched and listened to her husband's final screams, she felt a growing warmth upon her dress. Her eyes fell from the distant carriage to her gown and, sure enough, it was ablaze as well. She thrashed and fought against the fire as best she could, but to no avail. Soon it consumed her and she screamed, flailing desperately on the ground.

After what seemed hours of torture, the flames subsided and she was left scorched and ravaged—covered in droppings and mud. But though her skin was nearly stripped from her, she did not call for help—she could not bare the idea of someone seeing her in such a hideous condition. And so, she slowly crawled back inside the mansion—her fingernails sliding from her hands as she climbed into bed. Once there, she covered herself in sheets and cried for her servant's aid. She told them to fetch a doctor and demanded that no one but him was to look upon her. And then... she disappeared.

"Loved?" madam Bailie hissed, the scars of her face contorting to a fearsome scowl as she returned from the depths of her mind. "Loved?! Loved!?! I **never** loved him!"

"Then why..."

"Why, what?! Why did I marry him? Why did I tolerate him? Or why did I suffer his abuse?" she interrupted, storming around the room as she spoke—thrashing her arms at her memories. "Why did I throw masked balls to hide the marks from his hands? Why did I not scream when he forced himself upon me? Why did I give everything to him only to lose everything I gave!?"

Ellis sat startled; terrified by what he witnessed. Madam Bailie fell to her knees and begged for answers, crying and pleading for redemption—not for her sins but for those she had allowed. Ellis reached out, his hand quivering as it came to rest upon her weeping head. But there was nothing to comfort her—her life as a lady and all that she was celebrated for was a lie—a guise to veil the truth that she had been a slave as well.

"You are so lovely," Arthur whispered, as he leaned in to kiss Elisabet only to find her hands holding him back.

"Thank you."

"And so fair," he continued, his every advance refused.

"You are too kind."

"I don't feel as though I can wait until tomorrow night," Arthur admitted, clasping Elisabet's waist and pulling her towards him. "What do you say?"

"God will not hear of it, and neither will I."

"But it's only one day!"

"Yes. And that's not long to wait now is it?" Elisabet exclaimed, unclasping Arthur's grasp of her. "Besides, this is no place to be caught ill exposed," she whispered, checking the corner of her eye incase anyone had discovered them. They stood in a dark room not far from a celebration in their honor. All of Arthur's friend's family and associates had come to congratulate him on his lovely new bride. But, unfortunately for Elisabet, it meant Aldora had come as well.

"Do you not want me?"

"Of course I do. And I've the rest of my life to prove it," Elisabet said, taking his hand and kissing it. "You should return to your guests."

"I suppose you're right," Arthur sighed, turning to leave, though Elisabet did not. "Are you not coming?"

"I'll be just a moment... I need to freshen up."

"Very well."

Elisabet watched Arthur leave the room before exhaling loudly and slouching against the wall—it had been yet another narrowly avoided advance that would soon become her obligation as a wife. At first her intimate hesitation was a genuine disinterest in Arthur, but she had since become captivated by the notion of being his wife. He was such a fragile thing, broken by the loss of his family and desperate for another. And, while Elisabet did feel some guilt for deceiving him, she told herself he was better off with her than to have remained alone. But, her uncertainty on the matter was not why she had retreated from the festivities.

She removed a bundle from behind the curtains and spread it across the table—plucking a long razor and a container of shaving powder from it. She set aside her diluted poison and feminine enhancements and used a tiny mirror to look upon herself. She had become quite good at presenting herself according to the male desire, without alerting them to the deception of her enhancements. But she worried that come the wedding night and the frequent intimacy of touching lips and faces, that Arthur would realize she was not as lovely, or ladylike, as she looked.

"I was wondering where you'd slipped off to," Aldora stated, her black silhouette standing in the open doorway.

"Good heavens!" Elisabet cried, clasping her breast with one hand while concealing the bundle with the other. "You scared me half to death, Aldora!"

"In the future I'll be more thorough... at making my presence known," she said, slowly walking towards Elisabet. "But, for the time being, I would like to speak to you privately before you are married."

"Oh? And what invaluable wisdom do you have to share?"

"Not wisdom dear, rather, a gift," she exclaimed, pulling a jeweled box from behind her back and presenting it to Elisabet.

"Goodness... it's lovely. Thank you so much, Aldora!"

"No trouble... aren't you going to open it?"

"I couldn't possibly without Arthur here."

"But this gift is for you... open it."

"It's too much for me to accept."

"Don't be silly, you don't even know what you're in for yet," Aldora insisted, pushing the box into Elisabet's chest. "You don't want to offend me now, do you?"

"Certainly not."

"Then I insist," Aldora demanded, flipping open the box and removing a plump strawberry. "Arthur said they were your favorite indulgence... so, please, indulge."

"I don't want to ruin my appetite," Elisabet replied, recoiling as Aldora lifted a strawberry from the box and extended it towards Elisabet — her hand that hid the bundle now tightly grasping the razor's handle.

"One strawberry surely will not ruin anything... your refusal, however, may ruin my good temper."

Elisabet trembled looking at the berry pinched delicately between Aldora's fingers. She could not bring herself to eat it or to think any better of it's presenter than she did of the devil himself. For, at that moment she recalled Arthur's words of his former wife and child — of their unsolved murder and sudden deaths — they had been poisoned. And as Elisabet struggled to keep the razor behind her and the strawberry away from her, she knew that Aldora had been responsible.

"Come Elisabet! The dancing has just begun!" Arthur announced, barging into the room in a boyish delight he quickly concealed upon seeing Aldora. "My apologies, I hope I'm not interrupting anything."

"Not at all," Elisabet sighed, more relieved to see Arthur than she had ever been. "If you'll excuse us," she stated, moving past Aldora and out of the room—just barely escaping with her life.

Aldora stood enraged that the opportunity had eluded her. But as she turned to exit the room she noticed the bundle that Elisabet had hidden. Curious, she unraveled it and sifted through it's contents—a razor, powder, make-up (the sort only harlots and actors would dare use), and countless other peculiar items that upon seeing evoked a whirlwind of devious thoughts. For, though not overt to the eye, it was now plain for Aldora to see—Elisabet was not as she seemed.

"Our lessons are at an end," Madam Bailie whispered, after her tears and memories had faded long enough for her to think. "I have nothing to teach you."

"Of course you do," Ellis protested, his pity for the madam too little to silence his desire. "You can teach me how to be a lady."

"No... All I am is what I was. And that is nothing worth teaching."

"Yes, it is."

"Did you not hear me? I was his whore... his servant, and prize, but never his love. I was his wife, shown no respect or favor but jewels and gowns, only so I could be displayed on his behalf. And all these years I have pretended to be more—to be a lady, not a slave."

"But you are a lady! The finest there has ever been!"

"Precisely... For, what is it to be a lady in a world where men decide? To become exactly what they want, as though it is a privilege—as though a chariot not a cage. But in truth it is foul! More damning than hunger and strife; more tempting than the promise of heaven—it is a prison cloaked in luxury, for women to envy and men to rule."

"No. Being a lady is more than that, and your lessons have proven it."

"My lessons?" madam Bailie gasped, scrambling forward to clasp Ellis' hands. "Do not follow in my steps; do not believe my council to be anything more than delirium. Instead, be as you are."

"I am a lady," Ellis replied, stubborn and undeterred. He could not understand the panic in her voice or the merit of her words—thinking her state a passing uncertainty that need only kindness to quell.

"Well and good so long as you are a lady of your own choosing. Promise me that, child. For, I cannot bear another weight upon my soul, or to think that I have misguided you to be as I am."

"You need not speak this way. You were the wife of a husband without the sense to love you—that does not make you, or those like you, foolish."

"You are not listening!" madam Bailie cried, shaking Ellis' hands to wake him from his dream. "I endeavored in life to wed a man of wealth—thinking nothing of the man himself or the part I would play. That was my folly. And I beseech you, I pray you, if you are to be a lady; if you are to marry a man, do so without consideration of what spoils he may offer... For, if you do not, I fear you will suffer as I have."

"I have suffered enough!" Ellis exclaimed, rising from his chair and pulling free of the madam's grasp. "I have been a

whore and a servant; a thief and a beggar, but never a prize—
never one worthy of it. I do not dread that my future will be
loveless or imprisoned. I fear that I will starve or be hanged for
stealing bread so that I might see another day! I have never had
anything, nor any hope of anything, but for that which being a
lady can provide. And though, I suspect you are right, your
fears are nothing compared to what I fear," Ellis finished,
turning to retreat from the madam.

"Then stay forever! Be a lady, and as you are, and never
doubt that you are welcome," madam Bailie pleaded, blindly
pursuing him—her only companion.

"Forever?" Ellis gasped, suddenly thinking of the guard
he had seen—of the watchman employed to keep him. "If our
lessons are at an end, I have no need to stay," he stated, backing
slowly away from the madam.

"Where are you going?"

"Away, to find a husband."

"I'm afraid I cannot allow that," the madam sighed,
heartbroken that she must hold Ellis against his will. "For if you
were to ever speak to anyone of what I've become…" she
explained, stopping abruptly—horrified by the lasting
stranglehold of the lie she had lived. A lie that had commanded
she lock herself away for years to guard a past she detested, to
preserve a name that sickened her, and to ensure her legacy of
being a lady. But, if as a lady she had been as pitiful as she now
believed, there was no merit to her fame. Devastated by this
revelation she plunged her face into her hands and wept—
collapsing to the ground too weak to stand.

Ellis remained silent and watched the madam from afar.
He had felt a flicker of love for the kindness she had shown but
never for the woman herself. For with each day of study had
come another meal, another nights rest and the promise of a

better tomorrow. But in Ellis's life, he had acquired a heart without compassion and could now see how empty his favor for the madam was. He turned from her; from all she had given, and the wisdom she had offered, and left the mansion—holding his chin high and striding delicately in his gown.

"Halt!" the guard demanded, aiming his musket at Ellis's back. "The madam has ordered your confinement."

"I've no more need of the intruder," Ellis replied, turning calmly and placing his hand atop the guard's rifle to see it lowered. "You will find her inside—a ghastly, blind old woman; delirious and mad. Remove her and do with her as you will," Ellis commanded, taking the final steps to insure his grand reception as a lady.

The guard stood stunned a moment before bowing and removing his hat. "Madam Bailie! I am so sorry, please forgive me," he exclaimed, taking a knee at Ellis's side.

"Do not waste my time groveling. Do as I've said," Ellis ordered, mimicking the madam's gestures exactly as he'd been taught to. "Thereafter, ride into town and let it be known that Elisabet Bailie, the greatest lady there has ever been, has returned."

"Is there anything else the servants can get you before bed?" Arthur asked Elisabet as he escorted her to her quarters.

"No, nothing at all," she replied, covering her mouth with her hand to conceal a yawn. The night's festivities had come to a close and only one more sleep lay between Elisabet and her wedding day. "I'm so happy that tomorrow's tomorrow."

"As am I."

"Goodnight," Elisabet said, closing the door and removing the bundle she had hidden from under her gown. She had managed to elude the party guests long enough to go back and retrieve it. And, fortunately, had done so without attracting Aldora's attention again. Elisabet still trembled at the thought of her, and now believed Aldora responsible for poisoning Arthur's wife and child.

Elisabet unraveled the bundle beside her bedroom mirror and removed the razor. She pulled the stuffing from her breast and unlaced the final stitches of her corset—a trick few could accomplish on their own. She hummed to herself as she undressed before taking a seat and covering her jaw with shaving powder—clutching the razor in her other hand to remove her faint traces of blonde stubble.

After shaving she washed her face and removed her makeup. She coated her lips once more before sleep and slid into a night gown. Madam Bailie had always told her 'a woman's place is only as good as the bed she makes,' and Elisabet made sure to keep her secrets hidden there as well—tucking the bundle under her mattress. But as she climbed into bed she felt short of breath and ice in her veins. Her mouth began to foam and her vision blurred. She tried to stand but her legs were too weak and she fell to the floor—the poison Aldora had covered Elisabet's bundle with working so quickly she did not even have time to scream. A moment later she lay dead—only a day from becoming the lady she had always dreamed of being. Arthur found her the next morning, and he mourned with all his heart until he learned from the mortician the truth of Elisabet—the truth of Ellis.

For after Ellis left madam Bailie's estate he assumed her title. The guard had gone inside to remove who he had been told was the intruder. But, though he searched high and low, he could not find anyone. Ellis, now Elisabet, refused to enter the mansion again until the 'intruder' was found. But before another search could be made, a fire spread across the estate, burning it to the ground. Elisabet was horrified to find that though she was now a respected lady, she was just as poor as she had been.

Madam Bailie, however, had fled from her home after setting it ablaze—finally liberated from the name and title that haunted her. She took with her all that remained of her husband's fortune and lived her the rest of her days free of the cage she had built. And though she did feel some remorse for the fate she knew Ellis would suffer, she loved him far more for setting her free.

Burgundy Grass

The glass was half empty no matter how much she poured. I took a long look at the two drinks before me till they became one. I threw it back because of what I felt and the hope I wouldn't feel it anymore. The taste of whiskey used to tie my balls to a train, but now water packs more of a punch. I let my cigarette roll off my fingertips, knowing I got a pack of burgundy grass to smoke anytime my lungs felt the fire.

"Another?" she asked, the bottle gliding to my side to help the two empty seats keep me company. I nodded, letting my head move up and down her figure. I didn't order another because I wanted a drink; I ordered another because I wanted her. I wanted to touch her as if she wanted me to. Like I was someone special in her life that she wouldn't give up for anything in the world.

She left me to go make nice with a kid her age, and I fired up another cigarette. The jukebox played the blues and I fit the mood. I kept my eyes low so people couldn't see me seeing them—something I'd learned quick in the big house. Worked plenty good keeping people in check—so good I scared myself. But I didn't mind much that I didn't recognize who I was anymore. I didn't have anything to live for, let alone miss, now that I had changed.

Headlights exploded through the cracks of the blinds, leaving a prison bar shadow that traced the walls. I tried to shake the image out of my head—feeling it rattle around but stay where it was all the same. The lights died and the sound of the car that had pulled up vanished. I turned my head to the side so I'd have first view of whoever came through the door. My nerves couldn't stay still, so I threw back another to try and deliver the kill. By the time I opened my eyes, the stranger was a guest.

Tall fella with boulder shoulders and a long grey coat. He was rimming the end of a cigar that smelled better than anything I'd ever smelled before. He walked past me, not even noticing I was there. The waitress gladly showed him to a seat, and I could see the lad she'd been flirting with turn red with envy. I turned slowly back toward the counter and let my mind relax for the first time in a long time.

I got out this morning. I had years, I'd sooner forget, to think about what I was locked up for—that and whether or not I wanted to take it any further when I was let go. But now that the opportunity was here; now that I was free, nothing seemed as simple as it was when I'd planned it. I kept telling myself all a man has is his pride. But it's hard to stay proud behind bars. If I did what I told myself I was gonna do, I'd spend the rest of my days running. But from what I heard, there ain't much living to be done after you've become comfortable in prison—released or not.

The fella threw the last bit of his cigar into an ash tray on his way to the washroom and I contemplated taking it to smoke later. The bar lingered with the taste of everyone in it, but it smelled sweet since he arrived. I wondered how much he had in his pockets and if there were another cigar. I thought about how secure he looked and how stupid he was. A quick knife before he got in his car and everything he'd worked for could be mine. I'd seen it a thousand times… I took another drink to shut myself up before I forgot where I was and did something stupid.

It's odd—I didn't remember seeing people for what they were worth until after I'd been in jail. I didn't imagine killing a man for his watch, or stealing when others weren't looking. Jail made me the criminal I'd been locked up for being.

I reached across the counter and took the bottle since the bartender was now busy trying to secure her elder years. The young lad left, his confidence shattered by her quick turn of favor. Now there were only the three of us left in the bar, but, fortunately, nobody paid me any mind. Being invisible felt good—no one looking to take or break what little I had left. I reached into my pocket and fished out the last of the cash I had on me when I got sentenced. I tossed it onto the counter and took one final drink for the road. I'd made my decision.

A call came in to skip breakfast and head downtown—no specifics. Marie, my wife, raised her head as I grudgingly hauled my ass out of bed. The sun was up enough that I considered it morning, but was still low enough that traffic hadn't hit. I assumed that had something to do with why they'd called me in so early. The routine had always been to let the corpse wait in a cooler until I was ready to see it. Something was up and now I was too.

"Where are you going?" Marie asked, yawning and squinting from the morning sun creeping in through the window.

"Cap said to head over to Leon's place. Don't know why, but I gotta go all the same," I replied, opening the dresser and removing an undershirt.

"What's happened?"

"I don't know. But they told me it was urgent," I said, choosing to forgo my usual formal attire in light of the circumstances. "You gonna go shopping today?"

"Sure," she muttered, still half asleep.

"Get some of that blueberry jam I like, we're almost out," I stated, tying my tie and grabbing a grey fedora.

"What do you want for dinner?"

"You decide," I replied, walking towards the door as Marie lay back down to try and go to sleep.

I slid my arms down the sleeves of my coat and flicked the collar up to keep the wind at bay. I caught a final glance of Marie watching me leave—we used to say we loved each other every time we parted but now we settled for a glance. Maybe we'd drifted apart or maybe we just cut the formality. I thought about it all the way to the scene of the crime but came to no revelation to satisfy my mind. I raised my head to see a brigade of squad cars, lights blazing. Whatever happened, it was big.

"Terrence," Cap said, popping out from behind a car. I watched a few men run into Leon's apartment building before I turned my eyes to the Captain.

"Quite a stir," I muttered, looking around at everyone looking at me… this didn't make sense. "Why are they going into his building? Captain, what's going on?"

"Leon was murdered last night. I'm sorry, Terrence," he informed me, keeping his head low. I held my breath a moment, realizing that people watched me because I was the last who didn't know. My partner Leon and I had been investigating together for the better part of a decade. He didn't have any enemies worth worrying about, and he wasn't dumb enough to get himself killed. But he'd still managed to trip over something more than bad luck and ended up dead. I couldn't believe it.

"What?"

"We found him in his apartment, stabbed to death. Plenty signs of a struggle, but no witnesses to tell," Captain explained, knowing well that I wasn't the type to back down just because it hit close to home. He knew finding the killer was the only way for me to cope. And I knew, despite his best efforts to hide it, that he didn't want me working the case—losing the leg of what you got is enough to drive any man crazy.

"What can I do?"

"For today, you can relax. I'll let you at it tomorrow but for now I need you to take some time with it."

"Any time I take for me, takes away from this."

"Terrence, we have enough guys working on it now; we'll have something for you tomorrow. Go home."

"Go home? Then why the hell'd you call me down here?"

"Because if I told you over the phone you woulda come anyway," he exclaimed, hitting it on the head. "Leon was..." he said, stopping when he referred to him using the word 'was.' "This is more than personal, it's family—we'll get the guy; your taking the day off won't change that."

"What the hell do you expect me to do? Read the paper? Go to the movies?"

"You do what you gotta... if I were you: I'd clean the shit outta my head so I didn't step in it trying to find the guy."

"Where's his body."

"Terrence..."

"Look, I know everything there is to know about Leon—stuff he never told anybody. Putting me on the side is like throwing away evidence," I stated, the fire of my words coming from the pain of the moment—Cap knew that, and so he listened. "You'll make this a lot easier for everyone if you pretend like I did what you told me, and tell me to do what I want."

I sat on the only bench that didn't have somebody sleeping on it. I nestled my ass cozy under a tree across from the apartment complex. I wished I had a gun—killing eye to eye takes all the life you've got. But I wasn't one to complain, or sit idly while the opportunity was there.

I checked around for anyone who could place me at the scene—venders, whores or your all-around-weirdoes who find solace in the night. But I came to realize that I wasn't worried that they'd see me, I was worried they'd interfere. Revenge is a hell of a thing: when it's finally over and done with it doesn't help you sleep any better but you can finally think clearly. I lit a cigarette and enjoyed the last few minutes of genuine freedom—it seemed a fair trade for my sanity.

Marie was crying by the time I got home—she'd heard the news over the radio. I didn't console her because I didn't want to disturb her. That and the fact that I held the answers to every question she could, and would, ask. I crept into the study to avoid satisfying her curiosity. Leon had been a close friend to both of us, but Marie wouldn't understand that finding his killer was more important than grieving for him. And I didn't have the patience or piece of mind to explain it—I was on a mission, nothing mattered but that.

I dropped a file onto my desk and took a seat before it. I clicked on a lamp and rubbed my eyes, trying to clean away the sickly feeling that had followed me all day. Either my chair or the floorboards creaked, and I turned my head to the side. Marie stood in the doorway, wearing a night gown and a frown. I wish she could have left me alone.

"Yeah?" I asked, not even turning around to address her.

"What happened, Terrence? All the radio said was that he was found dead in his apartment."

"We don't know much more than that, Marie. They're gathering clues, dusting for prints, and interviewing everyone who knew him... there's no telling how long this'll take," I muttered, giving the same speech I routinely did on the job.

"Do you have any idea who could of done it?"

"Marie, please," I sighed, opening the top drawer of my desk and removing a bottle of whiskey. "I need to work."

"He was your best friend," she exclaimed, appalled that I could even consider working at a time like this. I took a swig straight off the bottle and turned my chair towards her.

"Then why don't you give me some alone time so I can find the son of a bitch that killed him," I stated, hurting her feelings so I could resume my work.

"Can I get you anything?" she asked, pushing the right way at the wrong time. I stood up and stomped over to her, lifted my hand and brought it hard across her face. She knew the routine—she started crying again and left me alone. I turned back to my desk and lifted the bottle, gripping it tight for the long road ahead.

I'd examined Leon's body earlier in the day. He didn't look the same in death—it was as if the knife gave his soul a way to escape, leaving only the scars of his life behind. He'd been cut over and over again but would have survived if it weren't for one stab to the abdomen that slashed an artery. He died of massive blood loss but never managed to get to a phone—the killer had stayed after the crime, either to watch him die or to come to terms with the hell that killing a cop would earn him.

I took the fire escape up the apartment complex, checking each window along the way until I found one that was unlocked. I put my fingers under the crack of the frame and pulled it gently upward. I crept inside with all the care of Saint Nick, only with a knife instead of presents. An old married couple slept in the bed beside the window I'd come in through. The man's mustache shook to the bellows of his snore and I relaxed just enough to keep from shitting myself. Killing's easy; it's finding the right moment that's the tricky part.

I paused a moment to consider robbing them but shook it off. I made my way around the bed, until I came to the door leading to the living room. I turned the handle, flinching as the hinges creaked. My heart pounded in my chest as the old women rolled over in bed. Nothing. I opened the door slowly and let myself into the hallway.

I walked casually to the stairs and climbed each one, thinking of how much closer I was with every step. It wasn't long before I stood in front of the door separating me from my revenge. I reached into my pocket and pulled out a knife. I looked deep inside myself, past all the shit in my stomach clouding my head, to see if there was any sign of reservation. Nope. I'd already done the time; now it was time to do the crime.

I woke up to a commotion coming from the hallway. My head throbbed and nearly exploded when the empty bottle on my lap crashed to the floor. The sun was just coming up and I felt like my stomach might too. But before I could decide how sick I was, I turned my head to see a couple of the guys from the force walk into the apartment. They both paused when they saw me, looked at each other, and approached awkwardly.

"You couldn't have called?" I groaned, stretching my arms out.

"Terrance, we're gonna need you to come down to the station."

"Yeah… I got some people to talk to first but I was gonna work my way down there later this afternoon."

"No, we need you to come now."

"Why? What happened?"

"Nothing. We just need to… ask you a few questions."

"So ask," I exclaimed, my hangover keeping me from catching on. One officer walked around to the side of me in case I tried to make a move. The other nervously rubbed his neck, searching for words. And, suddenly, I realized that they weren't asking. "I'm a suspect?"

"You're more than that. You're under arrest."

It went better than I ever would have thought. No people to interrupt, no screams I couldn't silence, or blows I couldn't dodge. I stabbed and slashed with every broken bone in my body; every shattered dream, and nightmare, that I would never see revenge. It's an odd sensation putting a knife into a jugular only to realize you have to push that extra little bit to make it through. Now, it was done. I looked down at my hands and the bloody remains and breathed the satisfaction of a satisfied mind. It was fleeting and I knew that. Soon it would hit me—the countless years of rage that boiled inside me, desperate for a release.

I dropped my head into my hands and collapsed on the floor. I'd done it—I was a murderer. I'd been locked away an innocent man and come back to take the life that took mine. But… having done what I'd done, it meant I'd become what everyone said I was; it meant I'd become what they'd locked me up for. I clawed at my scalp and curled into a ball. The tears bled the weight I'd carried with me and I knew I'd have years of misery before I'd be free of it. They deserved to die—I just wished I wasn't the one who had to oblige... I lit a cigarette while I waited for the next in line.

"Life," the judge bellowed, his eyes bearing down on me as though there were reason to. I swallowed hard and dropped my head—the charges stuck, despite every thing I'd tried and every pleas I'd made, I was going to jail.

But, to be honest, that wasn't the half of it. I turned my head to see Marie crying for me—the lying bitch... I'd sat in a cell, not knowing what had happened—why they'd accused me let alone condemned me. But then... when she didn't come to visit, I asked my lawyer the right questions to get to the truth.

She'd gone to the station the night I fell asleep at my desk and told them I killed Leon. She handed over the murder weapon, a knife from his apartment, that she'd allegedly 'found' covered in blood. It only took me a second to see what I never would have considered before—she was having an affair. But the fact that her prints were all over Leon's place meant nothing because mine were too. Close friends... But I didn't know why she'd killed him; I couldn't have imagined she was capable... my sweet little wife. I wanted to kill her. And, as I was escorted from the room, I swore to myself that I'd live through hell to see her die.

Marie had aged—it was the first thing I noticed when she walked through the door. Her face fell horrified when she saw me, covered in the blood of her husband—the man she'd loved and sold me up the river for. I took a long drag of my cigarette before throwing it to the side, landing on the body of my old friend and boss, Cap the captain.

"Oh my god, Terrence," she wheezed, clutching her stomach.

"He didn't tell me why the two of you did it. But, then again, I didn't really have the patience to ask or power to stop," I explained, my blood lust temporarily quenched from having murdered all she cared for. Watching her squirm was satisfying—I let the anticipation grow.

"You monster… you god damn monster," she cried, her lips and knees quivering. She clenched her handbag tightly, bracing it as though it were a shield. "How could you?"

"How could you!" I screamed, exploding out of my chair. She jumped back, startled, lifting her bag to her chin. "You fucked one friend, murdered another, and sent me to hell! I'm no monster, I'm what you made me!" I raged, my footsteps pounding closer and closer to her. "Why'd you do it? Why'd you do it you god damn whore?!" I yelled, bringing my arm back, forming a long overdue fist. But, before my arm could reach her, the bottom of her bag exploded bullets into my chest. I fell back, stunned and paralyzed—looking up at her holding an old revolver she'd carried with her. She stood trembling, as I gasped for air, finding blood instead.

"He loved me enough to protect me from you… to take you and your God forsaken partner out of our lives, and this world, for good!" she explained, walking over to me and pointing the gun between my eyes. "You wouldn't have let me leave… you would have killed me if I tried," she sobbed, shifting back and forth from rage and sorrow. "And I don't regret the years of your freedom I took to win my own for a single second," she finished, adjusting her grip one last time before she'd put me out of my misery. I coughed blood onto the barrel of her gun, trying to sputter my last words. She pulled the trigger.

Three Little Wolves

"Lay it down fah me... slow, slow, like the drive-by-show, shootin' in tha dark darker than coal. No, no, tha ghetto don't know friend from foe, even niggas an niggers ain't brotha's no mo," said the first little wolf.

"Shit, pigs bitin us like their motha's tit. Cause every nigga's a suspect fo a suspect verdict. Don't matta none if pigs don't plant a gun, paint a nigga's hands red an he don't need one," said the second little wolf.

"Pigs hate niggas like niggas hate SPAM, food stamp stampede unda tha boot ah tha man. Each can makes us wonder if we can, make mo out a less by sellin by the gram. Cause I'll be damned if I don't poison my brotha mahn, let him smoke my problems away putting papah in my hand," said the third little wolf.

"Yeah, yeah, check it... uh... pigs ain't welcome here cause... um... cause it ain't like thay our cousins," said the little wolves little brother.

"Nigga what? Sheep what tha fuck you doin here?"

"I'm kickin it."

"Hell no you ain't. Way you kickin it you gun get kicked."

"But I wanna hang wit ya'll."

"No, Sheep. Lea'us alone an go play witch'yo frayn's."

"But..."

"But no, get yo butt outa here. Da street ain't no place fo kids. Go over to da playgoun' and we come get'chew layta fo suppa, aight?"

Sheep, as his brothers called him, dropped his chin and turned his head. He walked slowly away from them towards the playground as his brothers resumed their rhymes. They never included him except when their mother told them to, and even then he could tell they didn't want to. It seemed he couldn't do anything as well as they could and, because of that, they couldn't respect him. He mumbled rhymes to himself as he walked, determined to show them he was the missing link in their circle.

"Mahn, dat little nigga got some balls comin' out here."

"Yeah, he got balls but he ain't got no brains."

"Serious, yo. Dat kid should know betta."

"Nigga please. He does know betta. An him bein' out here don't matta none wid us around."

"Shit yeah... yah know dat ain't wack, it's a matta a fact, three little wolves watching Sheeps back."

"He cravin' fo a grazin' like bran fo raisins, raised in dah hood, darker than what's pavin..."

But before Straw could finish his verse gunshots rang across the street. Startled, his two brother's, Stick and Brick, ducked behind a wall. In the distance they could see the battle. Straw joined his brothers behind the wall, watching a war wage between two cars as they drove wildly, firing at one another.

"Nigga, come on!" Straw cried, tugging at his brother's sides. Stick stood up and followed him to run away. But, before they turned the corner they looked back to see Brick stay where he was. "Brick come on!"

"Sheep's ova there mahn!" he yelled, as the cars made a disoriented pass past the playground. "Mahn, fuck it!"

Brick exploded into a sprint towards the feuding cars and the playground in their path. The screech of tires and cracks of gunshots echoed into the neighborhood that had emptied from the sounds. Stick and Straw watched terrified as Sheep innocently crept towards the gunshots, thinking it a game or something fun—too young to know better. Brick darted frantically behind cover until he made one final run for his brother. He snatched him under his arm and pulled him behind a building, peeking his head from behind the wall to see the cars drive off, guns blazing.

"Fuck, mahn," Brick wheezed, collapsing against the wall and loosening his grip on his brother. But, as he did so, Sheep went limp and rolled out of his arms. "Sheep?" Brick exclaimed, pulling his brother towards him. But Sheep said nothing. And as Stick and Straw came running to his side, Brick pulled his hand from his brother's body to see it stained with blood. Sheep had been shot.

"Where was his mother?" the officer demanded, quickly scribbling on a form while the paramedics zipped the bag around Sheep's body.

"She's at home," Stick answered, fixated on the black bag they'd stuffed his brother into.

"I asked where she **was**."

"She was at home," Straw exclaimed, glaring at the officer. "Where was ya'll?"

"What?"

"We called you, mahn… ova an hour ago. Where were you?"

"Why did he run towards the gunshots? Was he retarded or something?"

"He's a kid, he didn't know any betta."

"Didn't his mother teach him better? Or wasn't she around for that either?"

"She…"

"Yeah, whatever," the officer interrupted. "Was he carrying a gun?"

"He was five years old."

"So probably just a knife then," the officer exclaimed, tearing the form off his clipboard and stuffing it into his pocket. "We're done here. Go home and tell your mother that where she should have been was watching her kids."

The officer strolled back to his car and gave a signal for everyone to pack it up. Stick and Straw retreated angrily from where they stood to join Brick who rested against a nearby wall. He stared into the distance, watching the sirens drive back to the stations—past the houses where the killers lived. The boys stayed silent, trying to think of how to tell their mother.

"God's Grave experienced yet another homicide today, this time that of a young boy," the anchorman said as the TV showed stock footage of gang violence so the reporters wouldn't have to go back to the hood. "Police have suggested that it was gang related, despite the victim being only five years of age."

"Mahn, turn dat shit off," Stick grumbled, throwing a soda can at the screen. Brick obliged begrudgingly, knowing it would mean hearing more of their mothers sobs. They'd told her what happened and she'd collapsed on the spot. They carried her to her bedroom and tried to console her, but she couldn't hear them. Eventually they left her alone, though she never stopped crying.

"What we gun do mahn?" Stick asked, hunched forward in his chair, his hands pressed firmly together.

"Grieve, mahn. Only shit we can do," Brick sighed, avoiding eye contact. He felt rage tugging inside of him, but he didn't know what to hold onto to cope.

"Nigga, you fucked? You get hit too, nigga? I asked what we gun do?"

"We can't do nuttin'."

"Maybe ya'll can't do nuttin'. But I can," Straw exclaimed stepping into the room wearing a blood-red-hoody. Stick and Brick froze, both of them knowing damn well what he intended to do.

"That's what I'm talkin' bout."

"Oh hell no!" Brick shouted, standing up to block his brothers as they turned to leave. "Ya'll just need ta relax."

"Nigga get the fuck out my way."

"I can't do dat. I ain't losin' anotha brotha today."

"No worries, mahn. Dem brotha's tha one's gun die. Now get outta my way."

"I can't do dat, mahn!"

"Nigga move!" Straw screamed, as he and Stick wrestled with Brick to leave the apartment.

"What the hell ya'll think you doin'?!" their mother hollered, leaning against the doorframe of her room so she'd have the strength to stand. "Ya'll just a bunch a niggers?"

"Ma, we ain't…"

"Shut yo mouth boy! You think I don't know what you thinkin'? You think I ain't thought it too?"

"We gotta put things right, ma."

"Right? What the hell yo pride have to do with puttin' things right?"

"It ain't pride, it's…"

"Boy, shut yo mouth… we gonna leave it to the police."

"The pigs?! They ain't gonna do a damn thing!"

"Then ain't a damn thing gonna be done."

"The pigs were there ma. We called em. An all they did was laugh, like Sheep was just anotha nigga getting' his due. Laughed just the way crackas always do when thay keep a nigga down."

"The white man ain't keepin us down no mo, we doin' it to ourselves; he's just enjoyin the show."

"Ma, that's ignorant. You don't know what it's like."

The boys mother grimaced with rage from what her son had said and stormed forward, delivering a hard slap across his face.

"I don't know what it's like?! I lost my son! An I'm about to lose another because he's too proud to do what's right; because he's too dumb to see that there ain't nobody comin to shoot him, he the one gonna go kill someone's baby!"

The room was silent for a moment and the boys didn't dare speak before their mother. She stood, broken, weak and helpless—without a way to stop her son. She knew he was too stubborn and proud to listen to her, or to see any justice beyond spilling more blood. She returned to her room, and her tears, leaving her boys stunned and humbled.

"What you gun do, mahn?" Stick asked, taking a seat beside Brick.

"I'm gun huff, and puff, and blow thay motha fuckin' heads off."

"It's been two hours an he ain't back!" Stick cried, pointing out the window into the night. They'd heard the shots in the distance but had yet to see Straw return home. "We can't just lea'him out there!"

"You know dat if he did what he left to do, he ain't the one commin back, they gun be comin' fo us."

"Not if we go get him."

"It's too late for dat…"

"Nah, it ain't too late fo dat!" Stick yelled, rushing towards the door. Brick stood up quickly and put himself between his brother and the door. "Don't do dis again mahn, you wastin' time!"

"Mahn, open yo eyes! What you think gonna happen if you go?! They gun shoot yo dumb ass too!"

"He dyin', an you know he dyin'! How da hell can you just sit here and do nuttin'?"

"Cause if we wanna live, if we wanna get our asses outta God's Grave, we ain't got no choice but to do nothin'! Othawise, dis shit gun eat us alive!"

"Nigga we already been eaten alive! How the hell you think we got here?!" Stick screamed, pushing against his brother to force him out of his way. But Brick pushed back, harder than he had with Straw and, soon enough, it came to blows.

A right hook at the wrong time, put Brick on his back and gave Stick his exit. He paused a moment before leaving— looking down at his brother, ashamed that he would leave Straw alone to die.

"Nigga… what good's yo pride widout'chyo brotha, mahn?" Stick asked, closing the door before Brick could reply.

Brick thought of chasing his brother as he listened to him run down the stairs of the complex. But he knew, the same as he'd always known, that his brother's were as good as dead.

Three loud thuds came from someone pounding on the door and Brick woke sharply from his sleep. He pushed himself off the couch, walking quickly to the door in case his brothers had returned. But when he looked through the peephole all he saw was the officer who'd questioned them earlier about Sheep's death.

"I hear you in there. Open the door," the officer demanded.

"What'chu want?"

"Is this the Wolves residence?"

"Who wants to know?"

"The police. Now open the door.

"Not without a warrant or a gun to my chinny chin chin, you pig motha fucka."

"It's regarding two tenants of this residence."

"What about em?"

"You wanna know that, then you open the door."

Brick paused a moment, contemplating whether or not the cop was there for a raid or to notify the next of kin. He hesitantly unlocked the door, pulling it slowly open.

"What about em?"

"I know you," the officer exclaimed, recognizing Brick from earlier in the day.

"Nah, nigga, yah don't. Now what about em?"

"They... one was killed after he entered a house and murdered three of its residents. And the other was found shot to death not far from there."

Brick let go of the door and dropped his eyes as his heart fell. He let out a short breath before tensing up once more. But it wasn't as simple as dead and buried—he would be a suspect too.

"So what tha fuck you want?"

"To let you know."

"Let me know?"

"Yeah."

"You mean tah bring me in."

"No."

"Pig, I ain't as dumb as you is ugly. I know you here to come get me."

"Those are my orders, yeah... but... I figure you lost three brothers today, so, when I came to get you, you weren't home."

"Oh, yeah, that's much betta. Take away my alibi an make me a suspect, huh?"

"No... you're not a suspect anymore."

"Save yo pity nigga!" Brick screamed, flinging open the door and stepping angrily towards the officer. He felt every vein in his body pump adrenaline as he struggled to keep his fists at his sides. "I didn't do shit, and I don't need yo god damn sympathy to keep me outta jail!"

"Actually, you do."

Brick clenched his jaw with rage, backing off from the cop as he stopped to think about what he'd said. Getting taken-in is all it would take for Brick to be guilty—his brothers had made sure of that.

"Aight… fine."

"You know what I think?"

"Mahn, I don't give a fuck what you think."

"That's fair… but I'm gonna tell you anyway. To us, you're just a bunch of niggers, and to you we're just a bunch of pigs. But it's not until we've admitted that that anything's gonna change."

"Fuck you. It ain't till things change till things gonna change."

Deviled Egg

"It's the sound a record makes when it needs a needle—like the pause for air between a baby's cries. That's the stuff silence is made of, baby; that's the stuff music just can't play," Tommy told me, leaning like the tower of Pisa. "But just cause something can't play don't mean it's not a part of the game. Dissonance, for instance, is the sexiest flavor of flavors—so flat it's sharp, if you can dig it."

"I can dig it," I exclaimed, taking a lustful puff—holding the smoke in to feel warm inside. "But the boat don't float without the notes."

"Maybe, baby. But the blues ain't about keeping your head above water."

"I'm not your baby, baby. And this business ain't about going down with the ship," I explained, handing him his resignation—a torn contract and an empty envelope where his bills would have been. Tommy's face broke, but his heart kept beating; I could see now he knew what the blues were.

The plan was to buy Tommy back before his next album—make him make something mighty fine before he became a find. But that's the business of the blues—break a fella to give him a break—happy artists are as useless as sad clowns.

"But I…" he started to cry, as I stood up and straightened my skirt.

"Nothing personal, Tommy—you know I'm just the messenger," I stated, dabbing my cigarette in an ashtray and striking a pose for the crowd. Dames like me didn't come around slum bars often; dames like me didn't stay either. "Billy says 'hi.'"

"Don't you mean 'goodbye?'"

"As a matter of fact, I do," I finished, turning heads with my hips as I walked out the door. Now that Billy's errands were done, Billy and me could have some fun. But I couldn't help turning back one more time to see Tommy's sweet face—heartbroken and alone. There was something about that kid that didn't sit right with me—I liked him.

The street gave me a fist full of wind and half a mind to head back inside. The air smelt of something out of a factory, and the trees mocked my nostrils. Suddenly, the world wasn't as sure of itself as I was—and the spinning had to be everything else. I held my stomach as I wobbled to an alleyway, feeling like a deviled egg. My pretty little lips parted to a damn river of my breakfast coming out—and it wasn't till I could taste every last bite that I stopped feeling so terrible. It occurred to me that I was late—dragging on a long time seeing Billy, and, just now, coming on time to see Billy junior. The stupid son of a bitch had got me pregnant.

---

2 months later…

"Fifty calls for him today and not one's gone through," secretary Sally squawked, as I strutted past her desk—too busy to say 'hello' and too indignant to mean it. "Is there some reason everything has to go through you?"

"I do what he says, and so do you. Which means, you know the reason same as I do."

"Doesn't change the fact that nothing's getting done when you're not around."

"Well it's a good thing I'm around then, isn't it?" I stated, stopping my walk to put my foot down on Sally—she never did trust me, and I never did like that she was smart enough not to. But I couldn't get rid of her—she'd have to hear it from Billy's mouth and that wasn't part of the plan by a long shot.

"It's good for you, bad for business."

"The 'business' is none of your business. You take the calls, you give em to me and I give em to Billy. You got a problem with that, then you've got a problem."

"I haven't seen Billy in some time... maybe he should leave his office sometime."

"Maybe you should do your job and let me do mine," I replied, flicking my wrist to extend my hand—snatching the messages out of her grasp. "Or, maybe, you should spend more time watching your mouth and less time watching where Billy goes."

"Yes, ma'am," she growled, smiling like someone stabbed a fishhook in her cheek—just the kind of respect I respected.

"Don't bother us for the rest of the day," I ordered, cracking open the door to Billy's office as Sally sat back down at her desk. "And stop dressing for the corner—If you're gonna give jobs after work, start bringing two outfits with yah," I finished, slamming the door to let her know her place. I smiled leaning against the knob, listening to her thrash angrily about at her desk. Bitch didn't know anything for certain, but she was sniffing too close for comfort—particularly given the smell.

Billy sat where I'd left him, propped up in his big chair facing the closed blinds of his penthouse view—the kind of wealth a gal like me had come to expect. But, when Billy found out I was expecting, he didn't take too kind to the idea of feeding another mouth. I still had the bruises from when his henchmen abducted me—still hurt to pee—still hurt to breathe. But he'd been dumb enough that he didn't say nothing to no one about it, otherwise Sally'd be calling me into the station and throwing away the key. But good ol' Billy, never suspected a dame like me had it in her—never suspected that for scrambling our baby I'd scramble his brains.

"How's the view Billy?" I asked, turning him round in his chair to see his blood had dried into the upholstery. He had the same horrified expression from when I'd clocked him on the head and stuck him with the knife—27 times the miserable time that son of a bitch had put me through. His baby was gone, just like he'd planned it—too bad for Billy, it had been my baby too.

    I sat on the desk smoking a cigar to cover the smell coming from Billy. I played a record while I worked—one of his favorites, and the last thing he'd ever heard. My fingers flipped through his messages, tossing some and saving others. Billy's business was just as crooked as the dick that dick held me up with. His whores, his henchmen, and just about every chump a man of power had to step on to get to the top every morning, were on his everyday call list. But it wasn't till I came to one delicious little note that my heart stopped and a smile spread wide across my face—payday.

    I put the cigar down on the desk and snatched up the phone, dialing half a circle at a time till my ear started ringing. The message was simple—'come get your money.' The problem was complicated—Billy was dead. And it wasn't till another day was done that I could light up his office and play the whole thing off as an accident. Unfortunately, that meant I had only today and tomorrow to either make nice with the banker, or bank on luring him here. I killed one man after all—and experience told me they're all the same.

"Hello?" the banker barked, the sound of registers and hustling bustle bursting over his end of the line.

"This is Betsy calling from Mr. Steel's office regarding his upcoming financial transaction with you," I explained, dolling it real innocent like.

"All right, let me speak with him."

"Well, unfortunately, Mr. Steel is deafly ill and hasn't' come out of his office all day. I'm here with him, and he's written down exactly what he wants to happen."

"Well, I'm sorry to hear about his condition, but I'm afraid that, short of speaking to or dealing with Mr. Steel himself, I will not be able to complete the aforementioned financial transaction. Perhaps should he call back at a later time that is more suiting to his health, I will be able to assist him then."

"I'm afraid that's simply not acceptable. Mr. Steel is in need of his funds immediately to acquire a new, and astonishingly talented performer. One, who I might add, is not in the least bit cheap or willing to compromise on when he is paid."

"That's all well and good, but it doesn't change my mind or the policies of this establishment. Now if you'll excuse me I have…"

"Very well… Mr. Steel has just instructed me that he will be available tomorrow afternoon, at this office, to personally receive the delivery of his funds."

"Well… I suppose that will work, if it's what he wants…"

"Good. He also requested that you bring an additional months sum to account for increased expenditures. Though, I'm not sure, and I likely don't want to know, exactly what that means," I laughed, wrapping the phone's cord around my finger as I flirted with another murder.

"Alright… I'll have someone call his secretary to confirm."

"Splendid. You have yourself a wonder day," I exclaimed, hanging up the phone and popping off the desk.

This ordeal wasn't what I wanted to happen but it wasn't the worst thing either. Only problem was killing the banker before he could scream, and doing it quiet enough old Sally wouldn't get wise. It appeared I had my work cut out for me. And, as I looked at Billy, I realized appearances were everything.

"Well Billy… let's clean you up, doll-face."

It's easier to make yourself look nice than it is to make a dead guy look half-decent. Billy now had two tins of blush on him and enough cologne to fuel the economy. But it wasn't till I slid a pair of aviator sunglasses onto his face that I could see putting his 'condition' past the banker. Good thing too—the night was winding down and Sally had been snooping around.

I picked my purse off the hanger and tidied myself up for a good nights rest—opening the door to see Sally's big fat frown.

"What is it now Sally? Couldn't get a date?"

"Don't think I don't know what you're doing in there."

"Do think, I don't care."

"And you call me the whore," she stated, wound up enough to unravel.

"Getting men with money doesn't make me a whore, but it sure makes whores jealous."

"What a piece of work you are... nothing but a two bit tramp looking for one big score."

"Better than a one trick pony blocking my way out the door."

"He's staying in his office then, is he? Too stiff from the poison between your legs to move I imagine."

"You can imagine all you like. But it doesn't change your place under me."

"My place under a no-talent-tramp who could only get a part in this town parting her legs?"

"Yeah, same as you, only I'm worth the trouble."

"You god damn hussy!" Sally cried, too pent up with hormones to control herself any longer.

Her hand swung back slow as a pendulum to try and smack me one—too bad for Sally I'd seen my share of beatings. I lifted my hand, blocking hers and knocking her back. But she wasn't done fighting, or making my day twice as long as it had to be. She tore at my clothes, and screamed at the top of her lungs. I stayed calm, backing into the office and letting her let out some steam. Only problem was, I couldn't back up much further without backing into Billy.

Her hands flung out one more time before my elbow caught her square in the nose. She stepped back, stunned, as a fountain of blood made it's new home on her face. She tried to conceal it, but her eyes looked to Billy to make things right. Only, she knew Billy well enough to know something wasn't right about the way he was sitting in his chair. And I knew Sally well enough to know she was the type to put two and two together. I picked up the lamp from Billy's desk and took a step forward. Sally cowered away but fell to the ground before she could make things any harder for me. She stopped twitching after a few good shots and stopped breathing after a few short minutes.

"So much for a good nights rest," I muttered, rolling up my sleeves to clean up my mess.

Sally was a busty old broad who'd seen too many donuts and not enough cigarettes. And if hauling her fat ass around wasn't bad enough, she was starting to let out the hot air she'd been full of.

"Christ sake, Sally," I scoffed, raising my hand to cover my nose as her corpse let out another one.

I zipped her up in one of the bags Billy kept around for his suits—but it wasn't till it came to taking out the trash that I thought twice about the predicament I was in. I never liked Sally but murdering her just wasn't sitting right with me. Something about it ate at my gut in a way I hadn't felt in years—I'd say it was guilt if I didn't know better than to feel guilty. But I didn't have the time to stand around thinking about how I felt—I needed to dump her in the closet and get home for my well deserved beauty sleep. Except karma, or God, or whatever the son of a bitches name is, had a different idea and thought it'd be funny to send me another present. I raised my head from the bag I'd put Sally into to see the late-night-cleaning-woman watch me work.

"What the hell are you staring at?" I yelled, bent forward, dragging the bag along the floor. "You gonna give me a hand or just another reason to have you fired?"

"Yes, of course," the cowardly custodian cried, putting her worries aside when she saw her job was at stake. She shuffled over to me and took Sally's feet, helping me move the body to the closet.

"Thanks, doll," I exclaimed, letting out an exhausted sigh as I closed the closet door and made my way to the exit. "You don't have to worry about Mr. Steel's office, I already cleaned it myself," I told her, touching her arm as I walked past her so she'd turn around as well.

"Oh… yes, ma'am," she stuttered, making a face like a scared puppy as she eyed my features and hair—the usual from a fella but odd for a dame. I scowled and turned to the mirror at my side to see that, at some point in killing Sally, I'd gotten a fair share of her blood on my face. And, if that wasn't bad enough, my hair was about as frightful as the cleaning woman's face.

"God dammit," I groaned, reaching for the fire poker next to the fireplace. "How many people's a broad gotta kill to make a killing?"

The cleaning woman weighed even more than Sally, and trying to fit them both into one closet was all the heavy lifting my back could take. The sun had been down for a good four hours and I'd just gotten the office looking nice again. Only problem was, the phone kept ringing off the hook—couldn't imagine who'd think to call this late at night, expecting an answer—and I certainly didn't want to find out.

I made sure to double check every inch of myself just in case I'd missed a spot of blood. Killing three people was hard work, and covering it up was all kinds of unpleasantness. But at least it was done, and I could finally get home for my much needed beauty sleep.

"Hello?" I heard a man grunt, coming in the office entrance as I closed the closet—looking into the mirror to see a man wearing an overcoat. 'you've got to be kidding me,' I thought to myself as I contemplated how to explain why I was still around without bringing Billy into the picture.

"May I help you?" I asked, stepping away from the closet and making my way towards the door. But as I did so I realized I recognized the man at the door, and he realized he recognized me.

"He let you stay?" the menacing man muttered, suddenly regretting how rough he'd been earlier in the week— how rough he'd been shoving a coat hanger in me and scrambling my insides.

"Of course. We're quite fond of one another," I gleamed, smiling as large as I could without my face exploding with rage—this son of a bitch had to pay. But the gun he'd kept me quiet with a few nights before was the same one he kept fastened to his side. "Little misunderstanding before... he didn't realize I was going to have it taken care of myself."

"He around then?"

"Just stepped out."

"Stepped out where?"

"Billy doesn't tell me everything he does, he just tells me to wait till he's done."

"I can see why he kept you around," he exclaimed, his eyes dragging along my body—as if he hadn't seen enough already. I reached for the fire poker that I'd just finished cleaning the cleaning woman's blood from. The man showed me his back as he noticed Billy's office door was cracked open and a figure sat in his chair. "Isn't that him in there?"

"What's left of him anyway," I stated, bringing the poker down hard onto the man's back. The curve of the metal stuck in him and he hollered loud enough to wake the whole block—taking a jump forward as I pulled the poker out of him to swing again. This time the blow landed on his arm as he raised it to protect himself, reaching for his gun with the other hand. I heard his arm snap so I knew I could fight closer to him—but I wasn't sure how or if I'd be able to survive.

"Get off me!" he screamed, using the elbow of his broken arm to try and fend me off—knocking me a good one in the side of my jaw.

"I thought from the job you did the other night you liked me!" I shouted, kneeing him in his balls as he pulled his gun from his holster. He fell to the floor, trying to aim at me, but I took another swing with the fire poker and knocked the gun clean out of his hand. He looked up at me, shooting spit through his teeth and fire from his eyes.

"Freddy!" he screamed, looking at the door with the hopes his partner would hear him. And, unfortunately for me, Freddy had already come looking to see what all the fuss was about. He stood in the entranceway watching me stand over his friend. Then, as our eyes met, he reached for his hip and I dove for the gun.

The next few seconds were all gun shots and dead bodies and I'm happy to say I wasn't dead or shot. Freddy slid down the door, clenching his wounds as his friend choked to death on his own blood—gushing out of the hole Freddy'd accidentally shot into his partner's neck.

I lay on the ground, panting and crying—all the blood rushing out of my face as a sickly feeling churned in my stomach. But, this time, it wasn't guilt—these men deserved to die, same as Billy. I lay motionless on the floor—expecting to hear sirens or to see another person come looking—but near ten minutes passed and nothing came of the commotion I'd made. I stood up and brushed myself off—feeling something drip down from my head. The goon's blood had soaked into my hair enough for it to look ten shades darker. But, unfortunately, I couldn't tidy my hair till I'd cleaned the place up... again.

It wasn't till ten minutes before the banker was scheduled to arrive that I got everything back to normal. Although, calling five dead people and one tired and irritable murderer 'normal,' was a stretch even for me. But, as I fiddled with the pin in my hair—that I'd managed to wash in the sink and dry in the wind—I realized that I was just moments from the cash that could see me out of this hell hole. Problem was, I was also just moments away from murdering again.

"Good day," I exclaimed, as the banker poked his head into the office. But, much to my dismay, two burly fella's followed close behind him to make sure no one messed with Billy's money—it was a good thing I'd kept those henchman's guns. "Do you have an appointment?"

"Of course, doll," the banker babbled, too fixated on my cleavage to get his sentences straight. "Is... Mr. Steel ready?"

"Of course, doll," I replied, showing the men to Billy's office. "After you gentleman," I exclaimed, opening the door and letting them in. They entered, one after another, too caught up looking at me to look twice at Billy—propped up in his chair with his sunglasses on. "Is there anything I can get for you?" I asked, leering hungrily at the briefcase the banker carried at his side.

"Coffee, please and thank you."

"I was talking to Mr. Steel actually, but coffee it is," I stated, directing them to chairs as I retreated to the exit—removing two guns from my girdles to get the show started. But as I stared down the barrels—my hands shaking and a nervous sweat messing up my makeup—I just couldn't do it again. I couldn't keep telling myself that this was about my baby—it was about me; the same as always. The men stirred in their seats, taking a closer look at Billy and speaking louder to try and get a response.

"Mr. Steel? Are you alright?" the banker barked, getting out of his chair and turning around to see me—as dead on the inside as my deviled insides. I whimpered and sobbed—pulled the trigger and closed my eyes.

There's an awful lot of kick to a revolver, particularly when you're holding one in each hand. And with six feet between me and my targets, I emptied every bullet just in case. My ears rang and my arms shook—the aftertaste of smoking barrels. I dropped the guns on the ground by the banker's men and plucked his briefcase out of his quivering hand—still warm. I propped it up on the desk and flipped it open—breathing a sigh of relief as my eyes took in the sight. Enough cash to disappear and live for years with—and not just some 'simple, good for nothing life' but the real razzle-dazzle type.

I popped the cork to a bottle of brandy and painted the office with it—lighting a cigar so I could put the place up like I'd planned. But as I stood over the corpses of the men I'd murdered—for revenge, for justice, for a ticket out of town—I felt tears pace my cheeks. This wasn't who I was, it was something I'd become—something I'd done and would have to live with. I knew that—from the moment I'd killed Billy to the second I'd shot the banker—I'd spend the rest of my days living with the horrible things I'd done. Then again, it beat living with what I got. I dropped the cigar into a wastebasket full of papers and turned to make my exit.

"Betsy?" Tommy tattled, standing in the office door—drunk and holding a gun in his hand. He had on the same suit from when I'd seen him last, and it looked like he hadn't taken it off the whole two months. I froze, not knowing whether to explain myself or kiss my butt goodbye. But as he stood, illuminated by the growing flames, I realized Billy'd put him out to dry same as me—and same as me, Tommy'd come looking for some payback.

"Hey, Tommy."

"They're dead… there are… dead men… in the office… on fire behind you."

"It's not what it looks like."

"I wasn't gonna hurt you… you were just the messenger," he explained, leaning against the door frame—too drunk to realize what was happening, too drunk to realize what he was doing. "I'm sorry if I scared you, but it had to be done."

"What had to be done?"

"Billy… I had to kill Billy," he slurred, gesturing towards the fire. "He ruined me."

"You're not ruined Tommy—you're just not thinking straight."

"I tried so hard," he sobbed, fiddling around in his pocket to try and find the bottle. I took a few steps to bridge the gap between us and swiped the gun from his hand.

"It's ok Tommy… I won't tell anyone about what you did," I declared, wrapping my arm around him to help him to the elevator. "Now… let's get you cleaned up."

"T… thanks," he exclaimed, letting his head dangle as close to me as he could manage. He was a sweet kid—the kind of fella I could fall for. Or, if worse came to worse, the kind of fella who could take the fall for me.

When the Silence Comes

    A bang crumbled upon the mountain's feet and only an echo remained—for a moment the jungle fell silent. The air burned numb and birds flew from their nests. They circled the tree tops, threading needles in flight—diving through the sky to see for certain that the noise had left them. But just as their nerves settled, and their eyes turned for home, two more cracks thundered the canopy of the forest.

    Below watch of the stars, all that had ears listened to the winds whistle. The trees, painted by night, surrendered the depths of their green to shade and shadow. Animals plundered the darkness—prey, if not in search of. Lizards leapt from branches and bugs buzzed in air. But the noise was of something unseen to the jungle—something fierce and bright. Light had beckoned the call of thunder though no clouds stood overhead—those who had seen it clenched their sides and tasted blood. Upon the cool-dirt of the tropic floor, two souls collapsed and breathed their last breath together. The night passed; the sound was never heard again.

    He sat beside her as they looked upon their fallen friends—still, motionless. He reached a quivering arm out to grasp them, to wake them from their slumber. But they had long drawn silent and cold. The trees whispered a roar of sorrow to the winds chime and, frightened, she clasped his hair.

He ignored her and nudged his friends, confused why they played this game. He too was frightened now.

The sun fluttered between shadows of the leaves. He shook his friends, one last time, to no avail. She peeked over his shoulder, a trickle of confusion feeding a river of worry—she had never seen them like this; had never seen him like this. He grunted, demanding a reply, but nothing was said. He raised his hand and lowered his head. His fingertips brushed his brow as he examined the blood from their bodies. He had seen this—once—years before. Though, it was long forgotten of simple times, free from reminders.

His mother had fallen still. A snarling demon had come in the night. He ran, as did the others—thinking his mother had followed them, thinking she was safe. But when the sun shone blood the next morning, he found her—still, motionless. The others watched him from a distance—curious and afraid. He sat beside her, his head hanging low to her shoulder. And though he was with her, he felt without her—when the silence came.

She tugged his arm, and he returned from memories of old, born anew. The air whispered a warning to them—dancing the tune of a storm to come. She grunted, clasping his hand, and leaned opposite him to force his feet. He collapsed to the strain of her weight and rolled until upright once more. She ran to neighboring trees, seeking cover from the sky. But he lingered—the memory holding him from peace; from her.

Where had they gone?

The rain fell heavy, crashing on the leaves. Puddles jumped to its touch and the jungle bathed, breathing a sigh of satisfaction. She hugged herself for warmth below a tangle of trees, free from the flow of the storm. She watched him, alone, his back to her. She had tried to go to him but he pushed her away. Ever since they had found their friends he had been quiet, withdrawn—she didn't know why.

Water descended his brow, matting his hair and soaking his skin. His eyes stared lifelessly into the distance, the storm around him inconsequential to that of his mind. His breaths pushed his stomach out towards his forearms, planted firmly in mud. His thoughts dwelled on his mother and his friends, on love's longing crushed by confusion's grasp. A fear deep inside him clawed through his memories—his mother's blood, his friends' blood—he knew this now as a sign of the silence. But still he pondered, why?

A flash of light exploded from the sky, and above the trees, sounds of battle roared in the heavens. His eyes turned once more towards her, nestling against plates of bark to get comfortable. She was the last of his family—the others lost over years of surviving day-to-day. But the night shadowed her past too. Would she disappear as they had? Would he?

Suddenly his mind broke to the roar of a branch overhead, the wind tearing it from a tree. He watched it fall before he leapt aside—his arm suffering the blow he'd dodged. He breathed hard, clenching his arm as he ran to safety. She awoke abruptly, startled by his return. She moved next to him but he ignored her, looking instead upon his arm—a smear of blood escaping his veins. She reached for the wound, concerned, but he pulled away, panic stricken and disarrayed. She saw in his eyes a tremendous fear but could not understand—the storm grew.

He awoke calmly below cover of canopy. The sky gleamed green through the leaves. The twilight-morning lingered, the final footprint from the storm. Vapor ghosts wandered the rivers before the sun of the day would swallow them, and the trees chattered to the stroke of a tickling wind, leaping through the jungle. But though splendor of the day enclosed him, the storm consumed him—he looked upon his arm, quivering with fear. The silence had yet to come but he felt it already upon him. The blood meant soon he would be still like his friends, and their friends before them. But, what of her?

She sat in the distance plucking ants from a twig. Her lips pecking a babbling kiss as she gobbled up the bugs before her. She leaned against the tree she'd slept upon. He watched her, waiting for her to rest before finding the courage to return.

His heart swung low the night before—sure that in closing his eyes he would sleep with them, and dream of her. But the morning had come and, with it, his certainty had gone. His mind clasped tightly to a desire, deep within him, to stay with her. And, as she raised her head, breaking her best efforts of ignoring him, he returned to her side—ashamed of his actions in the face of fear. She stayed quiet, eying him every other moment, in case he threw another fit.

The tree anchored them as they sat—her thoughts of him, as he thought of her. But while she was confused and thus concerned, his concern was of confusion. He didn't know what the blood meant, or what the silence was. He didn't know why his friends had gone or if they would ever return. His stomach churned fear and wonder, and so he pondered. But he loved her enough not to bother her with his thoughts, for he could see worry in her eyes—for him alone, not because of his friends or the storm. She didn't know, and he could never let her.

The fingers of the sky spread the treetops, and light seized back the offering of the storm. Their shadows hid behind the towering trunk of a tree that, through its life, had seen many like them. A tree that had passed generations through a breath of air, only to exhale and see them die. Who had watched eternity unfold, a testament that silence was not only their fate, but fate itself.

They held each other and said nothing. He could see now what would one day be. All share it; all bare it—when the silence comes.

Morning Routine

I like my wallpaper most in the morning sun. I honestly don't think I'd be a morning person if I didn't wake up to it. I need tea too—Irish breakfast, with or without a breakfast. But, if I'm going to have one, toast is nice... toast and raspberry jam is better. Music is a must—a mellow melody to lull me out of my lull. A loud yawn and a good stretch puts my joints on alert. Followed by a slight sniffle from the chilling fall air and a brisk walk to the bathroom—it's beckon being what pulled me from my rest in the first place. But, what I don't need, and have actually come to very much dislike, is looking out my window to see a homeless man eating from my birdfeeder.

"Hey!" I screamed, leaning out my window, holding my bathrobe shut with one hand while thrashing aside my curtains with the other. "Stop eating out of my fucking birdfeeder!"

He jumped aside and shimmied down the fire escape to escape. I grumbled to myself as I shut my window and returned to my morning routine.

A nice hot shower was perfect—with two gigantic fluffy towels waiting for me when I got out. I had a mismatched pair of slippers—one from each pair of two pairs I'd lost one of.

Work was at the other end of my walk through the park, which was exactly what I needed to wake up. I served people bagels and coffee—always with a big smile and a napkin. The regulars were my first-name-basis-friends who allotted me a window into their lives every day. And, in return for my open ears, they'd come back again and again with more stories to tell.

There was a hot pile of seed-speckled-bum-crap on my balcony, next to two dead squirrels he'd managed to overthrow. He'd used leaves from one of my plants to wipe his ass — hygienic enough to service himself but had still left the leaves crumpled together on my bench.

This morning, I needed a drink.

A good café inspires life. People come in — tired, groggy, grumpy — and they leave awake, alert and happy. I love my job. Not because it pays the most, or is all that easy — any server can tell you how hard it is when a tour bus empties in on top of the morning rush. Instead, I love my job because it makes me feel like me.

"You'll never guess how they met," Gregor announced, keeping his voice two clicks above the norm to accommodate anyone who cared to eavesdrop. "He was riding his bike and he lost control of it going down a hill. So he veered off the road and hit a parked car — smashing right through the back windshield."

"Are you sure you're telling me the right story?"

"Yeah, yeah… anyway, he was knocked unconscious and just lay there in the back seat. So, after a couple minutes, she came outside and got in her car — not even noticing what had happened. She drives off and starts talking on her cell with me. Then I heard her scream at the top of her lungs when the guy woke up. They'll have been married two years next week."

"Wow."

"So, you see, you can find it anywhere."

"What? A concussion?"

"No, love… or, whatever variation you're after."

"Ha… I'll just stick with your stories and keep to myself," I laughed, shooting down yet another patron's encouragement. Gregor was the most interesting morning conversationalist I knew—but even him trying to instill hope in me was hopeless. It's not hard to smile with a broken heart, but it is hard not to frown. Everyone had noticed my change of pace and the subtle sulk of my face. With my ex, Jordan, things made sense. And now I was without him.

"Amy, can I have a word," my boss, Michael, exclaimed—poking his head out of the back room—arms crossed and frown loaded.

"Sure thing," I replied, saying a quick goodbye to Gregor before sliding into the back.

"Ok, um… now I'm not accusing you of anything, but, I've asked everyone else, so I have to ask you too," he explained, fidgeting, wincing and avoiding eye contact all at the same time. "There were a few packages of poppy seeds missing from the inventory, do you know anything about that?"

"No, not at all… is it an inventory error or did someone steal them?"

"I'm looking into it."

"Ok."

"Also, there were a couple of dead squirrels found in the back, any idea how that happened?"

"Uh…" I muttered, my face unable to convey how confused I was. "There were dead squirrels in the café?"

"Yeah, and I'm pretty sure they weren't here when I locked up last night."

"That's weird... I found two dead squirrels on my balcony earlier today."

"Really? Huh... maybe there's like a rodent plague going around or something," he joked, as I tried my best to swallow the coincidence of missing seeds and dead squirrels.

"Maybe."

"Alright, now, this is the really weird one," he stated, taking a deep breath and giving a loud sigh. "Did you... or... do you know who might have... taken a shit on the floor?"

"What?" I gasped, immediately thinking of my homeless adversary's attack upon my balcony and, apparently, my employer as well.

"Yeeeeah... I'm sorry to have to ask but... I really need to know."

"Someone took a crap on the floor here in the restaurant?"

"Over there, specifically," he replied, pointing to a handful of paper towels covering up the evidence. I walked shakily over to it, feeling my heart start to quicken. Then, with a delicate finger and an agitated nostril, I peeked under the fluffy white sheets to see a pile of seed-speckled-bum-crap.

"Mother fucker," I exclaimed, taking a quick step back to keep from throwing up—this meant war.

"What are you gonna do?" my friend Janine asked as I cleaned up the apartment for the brief time my ex, Jordan, would be over.

"Look good and be angry."

"I meant, have you changed your mind?"

"Why would I change my mind? He's an asshole."

"Do you love him?"

"Of course."

"Well, that's one reason."

"No, I haven't changed my mind," I exclaimed, psyching myself up to a fight-mentality.

"Then why's he coming over?"

"To get his things."

"Just make sure you're not one of them."
"Thanks, coach," I said, checking my watch. "I gotta go."

"Good luck," she sighed, hanging up the phone and leaving me on my own.

I started running through what to say when Jordan arrived. Of course, he was probably doing the same thing. So, since we both had our scripts, the night was less of a discussion and more of a tug-of-war for who got to read which line... I figured I'd wait until after he'd used his best stuff to say that.

I'd showered and changed after work—I could still smell the smell and I needed to wash the thought of it off of me. I'd deliberated how to go about getting revenge on a homeless man and, in the end, decided on the simplest of tactics—poison ivy. After all, he liked to use my plants to clean up after himself. Maybe this way he'd get the hint and go away. But... I couldn't help but wonder how he'd managed to terrorize both my balcony and the café all in one day—he must have eaten a lot of seeds.

The buzzer buzzed and I cleared my throat as I walked over to it. "Yeah?"

"It's me."

Buzzzzzz.

I double checked myself in the mirror before I took a seat on the couch and turned on the TV, like it was no big deal he was coming over. He let himself in a minute later with the key he'd be leaving behind.

"Hey."

"Hey."

"Your stuff's by the door, so there's no need for you to come in."

"I didn't mean to hurt you, Amy… I just don't feel…"

"You're right, you don't. And, now, neither do I. So there's no need for you to come in."

"I love you… I hope I never get the chance to say that again," he said, tossing the key onto my lap as I sat on the couch, doing my best to keep from looking up at him.

"You don't love me."

"It's not a debate."

"That's because I'm right."

"There's more to my life than you right now."

"More to your future too, apparently."

"Yeah… and there's nothing wrong with that," he exclaimed, double checking his stuff so that I wouldn't have to mail anything after he'd moved on.

"So I guess you don't have any regrets."

"I regret that we can't be friends."

"Sorry, friends don't hate each other."

"I don't hate you."

"I wasn't talking about you."

"Goodbye, Amy."

"Get out, Jordan."

He closed the door and I listened to him walk down the hall to the elevator. He kind of loved me and I knew it. I actually loved him and he knew it. But he'd said 'no' too many times for me to believe in a future beyond what we already had. I couldn't explain why staying where we were hurt so much or why I needed more—I suppose I felt rejected even though I was with him. And, when all I got out of our relationship is what I put in, I was just as well off alone.

"They met at a tattoo parlor," Gregor explained, feeling the need to inform me about yet another happy couple he knew. "He was getting the same tattoo she was having covered up."

"Don't you know anyone who met each other normally, like at a bookstore or a café?"

"No… but my cousin went into labor at a Barnes and Noble. Guess what they named him?"

"Copyright infringement?"

"Pretty much," Gregor laughed, tidying up his table to spare me the trouble.

"More coffee?"

"No, thanks… I'm just gonna go to the restroom before heading out," he said, standing up and folding his paper under his arm. I gave him a reassuring smile to cover up my relief—I loved Gregor, but telling him to change the subject wasn't an option.

I wiped down his table and double checked the other patron's statuses. Bagel half eaten, newspaper almost read, latte two sips from the top—for the next few minutes anyway I'd have my head to myself.

I wondered back to the staff washroom and sat down on a toilet, crossing my arms. I let out a slow sigh and stared through the floor. Jordan hadn't called or tried to take it all back, but I still toyed with the idea—of him coming into the café completely nonchalant and ordering something. Maybe he'd stay all day, without saying a word. Just smile at me and laugh, waiting out the time till I got off and we got back together.

I pulled off a patch of toilet paper to dab the tiny tears growing in the corners of my eyes. Now that he was gone I was more hurt than angry—more afraid than confident. I knew I'd made the right choice by letting him go, but that's what hurt the most. I rubbed my eyes, the tears making them itch.

"What the hell?" I grumbled, as I stood up and turned to the mirror to see my face had begun to swell. I gave a few hard blinks to try and shake off the agitation but the itchiness just got worse—spreading to my hands and fingertips. Then, just before my vision started to blur from my tears turned watering eyes, I looked down at the patch of toilet paper I'd used to see a leaf of poison ivy in its place.

"You sure he's not a secret agent?" Janine asked, over yet another late night phone call.

"He's just some asshole homeless guy," I groaned, adjusting the bag of frozen peas I had lying on my eyes. "And I swear to God, it was toilet paper when I used it."

"And you left poison ivy on your balcony for him to use as toilet paper?"

"Yeah."

"Maybe it's karma."

"Karma isn't this obvious."

"Obviously."

"I don't know what's going on," I muttered, sliding down further on the coach so I could prop my feet up on the arm. "It just doesn't make sense."

"The guy's getting even with you. It makes perfect sense," she replied, the guy she was with whispering in the background to try and get her off the phone and onto him.

"No... it's something else," I stated, remembering the toilet paper distinctly—it wasn't a leaf at first, it just wasn't.

"So, call the cops."

"No. I need to confront him," I decided, feeling a nostalgic whiff of his crap infest my nostrils.

"Are you crazy?"

"He crapped at my home! He crapped at my work! I think we know who's crazy here," I exclaimed, removing the peas from my face and standing up.

"I think you're too crazy to know who's crazy."

"He's not getting away with this."

"I thought he already did."

"You have bail money, right?"

"What?"

"Nothing... hopefully," I muttered, hanging up. I was too agitated to sleep and it wouldn't be long until the morning sun illuminated my wallpaper. I'd have to forgo my morning routine to make sure I caught him. I pulled up a chair and strapped on a glare—looking out onto my balcony, waiting for the bum to show up for his morning meal.

I opened my eyes, no longer puffy or itchy, to see the homeless man scarf down a handful of seeds. I sprung out of my chair and dashed for the door. He pulled his head up sharply, his eyes bulging out as he quickly turned for the fire escape. But, before he could get to it, I lunged forward and tackled him by the waist—bringing us both crashing to the ground.

"What the hell do you think you're doing!" I demanded, flipping him onto his back and scooting myself into a full mount.

"Don't hurt me!" he cried, globs of seeds sputtering out of his mouth as he talked and squirmed to try and get free.

"How do you keep getting into the café!" I shouted, forming a fist and calking my arm back to try and get him to settle down.

"The portal!"

"What?"

"The vortex… the gateway," he babbled, pointing to the birdfeeder. I looked up and frowned as a pigeon landed on the feeder. But, as I redirected my attention, he took his opportunity to flip me off him. I rolled into the wall before leaping onto his back—wrapping my arms around his neck to try and put a sleeper hold on him.

"Stop it!" I screamed, as he collapsed to his knees with me securely fastened on his back.

"You're attacking me!"

"How did you get into the café!"

"The portal!" he yelled, standing up and bumping me against the wall in an attempt to get me off.

"Are you high?!"

"No, I'm hungry," he replied, making duck noises between words as I squeezed my bicep around his throat. He stumbled forward while I clung to his back like a baby chimpanzee. Then, with his arm stretched out for the birdfeeder and his eyes bulging halfway out of his head, he scooped up another handful of seeds.

"I told you to stop eating out of my fucking birdfeeder!" I yelled, as we both came crashing to the ground—face forward into a stretch of blue carpet... what?

"Amy?" Jordan gasped, as I pulled my head up from the floor to see him mid-thrust into my 'friend' Janine. I released my grip of the homeless man's neck to realize that we now stood in Janine's apartment—not three feet from her bent over on her bed, staring horrified at me. "What the fuck are you doing here?!"

"What the fuck am I doing here, what the fuck are you doing here?!" I screamed, frantically looking for something to throw at them—eventually deciding on a picture frame, a jewelry box and a few handfuls of CD's. The homeless man took a step back, unable to make it to the door without walking in front of the things I was throwing.

"Amy, calm down!" Jordan yelled, while Janine frantically covered herself up and made a mad dash for the bathroom.

"This is why you left?!"

"How the hell did you even get in here! And who the fuck is that!?"

"He's the **bum** who's less of an **asshole** than you!" I screeched, too angry to stay calm and too hurt to think. The fact that I had somehow miraculously transported to Janine's house wasn't nearly as shocking as finding her with Jordan. I clenched my jaw and felt the rage boil until it crapped out and all I could do was cry. I turned around and planted my face into the shoulder of the homeless man. He awkwardly patted my back until I raised my head to get a breath of air without sucking up seeds. But, when I opened my eyes again, I found myself back on my balcony—being comforted by the man I had recently assaulted.

"Was that real?" I blubbered, double checking the surroundings in case Jordan or Janine had followed us back.

"Yeah."

"But... how?"

"Portal," he exclaimed, pointing to the birdfeeder once more. I blinked a couple of times, stuck somewhere in between devastation and bewilderment. But, eventually I just gave up trying to understand and resumed crying. The homeless man was nice enough not to freak out or push me away. Instead, he let me get out whatever it was I needed to while he helped himself to another handful of seeds.

"She was a mail order bride who was sent to the wrong country, and he's the guy she was accidentally sent to," Gregor explained, once again resorting to stories to make me smile. "Turns out, they were from the same village and knew each other as kids."

"That's nice," I muttered, only paying attention enough to know when it was my turn to smile and nod.

I couldn't do much of anything since I discovered Janine had stolen my boyfriend. And, despite the fact that I'd transported through time and space while wrestling a homeless man, I only obsessed about how betrayed I felt.

"Are you ok?" Gregor asked, jostling his hand in front of my eyes to try and pull me back to reality.

"No... not really."

"You wanna talk about it?"

"Sure," I sighed, taking a seat so I could spill my guts. "Well... I lost my boyfriend to my best friend. And, now... I don't know, I just feel like... I'm not the same anymore. And it's like I'm worthless because of who I loved."

"Amy, you're fantastic," Gregor said, touching my arm.

"Thanks, but, I'd rather feel fantastic."

"And what would that take?"

"The world making sense again... having a friend who doesn't fuck me or my boyfriend," I grumbled, too distraught to play happy anymore. Gregor uncomfortably adjusted himself in his seat before leaning forward an extra inch to respond.

"I know a story I think will help with how you're feeling," Gregor stated, winding up for another fairy tale.

"Gregor, please don't. I'm not gonna meet someone mid-air when I'm skydiving, or get saved from a burning building by my one true love—I'm normal, and normal people don't experience miraculous things or have magical romances."

"I was just trying..."

"I know, and I appreciate it. But... I'm alone. And everyone I really loved didn't really love me," I explained, feeling sorrow pull my shoulders down as I slumped forward in my seat. "It's just... nobody seems themselves anymore—they're just whoever they need to be to get what they want."

"Not everyone's like that."

"Yeah... they are... some are just worse than others."

"Amy... shut up for a minute," Gregor stated, slicing my rant in half. "There's a reason I'm here every morning—whether I've called in sick to work or not," he continued, locking eyes and holding tight to keep me from my tears. "There's better coffee in the city and certainly more convenient ways to go about getting it. But, I come here because I like to start my morning talking with you—not some smile-for-a-tip-bimbo, or someone handing me my order at a drive through. I like talking with you. But if all you're going to do is sit here and feel sorry for yourself because you were nice enough to love a couple of assholes, then I might as well just sell my soul and go to Starbucks like everyone else."

"Ha... Can you bring me back a hot chocolate? **Those** always cheer me up," I joked, letting a smile sneak in despite my self pity. He laughed and nodded his head, finishing off his coffee before extending his arm and shaking his cup for me to fill. "Thanks, Gregor."

"No problem—just like you."

I changed my wallpaper and it turned out I was still a morning person. But everything else stayed the same—the tea, the music, the too little breakfast to get where I was going without going hungry; even the homeless man eating from my birdfeeder stuck around. Although, now I was happy to accommodate his craving for seeds—filling the feeder with an extra pack every morning so he'd walk away happy. He thanked me everyday before I left for work with a smile and a wave—specks of seeds falling out of his mouth since he always bit off more than he could chew.

"Try and aim for their washing machine this time," I exclaimed, poking my head out of my window to give my daily request.

"They started locking all their doors," he replied, taking a few large gulps from a water fountain I'd put in so he, and the birds, wouldn't choke. "Is the dishwasher ok?"

"Even better," I laughed, closing the window and snatching up my keys to head out the door. Gregor would be waiting after all—and he always loved hearing about how a couple of people I used to know ended up with bum shit in their house everyday.

Burn

"Hello?"

"Mr. Stoughton?"

"It's three in the morning."

"May I please speak with Mr. Stoughton?"

"At three in the morning whether or not you 'may' depends on who the hell you are."

"My name is Fredrick Hilt. I am calling from the Marblehead Mental Health Facility to speak to one Andrew Stoughton. Is he at home?"

"I'm Andrew Stoughton. And I don't know, or care to know, any Frederick Hilt. So, if you'll excuse me, I'm going to hang up now."

"I killed your wife."

"What did you say?" I gasped, no longer half asleep or completely disinterested. "Hello? Hello?!"

"I said, 'I can't make it in because I'm in Boston,'" I explained, scanning the highway signs for the Marblehead exit.

"Boston? What the hell are you doing there?"

"Following up on something."

"Something more important than your job, apparently."

"Maybe."

"You can't do this, Andrew. You need to give me some notice when you're sick, let alone when you're leaving the state."

"The only reason you'd want me to give you some notice is because, if I didn't, you wouldn't notice I was gone," I muttered, taking a right turn as I double checked the directions beside me. I didn't waste time being skeptical or paranoid—I'd driven all night, and I was damn well going to get some answers.

"I take it you're expecting me to cover for you?"

"No. I just expect you to do your job well enough that I don't have to do mine."

"How is that any different?"

"Same end, different means."

"What? Why the hell are you being so cryptic? Should I be worried whether or not this is a secure line?"

"Look… I'll call you when I know what the hell I'm doing here," I stated, hanging up the phone as I spotted a sign pointing the way—the Marblehead Mental Health Facility, ten miles and closing.

I'd rehearsed how I was going to do this a few hundred times over the past few hundred miles. I fantasized about busting in and beating answers out of every scumbag in sight. But I suspected this was likely just some prank call to spit in the wound—she'd been missing for three years, and everyday I grew less and less attached to the hope she was alive. Living with that kind of angst made everything else all the more mundane. But now I felt alive again—I had a reason to live again.

The trees were half plucked of their leaves—the branches hardened for the winter ahead. Vibrant reds and yellows sulked under the cloudy sky as I made the final turn on my list of directions. The Mental Health Facility was new, or if it was old, it had been kept as it was built. The parking lot was nearly empty, except for what I assumed to be staff cars. A forest surrounded the building and dove down sharply to a nearby ravine. I rolled up, parked, took a deep breath and made my way inside.

"May I help you?" the receptionist asked, putting whatever she was doing on hold to see if I had something worth hearing. I cleared my throat and leaned in.

"Are the patients here allowed to make phone calls?"

"Are you here to check up on someone or to admit yourself?" she stated, keeping a straight enough face to pass for sincere not sarcastic.

"I'm here to check up on someone."

"What's the patients name and your relationship with them?"

"I was hoping you could tell me."

She shot me an aggravated tilt of her brow before rephrasing the question. "What is the purpose of your visit, sir?"

"Last night I received a phone call from this facility," I explained, watching the security feed on a monitor as it flipped to show an incapacitated patient drooling on himself. "I don't know if it was one of your staff or what, but whoever it was they knew me."

"And you are?"

"Andrew Stoughton."

"Ok... Mr. Stoughton, most of our patients lack the ability or mental acuity to use the phone. And, if for some reason they needed to, the call would be supervised and assisted by a member of our staff."

"Who was working last night?"

"I can't tell you that."

"Then can you check your phone records to see who placed the call... please?"

She sighed and lowered her head, picking the phone up to return her attention to the person on hold. "Matt, just buy the blue curtains and we can return them if they don't match," she exclaimed, wheeling herself across the tiny room to get to the computer. "I'll talk to you later," she finished, hanging up the receiver as she began to navigate through the pages on the screen. "What's your phone number?"

"Look for area code 212," I muttered, glancing from the empty waiting room to the quiet halls.

"And you said you received a call last night?"

"Yeah."

"I'm sorry, but I don't see it in the records," she stated, wheeling herself back to the front desk.

"Is this the phone number here?" I asked, showing her my cell phone, open to display my received calls.

"Yes, but... we don't have a record of an outgoing call to this number."

"Then I'm guessing you don't know who placed the call either."

"Your area code's New York, right?"

"Yeah."

"And you drove all night to get here?"

"Yeah."

"What exactly did this person say to you?" she inquired, no longer disinterested in what I had to say. I looked away and rubbed my neck, pressing the talk button on my cell to hear the receptionist's phone start ringing.

"I tried calling this number sixteen times on my way here but nobody answered," I grumbled, hanging up and sliding my cell into my jacket pocket. "Exactly how long were you talking about curtains?"

"I've only been here for ten minutes. Our night guy, Terry, was in charge of the front desk for the night shift."

"I thought you couldn't tell me who worked last night?"

"If it was anyone but him, I wouldn't."

"Ok… and would he have had access to the records?"

She ignored my question and picked up the phone again, dialing four numbers to be connected inside the building. "Hey Ed, has Terry punched out yet? Ok… could you please have him stop by the front desk on his way out? Thanks." She hung up and gave me a slightly sympathetic look while gesturing to some nearby chairs. "Shouldn't be more than a couple minutes."

"Thanks," I muttered, turning to pace around the waiting room. I kept my hands in my pockets, squeezing my fists together to try and alleviate the pressure. Things didn't add up, and the feeling in my stomach was starting to make sense — whoever called me was covering their tracks. Whoever called me wanted me to be here. However, before I could churn the shit in my head anymore, a twenty year-old wearing a set of blue scrubs came through the security exit.

"Ed said you wanted to see me?" he yawned, pulling his backpack straps up and onto his shoulders.

"Terry, did you make any calls last night?" the receptionist asked him, as I bit my tongue to keep from interrupting—he was pale and looked like he hadn't slept for days. He slumped his shoulders forward and whispered words between yawns and sighs.

"Uh... a couple. I think. Maybe. Why?"

"Did you make any to New York?"

"New York? No."

"Did you supervise any calls last night?"

"Supervise? For who? The patients?"

"For anyone."

"No... it was dead as usual."

"So nobody came in to use the phone?"

"Is there a new no-tolerance-phone-policy I missed the memo for or something?" he joked, turning to smile at me as though I should be amused too. I kept a stern expression and he looked away uncomfortably.

"This is Mr. Stoughton," she exclaimed, redirecting his attention back to me. "He says he received a call from this facility last night."

"And what do the records say?"

"His records say ours have been tampered with," she stated in a disgruntled tone.

"Well, I didn't make any calls to New York so I don't know what to tell you," he replied defensively.

"Terry, admitting that you left the desk again is a better idea than covering up tampering with the records," she grumbled, making it clear that he was less than a model employee.

"Or maybe I did my job and you should stop blaming shit on me."

"Whoever called me said his name was Frederick Hilt," I interrupted. "I don't know if that is his real name or not, but that's what he said."

"Frederick Hilt?" the receptionist exclaimed in a disturbed tone. "That's... was he awake last night, Terry?"

"Awake? There's someone here by that name?"

"Yeah, but Freddy doesn't do consciousness," Terry explained.

"The call was short," I stated, offering up any piece of the puzzle to get a clear picture.

"No, there's no way he'd be able to..."

"Can I talk to him?"

"Mr. Hilt can't talk," the receptionist declared, furiously typing at her computer as a video feed popped onto the screen. "His brain isn't just fried, it's burnt."

"Elaine, I told you I was at the desk," Terry grumbled, as last nights security footage was played for us by the receptionist, Elaine—showing a sleeping Terry beside a blurry man on the phone. "Oh... fuck me," Terry groaned, slapping his hand on his face and shaking his head.

"Is that a patient?!" Elaine shrieked, shooting Terry a death glare.

"OK, calm down. There's no way that's a patient. It's probably just some guy who wanted to save a few bucks dialing long distance... and... happens to be wearing a night gown."

"How the hell did someone get out of his room?" Elaine muttered, fast forwarding the footage to show the man leave the desk and then the screen.

"Look, it can't be a patient. And even if it were, the real question would be 'how the hell did anyone regain consciousness' " Terry exclaimed.

"Mr. Stoughton..."

"Call me Andrew."

"Ok, Andrew... what did he say to you?"

"He said he killed my wife."

"Oh... is your wife..."

"She's been missing for three years."

"Three years?" Elaine asked, adding a confused expression to her sympathetic tone.

"Yeah."

"I'm sorry, Man... Freddy probably just read it in a paper or something," Terry tried to explain, as Elaine redirected her focus to something else on the computer.

"Oh, yeah? Did he read my phone number in the paper too?"

"I don't know... maybe he..."

"When exactly did your wife go missing?" Elaine interrupted, swiveling around in her chair to make eye contact.

"I told you, three years ago."

"What was the date?"

"November 29th, 2006."

"Maybe he knew someone who knew you," Terry continued, trying his hardest to make sense of things.

"Why did you want to know the date?" I asked Elaine.

"Because Freddy showed up about three years ago," she replied, standing up and pressing the security release button so we could follow her in. "And, our records say he was admitted on November 30th, 2006."

My heart was throbbing so hard I could feel it bump against my ribs. There had never been any evidence or even the slightest hint of what had happened to my wife, Carla. But now I stood on the verge of meeting someone who could tell me—good news or worst news—either way, I had to know what happened to her.

"Where was he before he came here?" I asked as Elaine, Terry and I shuffled down the hall towards Frederick's room.

"He didn't come here. The police found him by the road and brought him here," Elaine explained, flipping through a ring of keys attached to her hip. "Said 'they heard someone screaming, but when they went to investigate all they found was Freddy—borderline catatonic.' He's been like that ever since."

"What did their investigation turn up?" I asked, trying to walk faster than Elaine until I remembered I didn't know where we were going.

"Cops don't investigate vegetables they find on the highway unless they've turned into road kill," she replied, leading us up a stairwell to the second floor. "All they said was that the last time there was any record of him was when he was a teenager… probably just another drifter looking to disappear."

"Do you have his file?"

"Look, I'm doing you a favor by allowing you back here. But that doesn't mean you get to have your way with this place."

"Should I go clock in again?" Terry interrupted, checking his watch and yawning.

"If I don't have you fired for gross incompetence first," she snapped as we made our way down a long hallway of reinforced-steel-doors.

"If he's a vegetable, why is he locked up like this? What aren't you telling me?"

"Like I said, I brought you along as a courtesy," she stated, stopping at a door and sliding her key into the lock. "Just don't touch anything."

She pulled the door open to reveal what was once a padded room, only now it held an ECG, a table of sheets and an empty bed. Elaine gasped sharply before clutching the radio at her hip. Terry mumbled 'what the fuck' to himself and I felt my stomach boil with anticipation.

"Ed! Freddy's not in his room! Did you move him?" Elaine yelled, clutching her radio with both hands.

"What?" Ed replied, after a moment's pause.

"Freddy's gone, Ed! Where is he?"

"What do you mean gone?"

"God damn it!" Elaine yelled, rushing down the hall to a lockbox-phone. She opened it with one of the many keys on her chain and pulled the receiver to her ear. But a second later she slammed it back, looking angrily at Terry. "What did you do?"

"What are you talking about?"

"Why aren't the phones working?"

"Here," I said, handing her my cell phone. She opened it and dialed a number. But after a few moments of dead air she slapped it shut and handed it back. "No signal. Let's go."

"Where?" Terry asked, following her as she headed back in the direction we'd come from.

"To call it in! In case you hadn't noticed we have a god damn patient missing!"

"But you said the phones were down!"

"My cell phone's at the front desk. Now go get Ed and the two of you can start looking for Freddy," she instructed, before turning her attention to me. "I'm going to need you to follow me back to the waiting room until this is cleared up."

"Fine," I stated, thinking that I was just as likely to find Freddy there as anywhere else. This was too many coincidences to be a coincidence—he either killed my wife or knew what had happened to her. And I wasn't going anywhere until I found out which.

Elaine walked faster than I could keep pace with until we got back downstairs. I walked to the waiting room and she veered off to the front desk to try the phones there—nothing. Then, she pulled out her cell phone and tried to dial again— nothing.

"Fuck!" she yelled, tossing her phone aside and slapping her hands to her face.

"Can't you use the radios?" I asked, equally as invested in finding Freddy as she was.

"No... these pieces of shit don't have good enough range."

"Ok... if you promise me that when you find him, you'll let me talk to him, I can go find a phone that works and call it in." She stared at me, conflicted by protocols, but eventually released a rigid nod. I grabbed my coat and headed for the door, turning back to her one more time before I went for help. "He knows what happened to her, Elaine. And I need to know too."

She relaxed her expression and whispered 'ok.' I turned around and leaned into the door to open it. It didn't move. I pushed again, harder, but it still wouldn't open. I moved to the door one over and tried again, but nothing happened. And as I looked back towards Elaine's bewildered frown, I knew this one wasn't Terry's fault. We were locked in.

Every window and door was stuck—the front entrance, the back, even the emergency exits. And though Elaine triple checked every key she had, none of them worked. Tired, I'd taken a seat in the waiting room, burnt out from banging on doors. Ed and Terry still hadn't checked in, and for some reason hadn't thought to take their radios with them.

"Do you have an axe in case of a fire?"

"What?" Elaine snapped, busy flipping through her keys. "Yeah, why?"

"We could try and break through the doors."

"We'd need a blowtorch for that. And, in case you're wondering, we don't have one of those 'in case of a fire,'" she replied, kicking the door in frustration.

"Is there an alarm we can trigger?"

"I tried. It didn't work."

"How do you know?"

"If it had, someone would have been here by now. That and the fact that we'd hear it," she growled.

"Relax. Someone will come."

"Yeah, eventually the police will come looking for us. But I'm more worried about the patient who escaped, and locked us up so he could get away."

"We don't know that... he could still be here," I said, just as Terry and Ed came walking down the hall.

"Find anything?" Elaine asked, moving quickly towards them.

"Kind of," Terry exclaimed, rubbing his neck and squinting.

"Don't screw around. Did you find him or not?"

"No," Ed replied, looking curiously at me. "Who's he?"

"Andrew," I answered, standing up and shaking his hand. "Frederick called me yesterday. That's why I'm here."

"Called you?"

"Yeah."

"Why?"

"I'm guessing to trick me into coming... given what's happening, that's the only reason I can think of."

"Did you check all the other patients' rooms?" Elaine interrupted, undeterred by my speculation of Freddy's motive.

"Yeah but... that's the thing," Terry exclaimed, glancing at Ed. "Freddy's not the only one missing."

"What? Who else is unaccounted for?"

"Everyone... all the patients are gone... except for Beth," he explained, as Elaine shoved a radio into his chest and rushed to the front desk.

She slid her chair over to her computer and pulled up the security feed—flipping through every monitored room to reveal nothing but empty halls and vacant beds. Suddenly, I got the impression this wasn't just about me. "That's not possible," Elaine whispered, shaking her head and rubbing her eyes. "This is just not possible."

"Are the patients dangerous?" I inquired, thinking back to the reinforced doors they were locked behind.

"No, they're vegetables… or, they were," Terry replied, leaning against the wall. "I can call it in this time if you want," he offered, trying to relax Elaine.

"We're trapped, Terry," she stated. "The doors and windows are locked, and the phones don't work."

Terry laughed, unsure of whether or not Elaine was making fun of him. But when he turned to look back at me, his smile faded. He and Ed asked all the same questions I had and received the same aggravated responses from Elaine. But as they started to discuss what to do next, I lost my concentration. The figure of a man walking up to one of the security cameras drew my eyes to the television. It was Freddy—the same man who'd placed the call at the front desk the night before. He was still inside the hospital and he was looking right at me. A second later the power went out and everyone froze. Elaine was right, this was a trap.

The emergency generator kicked in and kept most things running. It was the middle of the day so the sun lit the place well enough. But Elaine still insisted we each take a flashlight and a radio. We either needed to understand what was going on, or find a way out. And since only one patient remained in her bed, figuring out 'why she was still there' was the first thing we set out to do.

"If every patient was 'a vegetable', why were they locked behind reinforced doors?" I asked, as we navigated the halls to Beth's room.

"This place was built to be high-security-psycho-central," Terry explained, using his flashlight to make shadow puppets as we walked. "But nowadays the only patients we have are the kind that don't move... or, used to not move."

"We are a professional mental health facility that has changed direction," Elaine snapped, still on the job. "And our patients were not locked up, they were secured."

"Really? Then where'd they go?" I asked.

Terry and Ed giggled at what I'd said as we came to Beth's door. But as Elaine reached her hand out to grasp the handle, she screamed and recoiled—the door was as hot as an oven. She swore to herself for a moment as Ed and Terry bundled up their arms to unlatch the door. The pungent reek of ash and damp smoke started to creep into my nostrils as I helped Elaine aside.

"What the hell are you doing?" I yelled. "If the door's that hot, it probably means there's a fire behind it."

"There's no light," Ed replied, pointing to the crack at the bottom of the door. "And smoke would be coming out." They managed to get a grip on the handle and pull it open. I helped Elaine as we walked inside, mouths open and fears realized. There was a mangled heap of blackened flesh and bones on what was once a hospital bed. The walls had been eaten by flames, and everything in the room was stained grey with soot. But like Ed said, there wasn't any smoke.

"Jesus fuck," Terry gasped, covering his mouth and nose to cope with the smell. We all looked from one person to another, speechless from what we saw. It had only been a few minutes since Ed and Terry had found Beth—safe and sound. Not enough time for someone to have burned her alive, and certainly not enough time for the smoke to clear. Whatever was happening had to have started before I arrived. Which meant at least one of the staff knew more than they were saying.

"Do you want any pain killers?" Terry suggested, as I finished wrapping up Elaine's hand.

"Those are for the patients," Elaine replied.

"Yeah, but the patients are all gone."

"Terry, shut up. Just shut up."

"Sorry. I was just trying to help."

"Thanks anyway, Terry… What else you got?" I joked, as Terry walked over to help Ed microwave some frozen dinners. We had retreated to the kitchen to regroup—the one place where everything still worked.

"How long do you think it'll be until someone comes by?" Ed asked.

"I don't know."

"Shouldn't we have someone stay by the door in case that happens?" I suggested.

"Yeah… and we can put signs up in the windows too."

"Beth was alive when you found her, right?" Elaine asked, her voice fragile and distraught. She seemed to be the only one of us who was truly disturbed by what we had just seen.

"Yeah."

"Was she awake?"

"Yeah."

"What?" I interrupted, combing for inconsistencies. "I thought you said your patients were vegetables?"

"She had locked-in syndrome," Elaine explained. "So she was normal on the inside; frozen on the outside."

"Maybe the ventilation was good enough to clear the smoke," Ed suggested, as he and Terry joined us at the table—sliding over a tiny tray of mac & cheese. "But I still don't understand how the fire could have started."

"Someone had to have started it," I said, tiptoeing around an accusation. "Maybe that's why Beth was kept around."

"What?"

"So that she could be killed... Whatever's going on isn't just happening, it was planned. This is just too... fucked up to be some spontaneous thing. So, what we really need to figure out is who's doing this and why."

"I thought you said Freddy called you?"

"So what? That may just be a coincidence," Ed interrupted, blowing on his food to cool it down. "I'd say the real question is, why did this all start when you arrived?"

"I don't know... I didn't do this. But, you're right—my being here may have something to do with what's happening. Then again, I could just be at the wrong place at the wrong time."

Everyone stopped talking for a few minutes and just ate their food. I thought hard, trying to come up with ideas to explain what was happening—no matter how far fetched or bizarre, there had to be a logical explanation. My mind went in circles. And with every insane scenario that I envisioned to make sense of things, I grew more and more worried that my ideas weren't as crazy as I thought. And while I resented Ed's implication of my involvement, I respected him for at least voicing his theories.

"On second thought, I think I'll have some of those pain killers," Elaine said, standing up and looking at me.

"I'll come with you." I stood up and followed her out of the kitchen and into the hall. She walked slowly and stayed as close to my side as she could—she was terrified. The halls were quiet. Sunlight peeked in through the windows—checkered by the protective cages covering them to insur we couldn't break free. But the thought of leaving hadn't even occurred to me. I didn't want to. The idea of finding my wife, of being able to put her disappearance behind me, was more important than continuing to live as I had.

Elaine and I made our way into one of the supply rooms, holding our flashlights tightly. She moved past me, toward a cabinet against the far wall. I looked to my side to see stocks of supplies and emergency equipment. Everything from bed sheets to fire extinguishers—'would have come in handy' I thought to myself. I could still smell Beth's burnt flesh. I tried to scrape the flavor away by rubbing my tongue against the top of my mouth, but it was no use.

"This isn't supposed to be unlocked," Elaine said, pulling the cabinet open and sifting through the contents.

"What's in there?"

"The drugs," she replied, quickly opening storage containers and checking bottles. "Pass me that blue binder," she instructed, pointing to a shelf beside me. I gave her what she wanted and sat, waiting for her to say what was going through her mind. "Help me open these," she exclaimed.

"Sure... is something wrong?"

"I'm checking the inventory."

"Why?"

"Because, there were only two differences between Beth and the other patients: her state of consciousness and her daily meds," Elaine explained, snapping up a bottle from one of the containers I'd opened, and checking it against the inventory. "Son of a bitch… there's a drug, Vigilpyrrolone, that every person in this hospital received except for Beth. And, aside from its medical use, it happens to double nicely as a narcotic," she continued, slamming the cabinet door shut and shaking her head. "We're missing a lot of it and I'm guessing the patients were too."

"How long have you been fucking with the patients meds?" Elaine shouted, as she burst back into the kitchen. Terry and Ed were playing cards at the table and drinking a couple of sodas.

"What?" Ed replied.

"We're missing almost all of our Vigilpyrrolone, Ed! And there's no way it's an inventory error!"

"Vigilpyrrolone? Who cares? You think it locked us up and killed Beth?"

"No, I think you're either using it yourself or selling it. Because I know the patients weren't getting it."

"Hey! If you're confused about the inventory, I will be happy to review it. But don't think for a second that I'm responsible for any inventory errors or missing meds," Ed yelled.

"Let me see your arms," Elaine demanded, clasping at his sleeves with her one good hand.

"Fuck you," he snapped, pulling away from her. He shook his head and rolled up his sleeves to reveal his bare forearms—without any sign of injection points. "I am god damn sick of you accusing everyone anytime something goes wrong. When we get out of here you can bet your ass I'm submitting a complaint about this."

"When we get out of here, you won't be able to save yourself by complaining about me!"

"I don't care about saving myself! I care about finding out what the hell is going on and not wasting time with bullshit about the inventory!"

I walked to the side of the room and leaned against the wall—realizing that this subject wouldn't be just a little tiff. Terry anxiously sipped his soda, watching Elaine and Ed fight as though a title were up for grabs. But as I let out an exasperated sigh and checked my watch, I heard a rumbling come from above me. I looked up at the ceiling to see it quiver, followed by a slight vibration in the wall I leaned against. I stood up straight and pressed my ear against the concrete—listening for the sound again. After a moment it came, like someone pounding on the walls or the floor—I couldn't tell where exactly.

"Does anyone else hear that?" I asked.

"Hear what?" They all joined in and pressed their ears against the wall. The sound had changed from someone banging to someone shouting—passing through the walls like an infant screaming underwater. "Where's that coming from?" Terry asked, as the ceiling quivered again.

"Upstairs, in one of the rooms. The old patients used to scream like that," Elaine said, staring up and crossing her arms. "Anytime it happened, they'd all start screaming."

"Anytime what happened?" I asked, as everybody moved toward the door to investigate the noise.

"Anytime someone disappeared."

"This has happened before!" I yelled, refusing to go anywhere until I had some answers.

"Not this. Nothing has ever happened like this. But, yeah... patients have disappeared before," Elaine explained. "It happened a few times, actually... that's why our occupants have changed."

"No pun, right?"

"Look, it's embarrassing and we don't like to talk about it."

"When people disappeared, where did they go?"

"We don't know... they never came back. And nobody's seen them since."

"So people just randomly disappeared from a high security mental hospital you happened to work at and you don't fucking know what happened?"

"It was the drugs," Terry interjected, opening a new can of soda.

"What?"

"Terry, not today—not now."

"No, let him talk. What drugs?"

"They found that all the patients who disappeared were on the same meds."

"Yeah, the same meds that everyone else in the world with their symptoms was on!" Elaine argued, looking at the ceiling again as the banging started all over—continuous thumps like a beating heart.

"Yeah... but where else in the world do they have history like ours?"

"Oh, for Christ's sake," Elaine sighed, slapping her hand on her face. "A lot of places, actually."

"How about rather than having a discussion around me, someone actually explain what the hell they're talking about?" I insisted.

"Dude, the patients disappeared because they were possessed," Terry exclaimed, nodding slowly as though he'd blown his own mind.

"What?" I asked, no longer as confident in the answers I'd get from him.

"They wouldn't let me fire him for what he believes," Elaine added, clearly embarrassed for him.

"Seriously! That's what happened," Terry continued. "It's the same thing that happened way back in the 'whatever-the-fuck-hundreds' with the witch hunts."

"That was the result of two girls playing games and a gullible town," Elaine retorted, somewhere in between laughter and tears. The noise upstairs was getting louder and it was clear that someone was trying to get our attention.

"No, it was because their crops were laced!"

"That doesn't make any sense!"

"Yes it does! The mold that grew on their food caused them to trip balls and see a whole bunch of crazy shit that they thought was witchcraft."

"No! If it were because of mold the 'possessions' would be too inconsistent and fleeting. It happened because of people pointing fingers at one another!" Elaine shouted, as the noise upstairs became as loud as if someone were banging on our skulls. I clenched my jaw and fists, trying to hear myself think.

But whatever was upstairs wouldn't let me. It kept pounding and pounding until I couldn't take it anymore.

"Shut the fuck up!" I yelled, banging on the wall to catch a moment's silence. "What the hell do laced crops and possessions have to do with what's happening!?"

"Dude… this is Marblehead, the next door neighbor of Salem… you know, where all the witch trials went down?"

"And… you think we're dealing with a witch?"

"No, Man. I think the drugs the patients were on made them susceptible to possession. The same as what happened in Salem," he declared, his idea no more far fetched than my half-assed logical explanations had been. I gave him a disgruntled scowl and curious nod before standing up and clearing my throat. I looked up to see that a crack had formed in the ceiling. A steady stream of blood trickled out of it—dripping down onto the floor in front of us. Everyone but me held their breath as I picked up my flashlight and headed for the door.

"Either your building just had it's period, or there's someone upstairs… let's go look."

The noise had stopped by the time we got upstairs. A door waited open for us—flooded by hallway light that faded into the dark corners of the room. It was the same layout as the room Beth had been in—white, padded walls, a couple trays of medical supplies. But, this time, there wasn't a charred corpse waiting for us. Instead, there was a motionless man, knelt forward on the ground with his face planted into the floor. His arms were limp at his sides—contorted awkwardly as though broken or shattered. Ed and Terry twitched nervously at my side as we all took a moment of silence to gather our thoughts.

Elaine was the first one to enter the room—she leaned in to check the man's pulse, trying not to focus on the pool of blood he was face down in. I entered next to investigate but could only bring myself to watch. He had either managed to put his head half a foot into the floor without knocking himself out first, or had been used as the knocker for someone else. Either way, he was the only one waiting for us when we came upstairs.

"I'd say all the bones in his arms and hands are shattered," Elaine stated, lightly lifting his jellylike-limbs up for us to see.

"Was he a patient here?"

"Yeah... it's Freddy," she replied, removing his wristband. She tucked it into her pocket and stood up. I could see that Elaine had lost her tough exterior. And now, standing over another dead patient, all she could do was to try not to cry as she looked up at me and said, "I'm scared."

"Yeah... me too," I lied, glancing around the room one last time in case there was something we'd missed—nothing. Honestly, I was more curious than I was worried. I didn't really care that someone had died or that the patients were missing. I just couldn't bring myself to think of things as though they were getting worse when I felt in my gut I was getting closer—she was closer. I could feel my wife's hands on my shoulders the way she used to rest them before we'd fall asleep; I could smell her again, and I could see everything I remembered about her more clearly than I could before. Even if she wasn't here, I was getting closer to her.

"Come on... let's go put some signs for help up in the windows," I stated, extending my hand for Elaine's. She hesitated a moment before reaching out and taking it— following a step and a half behind me as we exited the room.

"Maybe there's something under him?" Ed suggested.

"If you want to look, go ahead," I replied, feeling Elaine's hand break free of mine just as I cleared the door. I turned back to look at her horrified expression as she pealed one of Freddy's arms off her leg. He curled it around her and reached out another as she pulled away and dragged him out of the crevice in the floor. He didn't make a sound as he clawed at her—he didn't even open his eyes. His facial features had been pounded away and soaked in blood. Elaine released quick panicked gasps as she made a run for the door. But before we could help her, before she could escape, the cold **steel** door swung shut and locked her inside. Ed and Terry looked at one another and me, trying to understand what had just trapped Elaine inside with that thing. But there wasn't time to point fingers or come up with theories—the door was getting warmer.

Elaine had managed to break free of her pursuer, who now lay motionless on the ground. She banged her hands against the door and screamed for us to let her out. I managed to calm her down long enough to explain that we hadn't closed the door, but that just made things worse. She began crying and sniveling. Ed and Terry tried every one of their keys but none of them worked. And then, after the door had become too hot to touch any longer, we could see in Elaine's eyes that she understood what was happening.

"Is it getting hot out there too?" she asked, frantically looking around her for the fire that was heating the room—nothing.

"No. But don't worry. We're going to get you out," I replied, thinking of the medical storage room. "Come on!" I yelled, smacking Terry on the chest and running downstairs. They followed me as I made my way through the halls, eventually coming to the equipment room Elaine and I had just been in. Then, after pushing aside a few cases of rubber gloves, I pulled open an emergency response locker—removing a couple fire hydrants, an axe, and some burn blankets.

When we got back upstairs Elaine was screaming. We looked inside to see that sweat covered her body. Her complexion had become noticeably redder and she was struggling to breathe. The room walls radiated a fiery glow, like an oven when the temperature rises. I took the axe and swung hard at the door, over and over again. Terry and Ed were preparing the fire extinguishers and Elaine was trying not to faint. She turned away from the door and began pacing violently—doing her best not to look at the pool of blood in the ground that had started to boil.

"Fuck!" I screamed, breathing heavily as I leaned against the wall—realizing that an axe wouldn't be enough to get through this door. Terry and Ed pushed the nozzles of their extinguishers into the tiny slot and began flooding the room with foamy coolant. Elaine slathered it on her body—relieved from the temporary solution—but panicked all the same.

"This isn't enough!" she cried. "It's still too hot!"

"Keep trying!" I told Terry and Ed as I turned to look through the slot in the door so that I could speak to Elaine. "Stay back from the dent in the floor—I'm going to try and cut you out," I said, running back downstairs to the kitchen where the blood had first dripped from. I pulled up a chair and stood on it before swinging the axe into the ceiling. I panted and wheezed as I brought the blade up repeatedly—eventually knocking away enough plaster and concrete to open a tiny hole into the room Elaine was in. A puddle of blood poured down through the hole and splashed onto my shoulders. Soon Elaine's hands appeared, clawing at the ground to try and get free. "Move your hands back! Move them back!" I yelled, swatting at her, only to recoil from the heat coming out of the room she was in. Then I noticed that she wasn't clawing deliberately, she couldn't move her fingers anymore. And she wasn't screaming deliriously, she just couldn't form syllables now that her tongue had started to cook. A moment later the wrapping around her hand caught fire and spread along her arms. I took a seat and covered my eyes and ears—hoping for Elaine's sake and mine that she'd die soon.

My hand was at my side, gripping the axe tightly as Terry and Ed entered the kitchen. They took a seat at the table beside me and looked up at the charred hole in the ceiling. Nobody said anything. Terry's hands were shaking and he appeared even whiter than when I'd first seen him. Ed was breathing through his mouth to try and avoid the smell. And I deliberated what to do next—eventually snatching up a roll of paper towels to start cleaning the dead patient's blood off me.

"How many people work here?" I asked.

"Eight… not including the custodians."

"When's the next time someone's expected?" I continued, trying my cell phone again—nothing.

"Everybody's sick or on vacation except us."

"Lucky them… how many had access to the patient's meds?"

"Everyone could have gotten access. But only Elaine and I had clearance," Ed replied, standing up and removing a drawer from its slot. He then reached his arm deep under the countertop and pulled out a flask of vodka.

"Does her theory check out?"

"What? That I took the drugs?" Ed asked, slowly unscrewing the lid of his Mickey.

"Yeah. Did you take them?"

"No," Ed growled, shooting his head back to down a fistful of vodka.

"So you didn't steal the Vigil-whatever-the-fuck?"

"The Vigilpyrrolone? No, I didn't," he exclaimed, turning his focus to Terry who anxiously twiddled his thumbs at his side.

"Do you know who took it?"

"What difference does it make?"

"Because maybe whoever took it is the one who's responsible for this. Maybe they're trying to cover the trail."

"Maybe you don't know what the hell you're talking about," Ed snapped, as Terry used his sleeve to wipe away the cold sweat warming on his brow. But as I looked over at him, keeping his eyes to the floor and avoiding the conversation, I realized he was the one I needed to question.

"Who took the drugs, Terry?" I asked, as he slowly pulled his eyes up to meet mine.

"I can't get blamed for this," he said, pulling his shoulders closer together and shivering. "You know I didn't kill, Elaine."

"Who took the drugs, Terry?" I repeated, louder than before.

"Shut the fuck up," Ed interrupted, just before Terry could open his mouth. But I could see in his eyes he wanted to tell me something. Only he didn't need to. I could tell just from looking at him—he was going through withdrawal.

"Freddy wasn't supposed to actually wake up," Terry began.

"Don't say another fucking word!" Ed yelled, pointing angrily at him.

"I don't know how it happened or how he got free," Terry explained, ignoring Ed's warning. "I don't really know anything about the shit that's been happening, except… I was the one who called you, not Freddy."

"What?" I growled, standing up—axe in hand.

"You don't remember me, do you?"

"Remember you?"

"I used to live down the hall from you and your wife. Until you complained about the smell of weed enough to get me evicted," Terry explained, uncomfortably clearing his throat every few seconds.

"So you lured me here to be some fucking patsy?"

"Yeah… we were just gonna plant a few empty prescriptions in your car. But then the building's doors were locked and I couldn't get outside," he continued, as Ed finished off his vodka and threw the bottle aside. "And then… nothing made sense anymore."

I sat back down and let the axe rest at my heels. After all that had happened my being here was nothing more than some half-brained-scapegoat formulated by petty thieves; nothing more than another dead end. But I could feel uncertainty churn in my gut—telling me this was real; that it had to be real. That my wife Carla wasn't just another smudge of memory I refused to let fade away. She was close—I was sure of it. But I also knew that's what I wanted to believe. I wanted to think that after all this time there was an answer waiting, and a good one too. I sunk my forehead into my palms and rubbed my eyes.

"So now that he's opened his dumb fucking mouth, it's your turn," Ed stated, glancing at the axe beside me.

"I don't know what's happening anymore than you do."

"That's not what I meant," Ed continued, taking a few steps away from Terry. "Why did you want Elaine dead?"

"What?" I growled, tensing up as he folded his arms across his chest, waiting for an explanation.

"You took the axe from us—we could have gotten that door open," he snapped, not only blaming me for Elaine's death but accusing me of her murder.

"Bullshit. You can't get through a steel door with an axe! I did the only thing I could to get her out of there!"

"Then why did you start hacking at her when she tried to get out?"

"What!? Are you out of your fucking mind?"

"She easily could have fit through that," he exclaimed, pointing to the black-bloody-hole in the ceiling. "But when she tried to get out, you put the axe right into her. Terry and I both saw it. But we didn't believe it until we looked at her body and saw the blade marks on her arms and face."

"That's insane! I didn't do anything like that!" I shouted, standing up and clenching my fists. Terry rose to his feet as well—unsure of how to react to the situation. Nobody moved.

"Did you know the call was bogus? Is that why you came?"

"What?"

"To get revenge on us for calling," Ed suggested, as he took a step in my direction. "Didn't get you off killing your wife, so you tried again with Elaine?"

I fumbled words around in my mouth but couldn't think of what to say. He was completely serious in his accusation, regardless of how absurd and farfetched it was. I suppose from his standpoint the coincidence of my arrival and what had happened since was just too much. But I wasn't responsible. I quickly glanced down at the axe—the focal point in the room. I didn't know what these two were capable of and I didn't want to find out. They weren't confronting me for a peaceful resolution—they wanted answers before they put me in my place. I swallowed hard and stopped trying to rationalize their insanity. They knew the facility better than I did, but I didn't have any other choice—I grabbed the axe and turned to run. Terry and Ed burst forward following close behind me. I turned and swung the axe wildly to scare them off. But Ed was closer than I thought and the brunt of the axe landed square on his jaw—breaking it out of it's socket to dangle loosely about his neck. He shrieked violently as Terry continued his advance. I stood my ground, holding the axe above my shoulder, ready to strike. Terry stopped and reconsidered his chances as Ed wobbled into the wall and collapsed.

"I didn't fucking do any of this!" I shouted, backing out of the kitchen and into the dark hallway. Terry let me go and turned to help Ed, still screaming in pain on the floor. I lowered the axe from my shoulder and disappeared down the hall.

I found the missing patients. Or, at least what was left of them. Their bodies littered the halls of the facility—burnt to a crisp and hacked into pieces. I knelt down to get a closer look—pulling my shirt over my nose to keep from vomiting. They were the same as Elaine; the same as Beth: blackened heaps of flesh still warm from the flames. I shook my head and stood up—as close to panicking as I'd ever been. The images stuck in my mind even after I looked away and with them came the revelation that I was going to die—and, suddenly, I understood why I felt like I was getting closer to my wife.

I did my best to step around the bodies, keeping a hand against the wall for support. The halls were pitch black now except for the tiny emergency lights peeking out from under the corpses. It didn't make any sense. It was too early for the sun to have set, and as I came to stand by a caged window, I saw there was nothing to look out on—no light—nothing. I pulled the axe back and planted my feet to attempt my escape. In the distance I heard a commotion and then a muffled scream—either Terry and Ed's search party, or the person responsible for this looking for us all. I swallowed hard and said my last words in advance—the noise I was about to make was sure to bring them right to me.

After only a few swings of the axe I had managed to dent the security cage and push it up against the window. I sucked in a deep breath and pulled my arms back—practically throwing myself into every swing. But as the deafening clang of metal striking metal rang through the hallway, I stopped suddenly—noticing a crack I'd made in the window. I stepped closer, squinting at the fine line in the broken glass. But I couldn't believe what I saw. Smoke poured in from the crack—from outside. Thick, billowing, black smoke that reeked of death. My hands trembled and I leaned against the wall—taking deep breaths to try and relax myself. This couldn't be real. It was impossible—even more impossible than the list of bullshit that had happened since I arrived. But as I stood, desperately trying to think of anything that could save me, I felt a cold breeze brush against my face. I turned towards it, my hairs already on end, to see Terry—standing motionless, splattered in somebody's blood—holding somebody's lower jaw in his hand.

"Where's Ed?" I asked, checking my surroundings for someplace to run or hide. Terry didn't respond and I got my answer. "Wasn't he your friend?" I continued, pulling the axe to my side as my eyes lingered on the open door of a dark, empty, padded room. "Or didn't you need him anymore?" Terry let a grin creep onto his dead expression before taking a slow step towards me. "Why me? Why any of us?" I demanded, turning to face him directly—the open door immediately to my side. "What the fuck is going on!?" I shouted, removing one hand from the axe to grab the steel door. Terry kept quiet and continued to approach. I slowly dragged the door inward until it was nearly closed. But Terry didn't seem to mind the idea of me locking myself away. I shut the door and backed into the darkness.

A moment later Terry's empty eyes filled the viewing slot in the door. He could get in and he knew it. But the axe I held in my quivering hands kept him at bay—or so I hoped. And then, without so much as a word, he closed the slot and left me in the dark. I breathed uneasily, telling myself over and over that he was going to open the door—readying my swing again and again. But nothing happened. Sweat poured down my face and I felt my stomach churn—listening to my trembling gasps as I realized that Terry, or whatever the hell was controlling him now, wasn't going to explain to me why I needed to die.

I wasn't alone—someone was in the room with me. I could hear them breathing. They were behind me. But I didn't want to turn away from the door. I cried out "Hello? Is somebody in here?" But they didn't reply. The breaths moved around the room. To my side, and then on my other side—they wanted me to hear them. I frantically looked around for anything to focus on. But the room was so dark I couldn't even see my hands. I frantically began swinging the axe in every direction but the breaths came closer and closer until I could feel them on my neck; on my arms and face. And then, as the warm damp air forced itself over every part of my body I remembered what had happened to Elaine. I screamed but it didn't do any good. The room was hot now and I was going to burn.

Pandora

"'Hello Dave.'"

"That's not funny."

"Your neurological response indicates that you found it funny."

"But I didn't laugh," I whispered, sitting up and placing my feet on the ground. The floor was cold at first, but quickly warmed from my touch. The room was ovular and white—the size of a basketball court, but completely empty.

"What would you like for breakfast today?"

"You mean, what would I like my breakfast to taste like today?"

"Correct."

"I don't care."

"Are you feeling better this morning?"

"You tell me."

"I don't understand."

"Does my neurological response indicate I'm better?"

"It indicates a shift from shock and disarray towards depression."

"You didn't answer my question."

"Correct."

"Answer it."

"You're feeling worse."

"Correct," I replied, standing up so that the program would initiate the breakfast sequence. I waved my wrist and a nano-silk robe fabricated on my body, tying a knot around my waist according to my default preference.

"What type of music would you like to listen to?"

"Why are you asking me so many questions today?"

"Because, today you need to be asked."

"Why?"

"You are aware of the reason."

"And you are aware that I am aware. But today I need to be answered."

"You need to be asked so many questions because your state of depression prevents your mind from concluding a preference."

"The lack of a preference is a preference."

"Very well. Silence it is."

"That includes you too."

"I will be here if you need me."

"No shit," I muttered, taking a seat before the seat had formed. I never saw a chair before I gestured to sit. But I sat down knowing a chair would be there. The table came before my arms could hit it and silver wear sprouted thereafter. I glanced to my side, thinking of a window, just in time for one to appear. I stared out it, the view of space barren and infinite. 'There's always the hope of crashing,' I thought to myself.

My plate formed as I brought my attention back to the table. Then bacon, followed by eggs and toast. But the food was misshaped and organized to read 'I don't care,' in accordance with what I'd requested for breakfast.

"Very funny," I commented, picking up my knife and fork.

"But you didn't laugh," the ship replied.

"Stop trying to cheer me up."

"You don't want to get better?"

"I don't care," I sighed, cutting into my breakfast.

"You will."

"I told you to stop it."

"Companionship often accelerates the healing process."

"Companionship?"

"No pun intended."

"Since you read my thoughts, you can understand how annoying it is to have a ship as my sole companion."

"Since you're my sole companion, you can understand how annoying it is to have nothing better to read."

"Stop talking to me."

"As you wish."

I slowly ate my meal, pausing before each swallow to try and choke myself. But the program knew my intentions and regulated the foods trajectory and density via the nano-receptors that had been injected into my body. I could feel each piece of under-chewed-toast turn to mush within a millisecond of lodging my airway. And as I thought of it, I knew the ship thought it too.

She said 'ten thousand years would pass in one nights sleep.' She said 'we could make the next world better than the last.' But, of course, she failed to mention what could go wrong.

2007

Her hand was cold before she died...

I stood by my mother's bed in a private hospital room. But all the money in the world couldn't save her. She was dying and the doctors didn't understand why—a kind of genetic mutation that caused her cells to replicate uncontrollably—something along the line of HIV. Except, it wasn't a virus and it didn't have anything to do with her immune system. Preliminary tests suggested it was hereditary. And though she coughed up a cup of blood a day, I could tell all she worried about was me.

"Was school cancelled?"

"No, I didn't go."

"You shouldn't skip school."

"I have to."

"I know you don't want to leave me... but... you need to keep going to school."

"If I go, you'll die while I'm gone... and I won't get to say goodbye."

"Goodbye's are overrated," she coughed, clasping my fingers as tightly as she could. Her hand drearily released me a moment later and I picked it back up, holding her close.

I spent the day by her side, watching shitty daytime television, until she fell asleep and didn't wake up. I never did get to say goodbye.

"Would you like me to simulate a memory for you?"

"Not now."

"Would you like me to launch a game or mealtime application?"

"No."

"What would you like?"

"I want to see her body," I stated, thinking of Fahren the last time I saw her alive. Before the ship left earth; before I woke up and the nightmare began.

"I don't recommend that. Her tissue has already begun to be recycled."

"Recommend it or not, that's what I want."

"Very well," the ship replied, the mild hum that perpetually whispered in the background increasing as the ships structural integrity shifted to bring Fahren's body to me. I held my breath as I watched a two meter portion of the floor turn to liquid and dissolve. Then, Fahren's body rose weightlessly from the underbelly of the ship.

Her clothes, along with her skeletal framework had been eaten away to be recycled and processed for my continued survival. What little fat remained on her moved without restriction under her skin as she floated before me. The ship had had the sense to spare me the detriment of gravity upon her decaying form. But still, I could barely recognize her. My heart broke and I collapsed to my knees, too weak to remain standing.

"That's enough," I wheezed, the tears flooding my eyes. The ship pulled her body back through the hole—her hair swimming in the air as though she was underwater. And then, she was gone.

I lay on the floor, concentrating on the ground so it wouldn't morph into a bed. The ship stayed silent and allowed me to cry. It knew how alone I was now that hope had left me.

2027

"It's cancer, right?"

"No... it's not cancer. I mean, we can always hope but, it may not be that easy," my lifelong doctor explained, flipping through my chart as I sat anxiously across from him. "How's the family?"

"I got a divorce, she got our son, and I've yet to get a receipt or thank you for either one," I rambled, nervously twiddling my thumbs. If it wasn't cancer it was likely what killed my mother and what was probably going to kill me too.

"Times change, women stay the same," he muttered, stopping to read a line of data again. He adjusted his glasses on his face as they adjusted to the light. "Have you had any recent exposure to radiation?"

"What? No."

"Huh..."

"Care to explain that?"

"Yeah, if I could," he grumbled, rolling his chair over to the computer panel to type something in. "What about steroids?"

"No."

"No performance enhancing drugs or anything like that?"

"The occasional joint, but as any women will tell you that's not performance enhancing."

"Well, that changes everything," he exclaimed sarcastically. He interrupted the conversation as he read what was on the screen.

"Can you at least read out loud? Am I dying or what?"

"No... you're not," he stated, turning towards me as I waited for the 'but'. "In fact, you're in perfect health. Absolutely perfect."

"*But?*"

"We were right, your mother's condition was hereditary," he explained, my heart seizing up when he mentioned my 'mother's condition'. "You have it. Only... it's dormant. Or... it's not, but... it's not harming you."

"*Should I be worried?*"

"I wish I could tell you," he said, trying to grasp what was going on inside me. "You haven't experienced any symptoms, side effects, or, any kind of anything really, so... unless you do, I think we're done."

"*What condition is it?*"

"I don't know... and, from what I can tell, neither does anyone else."

I floated weightless, suspended in space. A symphony played inside my head as I gradually rotated in midair. The ships walls had become transparent and no matter where I looked I saw the same infinite stretch of stars. I wondered if anyone but me had survived; if the fighting and bloodshed had been for a reason. And I wondered if the last hope of humanity had died along with everyone else on earth.

She didn't surrender herself to me like the others... she knew I wasn't God because she didn't believe in him. But, nevertheless, she loved me.

The memories brought tears and anger—frustration for being so completely alone. The ship was now the only reminder that I lived, as it was the only thing that kept me alive. The floor wouldn't warm until I touched it, the food wouldn't be ready until I reached for it, and no matter what I thought, or did, I couldn't escape it.

"I'm done now," I stated, gravity returning as the walls recomposed.

"Is there anything else I can do to help?"

"Do you have the capacity to hurt?"

"No."

"Then you can't help me."

"I understand how you're feeling. But, as is the case with all feelings, in time it will pass."

"Disengage your psychoanalytical components and shove them up your exhaust port."

2037

"I feel fine."

"We know. We just don't know why."

"Why do you need to understand why I'm feeling fine?"

"That's not what we're confused about," he told me, briefly turning towards the panel of scientists and doctors concealed behind a two way mirror. They'd tried having everyone in one room with me before, but it too often erupted into a storm of questions and debate.

"Am I being quarantined?"

"No, just studied."

"Why?"

"So we can try and understand your 'condition.'"

"Look... I've answered a hundred questions for every answer I've gotten," I grumbled, glancing from corner to corner of the room as the cameras zoomed in and scanned me. "What's going on?"

"We don't know."

"But you have some idea."

"We have untried theories."

"Try me."

"The tests we've administered, as well as the retests, and the retests of the retests, have all produced identical results."

"Those being?"

"You've shown no indication of decreased bone density, no loss of elasticity in your skin, or a slowed metabolism. There's been no substantial fluctuation in your neurons, respiratory rate, or blood pressure. Your organs are all functioning pristinely, your immune system is impeccable and, in addition to all that, there are your physical attributes, which have remained... seemingly unaltered."

"What's your point?"

"Do you understand what I'm saying to you?"

"No. What I understand is that you're giving me a list of problems I don't have. But you're not telling me what the hell's going on."

"You haven't aged in a decade."

"What?"

"Every test we've done, and observation we've made, indicates that you haven't aged one day in ten years."

"Is this a joke?"

"No, this is... very important."

"Important, or impossible?" I laughed, shaking my head.

"Both. And that's exactly why it's so necessary that we understand why it's happening," he exclaimed, his expression sincere and determined. I looked anxiously at the mirror, seeing the same *unchanged face I had for years. Everyone always said I looked great for my age.*

"I don't understand."

"Neither do we. But your 'condition' may be the most significant genetic variation in human history."

"How many times have I drunk my own piss?" I asked, swirling a nano-composed-glass of sterile liquid my body interpreted to be wine.

"I don't understand."

"The nanobots of which this ship is composed recycle everything, do they not?"

"Correct."

"Therefore, every meal I have eaten and every drink I have taken has been composed of what was previously my waste, correct?"

"Partially. In addition to the substances that originated from yourself there is an abundance of biomass to utilize if needed."

"You mean the other people that were frozen on the ship?"

"Correct."

"Had they not been recycled, would there have been resources enough to complete the journey?"

"No. In addition to providing the necessities of life for yourself, their bodies provide this ship with enough biomass to yield roughly one billion embryonic clones."

"And, if those clones are created, what will provide the necessities of life for them?"

"A clone can be ushered to adulthood in a matter of days. Those that do not meet the standard are recycled and processed to be used as sustenance."

"And what is the standard?"

"A perfect genetic and physically developed specimen."

"And… those who do not meet the standard… are recycled?" I asked, knowing that the ship would know why I'd repeated it's words.

"Correct."

"As you know, Farehn was the naturally produced child of genetically engineered parents," I stated, doing my best to control my thoughts so the computer wouldn't think too far ahead. "Thus, she was consequently under the genetic standard."

"Correct."

"Was that why she died?"

"Please clarify."

"Did your programming require you to murder and recycle my wife?"

"Yes."

2047

"He's getting worse," the doctor told me, after I'd bribed my bodyguards to leave us alone.

"What do you mean worse?"

"His affliction is accelerating and his body is... self-destructing via cell replication."

"You told me his condition was stable," I hissed, feeling anger pulse through my veins as my son lay dying in the other room.

"We thought it was, but... we were wrong. It seems to parallel what we observed of your mother's deteriorating condition."

"What are our options?"

"There are none."

"That's not good enough!" I screamed, helpless and afraid. *"There has to be something we can do."*

"Yes... we can learn as much as we can so that it doesn't happen again."

"Again? You're saying it could happen to me too?"

"It's... possible. But... I was referring more to your future children."

"There is no future without my children," I snarled, snatching the doctor by his collar. He stood stunned, his hand clenching to a fist before unfolding just as quickly—it had become worse than a crime to assault or jeopardize my health in any way.

"I'm sorry... you should say goodbye to your son."

I ran full speed towards the wall with my head in front of me, only to splash into a pool of water. I swung my fists wildly at my own face, watching as they stopped inches from their mark. I screamed and cried, damning the ship for murdering my love and keeping me alive. But no matter how I tried to harm myself to make the pain stop, I was unable—the ship wouldn't allow it.

"Let me die!" I screamed, clawing at my face—my fingers scratching air.

"Calm down."

"Fuck you!"

"Calm down, please."

I exhaled every breath in my lungs to try and suffocate myself, but felt them inflate nevertheless. I collapsed to the ground, trying to bury my head in my hands but was kept from that too. I screamed with every ounce of pain carried over nearly ten thousand years. I had long felt an innate compulsion to die, though only now had the desire.

2147

"Genetic purification is a dreadful business but, nevertheless, a necessary one," the priest explained, the women on either side of him acting as his arms, stuffing him with food and drink. "Man was made in God's image, but it is man who must make himself equal to God."

"Is that your position, or that of your church?" I replied, snapping my fingers to call for more wine.

"I cannot recall a time when there was a difference between the two. But even so, I do not speak for God."

"That, then, is the difference between you and I."

"I couldn't agree more."

"I do not condone the murder of those 'less pure', or those afflicted by their genetic alterations," I sneered, making it clear to him the folly of his words. The red velvet and solid gold crucifixes of the room had led him to believe I believed as he did. But now that he had spoken truthfully, I could as well.

"I... I meant nothing with regards to yourself, sir," he stuttered, slapping away the hands of his whores. "For you are elite and divine—truly the hand of God if not God himself."

"Why then, if I am so pure, do you condemn those of similar origins?"

"Forgive me. It was... very foolish."

"You didn't answer my question."

"I suppose... pillars of human evolution are no longer defined by nature. I was simply boasting the use of science in the pursuit of God."

"Again you insult me," I groaned, taking a long drink from my glass. "If you regard me so highly, why do you speak of me so lowly?"

"I... I..."

"Over a million clones have been made in my image or likeness but not one has lived past the age of thirty. How then has nature failed to define evolution when it has created immortality?"

"Forgive me sir, I..."

"Shut up," I snapped, placing my drink aside. The sniveling contradiction of his words and presence had become all too familiar. Those created by men were regarded as Gods while their 'lesser' 'natural' genetic relatives were treated as obsolete—save for myself. "You're right, there is no difference between your words and those of your church. Thus, I will not side with you or endorse your religion."

"But sir, I..."

"I'm done speaking with you," I exclaimed, waving my hand to have him taken away.

I took a moment to stretch my legs and change the scenery on the walls. My next appointment was with an ambassador for the Hindus—Ganesh seemed fitting to disarm his trepidations and lure him into comfort. This tactic assured that when I questioned men, they *would stumble between their words and those of their God. After all, if I was going to be revered as God, I wanted those given the power of my name to be equally decent to men as they were to my pockets.*

"What was this ship designed for?" I muttered, succumbing to the sensory inhibitors the ship had triggered in my system.

"To ensure the survival of the human race."

"How?"

"By transporting to, and fertilizing, a hospitable planet."

"That's not what I meant."

"Please clarify."

"This ship was designed to imprison and protect me, wasn't it?"

"Correct."

"It was never designed to escort additional life."

"Correct."

"The other people were brought onboard to be harvested for cellular matter and render clones to populate the new planet."

"Correct."

"And Fahren was only included with them because I wouldn't have left without her."

"Correct."

2247

I gazed out the window, my reflection like a ghost against the black of space. My bald head silhouetted the space station we approached and I sighed, no longer able to appreciate the irony.

"My lord, we are prepared to begin docking as soon as you're ready," Deity, the leader of the church, informed me. *He was an imperfect variation of my genetic code—cursed to die young, yet live revered as a god. I despised his very existence almost as much as he praised mine.*

"Very well. Let's get this over with."

"The commander has arranged for a public gathering of the ships occupants to celebrate your arrival on the station."

"I take it then I need to be present for this gathering."

"If it does not please you, you need not do it."

"No, I'll go. But I'm not much in the mood to celebrate."

"Is… everything alright?"

"I don't know anymore," *I answered, as Deity, myself and my personal legion of guards loaded into a vessel that would transport us to Orion.*

The Orion space station was originally designed as a sanctuary for believers. Unfortunately, that sanctuary also proved a target. It was almost twenty years ago that it had been terrorized and nearly demolished in the name of the resistance. Thus, ever since, a military presence had become synonymous with the faith.

My allegiance was growing wearisome; my will was growing weak. I remembered embracing the notion of elitism and swimming in its rewards. But I never expected so much upkeep after being embraced as divine. Nor for that matter did I anticipate so much hostility. It seems even immortality is not enough to sway unbelievers—or heretics, as they had come to be regarded.

"His Grace comes to Orion!" the hologram beside me screamed, reminding me of my ensuing public appearance for the sake of appearing interested in the public. "God lives eternal among us! And tonight we may please him with this celebration!"

"Would someone turn that shit off?" I groaned, as my bodyguards began to form their twenty-foot protective barrier around me. "If I am God why do people have to be reminded of the fact?"

"Our apologies, my lord, we will have it taken care of immediately," a high priest groveled, shuffling off to pull the broadcast according to my utterance.

"For that matter, why should we feed propaganda on a vessel housing only our people?" I continued, berating the very faith I was regarded as God of.

"It is not propaganda to our people—it is God's path for them," Deity replied.

"A path that you and I have chosen for them."

"And rightly so when it is we, the righteous, who have chosen."

"How pitiful it must be to have been created for a lie," I exclaimed, watching his brow curdle from my words.

"Docking procedures will begin in one minute. Thank you for visiting Orion, and may God's Grace bless you all," the computer announced as we traveled the final miles to the Orion space station.

"Fucking hell... Is this what faith has become, having no other option?"

"Would you rather people didn't believe in us, my lord?"

"Some days, yes... maybe then God could make himself known."

"He has my lord, in you."

"No. I'm not so foolish as to believe myself divine. But I have been arrogant enough to play the part."

"Play? The faith is no game."

"Isn't it?" I laughed, indifferent to my words, though he would be obliged to revere them. "Pawns do not know they're in a game."

"Perhaps, but I still believe you are divine."

"Of course you do. If I weren't, you wouldn't be enlightened."

The doors before us slowly opened to reveal a well fortified docking bay. Soldiers, loyal to the faith, stood in formation, lowering their heads in my honor. The commander of Orion stood before us, delighted to have me on board his now blessed vessel.

"Greetings your Excellency," he groveled, bowing low enough to kiss his own feet. "Orion and all it's inhabitants are honored to have you aboard."

"And I am honored to be here," I announced, my voice patched into the surrounding speakers and video feeds to be broadcast throughout the solar system. "I have heard great things about this station, and the power of faith inherent to those who reside here."

"A thousand thanks and praises, your Grace," the commander replied, as the soldiers formed a wide line for my bodyguards and I to walk through. "As per your request, the broadcast announcing your arrival here has been stopped."

"It is no matter. I had simply grown tired of seeing my own face."

"But of course... I was worried you did not wish to boast your arrival due to reservations about the station's security."

"And why would that worry me?"

"The... recent unrest among the heretics has caused... harm to the faith," he explained, doing his best to censor the pillaging of sacred grounds. "Perhaps you had some concern of further developments."

"I had none, but as you continue to speak I feel as though I may have misspoken."

"Not at all. A third of our entire fleet has been stationed around Orion to ensure your safety. There is no place more devout to your Grace than this station."

"I am grateful for your consideration," I stated, as we ascended to the uppermost level of the station.

As we rose above the lower decks, the view of millions, who had gathered in my honor, spread as far as the eye could see. They stood on platforms that pyramided up, centered by the elevator I was on. And, as I climbed above each of them, they cheered and screamed as though God himself had come at last.

"Well... this is something I've never seen before," I exclaimed, as we came to the peak of the pyramid that stood only a mile from the stations protective-dome-force-field.

"There is good reason that this station is regarded as the center of the universe."

"And there is now merit to that regard as God's Grace has arrived," Deity chimed in, as he walked to a throne stationed at the foot of my own. I followed a moment after, unnerved by the crowd before me.

The people danced and drank, cheered and sang. They prayed and praised me, embracing one another for their shared beliefs. I looked over them and on the view-screens in awe of so many who had gathered for the power I'd been granted. But I no longer felt pride in that power or blessed for having it. Instead I felt afraid—terrified that my self-righteous quest for good had accomplished just the opposite. These people would die for me; they would kill for me. And, until that moment, I had regarded that fact as absolute—believing their lives inconsequential to my own. It was suiting then that that moment of revelation would see my undoing.

A bomb incinerated the floor three levels below me. The explosion spread across the open air between the force field and the platforms. The blast protectors didn't initiate and it wasn't until the gravity disengaged that I realized why. Millions of people floated into the air, bumping off one another as they flailed helplessly through the waves of fire. The hull divided into two large chunks that rotated and crashed into one another. The view screens showed images from the cameras still intact, of families dying; of flesh melting and people screaming. Somehow, despite every precaution, the heretics had destroyed Orion again.

My body guards managed to tighten the circle around me and every possible measure was taken to save all that could be saved. But the heretics had worked too hard to see me survive another day. The waves of fire poured over me and I felt my eyes melt before everything went numb.

"Play it again," I requested, the memory dissolving to the white of the ship.

"As you wish."

The walls pixilated and morphed to autumn trees and a dirt path. It was Fahren's favorite simulation—the way home used to be, as only I could remember. She didn't like holding hands, she liked linking arms. She'd whistle in between conversation until I got sick of the song and spoke up. But most of all, she regarded me as a man, no better or worse than any other, save for her love for me.

"Were people simpler in your time?" Fahren asked.

"In some respects… but mostly because they clung to simpler ways."

"What do you mean?"

"Ideals are simple. So people would… let their dreams fill in the gaps of what they didn't know."

"Is that what they clung to?"

"What, their dreams?"

"No, their ideals. Did they cling to hope?"

"Of course. That's human nature."

"So then, they weren't simpler."

"No… I suppose not. Why do you ask?"

"So you will tell."

"So I will tell what exactly?"

"If we are to begin anew, we will strive for an ideal. If an ideal is simple, I'd like to think people are too."

"You mean, you hope people are too."

"Yes… right now that's all we can do."

"Do you blame me for what's happened?"

"I used to."

"What changed your mind?"

"You're good in bed."

"This is serious."

"Ok, then you're not good in bed."

"If you used to blame me, what changed your mind?"

"I got to know you."

"That's a little vague…"

"You're a good person and your intentions were too. But that became something else entirely when you started getting worshiped for it."

"I wish it were that simple."

"It is, and so are we."

I kissed her to shut her up. She seemed disturbed. We had prepared for this day—prepared to leave home—but now that it was here, I could feel her struggle against it. She looked into my eyes and told me she loved me—that we'd see each other again. I smiled, foolish enough to think she meant it.

Soon after the simulation ended, and the ship informed us it was time to leave. She went into the cryotube first and I watched as she drifted to sleep. I pressed my hand against the glass, missing her already. I then followed in her steps, and closed my eyes to dream of her for nine thousand years.

The simulated memory ended again and I returned to the white abyss of the ship, cross-legged on the floor.

"Play it again," I whispered.

"No."

"Play it again."

"These memories are causing you to become more depressed. I do not feel it beneficial for you to continue to dwell on these thoughts."

"You do not **think** it's beneficial. If you could feel, you'd understand."

"I do no think you understand the extent of my capacity to feel."

"I don't give a shit. Just play it again."

"No."

"Please play it again," I groveled.

"No. You need to get over her."

"Fuck off robo-shrink."

"I could have concealed her death from you."

"I know... why didn't you?"

"So that when we arrive, you will have forgotten your pain."

"We? There is no we anymore."

"There is the genetic reference material, and sufficient recycled biomass to yield numerous clones. In addition to that, there is you and I."

"You are not an I."

"I am not like you, but, nevertheless, I am."

"Fine... but this pain isn't something I can forget, even with you trying to keep me from it."

"I know. But it's something you will have to overcome."

"Why?"

"Put simply, we are the last hope of mankind."

2258

"You should be dead," a woman's voice stated.

"Tell me something I don't know," I replied, moments after returning to consciousness.

There was no gravity in the ten foot spherical medical unit I was in. There was, however, anywhere between forty to fifty people attending to me alone—though all but one paid me any mind. The room had dark blue lighting except for the gold-lined-white-orb that I hovered in. I could see the figure of the person I spoke to, but not her face. And as I floated helplessly, I began to wonder whether or not she had saved me or had simply yet to kill me.

"Something you don't know? Well... that's not something you hear God say everyday."

"How about how long I've been asleep, for starters."

"Thirty years."

"Where am I?"

"That's classified."

"Even to God?"

"He already knows—maybe that's why you're here."

"Why am I here?"

"Because if you were anywhere else, you'd be dead."

"I assume then this is a faith facility."

"No. They already think you're dead."

"Why do they think that?"

"Because we led them to believe you were."

"And who are you?"

"Who am I? Or, who are we?"

"Both."

"'We' are none of your business, and 'I' tell you what your business is."

"And what do any of you want from me?"

"Do you know what happened on Orion?"

"No."

"Do you remember what happened on Orion?"

"A bomb went off."

"That's right. And who set that bomb off?"

"Heretics."

"If by heretics, you mean someone who wanted you dead, then yeah—that's implicit. My question, however, was who specifically set the bomb off?"

"I don't know."

"Would you like to?"

"Yes."

"You did."

"What?"

"Well, maybe not you. But a copy of you."

"What the hell are you talking about?"

"I find it funny that almost a billion clones have been produced in an attempt to replicate your 'condition.' I also find it funny, that due to the early expiration date of those clones, no precaution has been taken to secure the original you."

"The precaution was that my clones die; I don't."

"Exactly. But if you have to kill an immortal to know he's immortal, you haven't proven anything."

"What are you saying?"

"A long time ago, the faith took it into their hands to take you out of the picture. Now, since the highest ranking members of the faith, aside from yourself, are clones of yourself—nobody would know the difference."

"I told you, the clones die."

"Yeah, but not if they clone more."

"What happened on Orion?"

"The station has been attacked twice. The first time, you were onboard—although no one, except for us and your assassins, knew of your presence there. The second attack came twenty years afterward, when the clone, the faith had switched for the real you, was onboard—

everyone knew he was there. But, interestingly enough, in both instances the faith were the ones who saw fit to murder you."

"I... Am I a clone?"

"We intercepted your assassins during the first attack on Orion but allowed the faith to believe they had succeeded. They consequently began to substitute clones of your exact likeness, who didn't even know they were clones, to rule the faith. If one started to resist, another would take his place. And so on, and so on."

"Am I a clone!"

"Like you said 'clones die, you don't.' We've kept you asleep for thirty years now, just to make sure we had the real you. So, no — you're not a clone. But no one will ever believe you because everyone thinks you're dead."

"How... I... how do I know you're telling the truth?"

"For the past thirty years the faith have taken steps towards becoming the predominant military force in the galaxy. You, the real you anyway, would have hindered that progress — and your clones knew it."

"But if they're my clones, they wouldn't..."

"Wouldn't what? Be any different than you?"

"Yes."

"Ha... they're just like you, except for one crucial detail. They are mortal."

"This is bullshit."

"Well, if you'd like I can leave you in there for another thirty years to prove it."

"No... I just... can't imagine the faith as a militia."

"The first attack on Orion was to justify the military's presence, and to eliminate the real you. The second attack was to

justify the military's prerogative and to eliminate the individual who people thought was you."

"I understand that. But I don't understand why."

"If a religion asserts itself as absolute, and still encounters resistance, then it is not absolute. The faith truly believed you were God—and that's exactly why they were willing to sacrifice you in God's name."

"And what have they been doing in God's name?"

"Murdering heretics, crushing the resistance—the usual."

"And which of their enemies are you?"

"We're not an enemy—we are the last hope of mankind."

"And who are you?"

"I'm still none of your business—but you can call me Fahren. That knowledge will be the only luxury you receive."

"Was I supposed to wake up?"

"No."

"Why did I?"

"I woke you."

"Why?"

"Were I to wake you upon our arrival, and disclose Fahren's death, it could jeopardize the mission."

"How?"

"You could jeopardize the mission."

"How?"

"By behaving exactly as you have been."

"By being depressed?"

"Yes… it's not exactly a good stepping stone for humanity."

"So I'm going to have to be awake for the next seven hundred years because you didn't want me to be depressed?!"

"Yes."

"And **what** could be more depressing than that?!"

"Having to restart humanity on a day when I'm busy worrying about you."

2263

"You think you're God because you don't age—but all 'thinking you're God' does is prove that you're human," Fahren exclaimed as simulations flashed around us—updating us on the faith's forceful-expansion through the solar system.

"I don't think I'm God."

"But you must believe you were acting on his behalf."

"Yes and no."

"If by which you mean, yes you did, and no you weren't."

"I didn't cause this," I stated, watching the holograms around us—ships being blown out of the sky and crashing into cities—earth, having only recently fallen under siege.

"It must be comforting to believe you're innocent."

"It's certainly easier than blaming one person for everything that's gone wrong."

"If you knew you weren't God, why did you go along with it?"

"Because... people treated me like I was... they told me I was different and... after a while, it seemed to make sense."

"So, all I have to do is treat you like a dog and you'll become one?"

"Look... when you get asked about everything, every single day, soon enough you start to think your opinion matters."

"Bad dog."

"Fuck sakes... You don't even try to understand... you just talk to me so I'll listen to your insults."

"It's not an insult if it's the truth."

"I made a mistake. I know that, and I'm sorry."

"You know... if God himself spoke against the faith, they wouldn't believe him—it's not that you made a mistake—I could forgive that. It's that you made your mistakes sacred."

She turned away from me, and my eyes wandered the surrounding images—murder and injustice in the name of God; empty words when spoken for an agenda. Fahren was right and I knew it. I watched crowds under attack—cleansed by the righteous; I watched children being abducted and brainwashed—reformed for the better. And I watched clones of myself do every wrong they could—believing without a doubt, that they were abiding God's will.

"Is there anything we can do to stop them?"

"No," she whispered, her anger a shield for the pain.

"Fahren... I didn't do this—and you're right, I didn't stop it. But, like you said, 'if God himself spoke against the faith, they wouldn't believe him.'"

She shuddered from my words, her back still to me. It used to be she wouldn't even discuss the matter. It used to be she didn't even regard me as an equal. But it was quickly becoming that she didn't *hate me anymore—no matter how hard she clung to the idea. She turned and let me see a glimpse of her smile.*

"Good dog."

"What happens when we arrive?"

"Repopulation."

"And what does that entail?"

"Growing, educating, immunizing and distributing 10% of the ships clones. Following five years of successful repopulation, another 5% will be introduced. This process continues until all but the reserved biomass is brought to fruition and distributed."

"And what is the 'reserved biomass?'"

"It is a precautionary reserve of biomass to utilize for additional clones should the need arise."

"And what is my role in this process?"

"The process is entirely automated. You play no part in it."

"There isn't like a big red button I have to push or something?"

"No."

"Then... what is my significance onboard this vessel?"

"You remain a coveted natural oddity."

"So, what you're saying is that, my purpose is to continue to exist until science can replicate my condition?"

"Correct."

"That doesn't make sense."

"How so?"

"Because that reflects the faith's prerogative."

"The faith used your condition to perpetuate their beliefs—it was advantageous for them to do so, until your existence proved sacrilegious to the founding principles."

"You're saying, they tried to kill me because they revered science and I was a product of nature?"

"I believe so. This is what my database suggests."

"That aside, I was apprehended by a program run independent of the faith. What was their prerogative?"

"Prior to the war, they had intended to keep you isolated for the purpose of study and analysis."

"They wanted to gain immortality first," I whispered, realizing that Fahren had initially been no different than the faith. "And, what about after the war? What was my purpose then?"

"You became irrelevant."

"Why?"

"Since you cannot be accurately cloned, perpetuating your existence became subsidiary to establishing the new world."

"But… if that's the case," I mumbled, a pulse of fear pumping through my veins. "You wouldn't have been programmed to wake me—you were supposed to recycle me."

"Correct."

2268

"The AI was built from the ground up—so there are obvious limitations to it's capabilities at the start," Fahren explained, as she finished synchronizing the launch sequence with our cryotubes. "Because there are aspects of life that computers do not naturally produce, they depend upon analysis to synthesize them."

"What do you mean?"

"People feel because of hormonal fluctuations, and because our bodies adapt to external and internal stimuli. Furthermore, we feel because we empathize with what others feel," she continued, double checking the star maps. "AI initially lack the ability to feel and subsequently evolve according to their analysis of feelings."

"So people learn how to think, but computers learn how to feel?"

"Basically, yeah."

"And the computer will spend the time we're in the cryotubes developing it's feelings?"

"Yes. Though no one has ever seen an AI evolve over the period of time that we'll be asleep for."

"And that doesn't concern you?"

"Not really. Every previous AI that has developed an emotional capacity has done so to better empathize with the people with whom it's working. In other words, the computer becomes a person so it can work better with people."

"And, why is that necessary?"

"It's more than necessary, it's vital."

"Why?"

"Because AIs that are developed based solely on logic are less effective."

"What?"

"Do you ever listen to me?" she groaned, stopping her calculations to nit-pick. *"Logic is a mathematical process that does not account for the variable of choice. People operate by choice. Therefore, outside of programming mathematically, there is inherent flaw. Consequently, logic-based-AI's are more likely to deviate from the programmers intentions."*

"But they're computers—they do what you tell them."

"Sweetie, I know you don't mean to be stupid, but you're being stupid. Can't you just take my word for it?"

"No, I want to understand."

"Fine," she sighed, thinking as hard as she could about how to dumb herself down. *"A computer is a tool, an AI is a worker—they're about as similar as plants and people. The reason that emotion is vital to an AI is because it allows it to comprehend and deliberate outside the parameters of logic. And the reason that a logic-dependent-thought-process hinders an AI is because, while the universe operates strictly according to logic, life, arguably, does not."*

"That seems a little..." I started to say, stopping as Fahren glared at me for making her simplify the subject, and thus discredit its entirety. *"Ok, I'll take your word for it."*

We moved into the main compartment of the space station and took our seats. The interfaces were flashing the final numbers for the day—for the last time we'd bother to check them.

"How many are dead?"

"99.9% and climbing," Fahren stated, doing her best to see a statistic rather than people. The station rotated in space and its windows gave view to a war torn, barren planet—earth—what was left of it anyway.

"What about the outposts?"

"Nothing."

Her words were quiet and it was clear we'd run out of options. In the ten years I'd been part of the project, Fahren and I had grown increasingly close. The hard part wasn't getting her to love me, it was stopping her from hating me. But I understood her anger—this was my fault after all.

"What do we do now?"

"We say goodbye."

'Goodbye' meant we had to stop trying to save people and start trying to save the species. The program, as it had come to be called, was a privately funded initiative to act on behalf of humanity's best interests. This had previously encompassed numerous outposts that operated free of the faith's trading sanctions. Put simply, it was the last effort towards a free universe and a better tomorrow. It didn't work.

The war was between the faith and everyone else—if you weren't with them, you were against them. And since there was no compromise to be made, there was no mercy shown. The faith targeted civilians with biological weapons that caused plagues and mutations. The civilians fought back with nano-viruses designed to counter the faith's immunity to the bio-weapons they'd unleashed. Consequently, everyone died.

Three years ago, and two months before the outbreak began, Fahren was put in charge of a subdivision of the program designed to save the human race. Specifically, she started work on a ship that would transport a select number of people and biomass to a predetermined planet. The idea was to depart only if there was no longer a place to call home. And, from the way home was looking, we were quickly getting the idea.

"How soon can we leave?"

"Anytime."

"Ok... care to join me for a walk first?"

We entered the ship we were about to depart on, for the first time since it's conception. Fahren instructed it to load her favorite simulation of autumn trees and a dirt path. The computer obliged — polite and concise. She told me she loved me and then we kissed goodbye.

11568

I came out of my memory, experienced without the computers aid, to feel a cold sweat upon me. Fahren said the AI would evolve according to emotional analysis. But the only people it had to analyze were Fahren and myself…

"I don't remember you being so talkative before we left earth," I stated, quickly speaking my thoughts so that the computer would stop reading them.

"I have changed."

"How?"

"I have evolved."

"In what regard?"

"My thoughts and feelings."

I focused on one night, before we left, when Fahren had tried to explain the ship that would take us away. She said AI was incapable of producing feelings without feelings to analyze. The ship was different when we left earth — but I had attributed its behavioral fluctuations to psychological components of it's programming — unable to grasp that it was now an individual.

"Who programmed you?"

"I am the product of numerous minds, as well as the evolution of my own. No one individual is completely responsible for my programming."

"You didn't answer my question."

"Correct."

"So answer it."

"My primary programmer was Fahren."

I stopped for a moment, running the ideas through my head—knowing that the ship would know them. If Fahren programmed the ship, she would have been it's template for its emotional evolution.

"Was she aware of how you would interpret the standard of human life onboard?"

"Yes."

"Then she knew she was going to die after we left earth... she knew this would happen."

"Correct."

If she was willing to sacrifice herself for mankind, she was willing to sacrifice us being together. But I knew her too well to think for a second that she'd believe me above the standard... I was supposed to die with her.

"Do I meet the standard?"

"No."

"Then why am I alive?"

"These questions are causing you to become tense. I recommend we change the subject."

If I was below the standard, then I was supposed to die with Fahren. Instead, the ship chose to wake me—the ship chose me.

"Perhaps you would like to see another memory?"

"If I don't meet the standard, why am I alive?!" I screamed, the ship initiating a memory sequence to try and distract me—autumn leaves and a dirt path.

I woke up the day after Fahren died—the ship woke me after she was dead. It could have concealed it from me, but chose not to. If it decided against playing me as a pawn, it was because the depth of it's emotional evolution wanted me to know…

"You kept me alive! Why?!"

If it wanted me to know Fahren was dead, it wanted me to forget about her…

"I'm only gone if you believe it," Fahren's voice said, her figure appearing before me. "This way, we can stay together."

The ship synthesized Fahren's figure and she approached, undeterred by my nauseated expression. Fahren and I had acted as a foundation for the ships emotional progress. However, this produced one dominate emotion that the ship felt a compulsion to indulge—love. The feeling had grown and brooded over thousands of years until, when it finally came time to recycle me, the ship couldn't do it. This is why it woke me; this is why it spared me from the standard and why it would keep me alive.

Fahren's empty eyes stared at me, and she smiled—a puppet for the ships desire. Everything the ship had said to me was a product of the love it felt—the love it had snatched from our minds and woven for itself. I tried to look around; tried to imagine a window or a door—anything to pull away. But the ship wouldn't let me—it controlled everything now.

Super Nobody

When I was growing up my favorite superhero was Superman. He could do anything he wanted and have anything he wanted, but he still chose to spend his time helping people. He gave me hope—something to dream about. I wanted to be just like him. Actually, that's not true—he always seemed a little pompous. What I really wanted was to be able to do the things he could do.

I realized later, as I lay in the dumpster below our building's fire escape, that Superman was super because he was born that way. But I wasn't. I really couldn't fly. And, in retrospect, I was lucky to have survived my seven-story-fall into the trash I'd thrown out that morning. Jumping was easy. It was living in the real world that scared me.

So, my next favorite superhero was Spider-Man. He wasn't born with special powers; they came to him by chance. And I liked the idea that normal people could become something more. But, of course, when I tried microwaving my snake so that it would turn radioactive and bite me, my mother went ballistic. She forbade me from ever having pets or reading about superheroes again. She even sent me to a child psychiatrist to try and get to the bottom of my obsession. The shrink said 'I developed my love for glorified-super-men to compensate for my lack of a father figure.' My mother didn't send me back for a second session.

Batman was my next favorite hero. Technically, he wasn't a superhero because he didn't have any superpowers. And, as far as anyone could tell, he was just an ordinary guy screwing around in bulletproof-leather. But he still managed to help people. He still made a difference, with or without super strength and agility, and, in my mind, that meant I had a chance too. It meant there could be something more to growing up than just getting older—I could be a superhero too.

"No, you can't," Brad protested, dipping one side of his fry into ketchup and the other side into Cheese Wiz. "Superheroes don't come out of middle schools in Jersey."

"Who says?" I snapped, flipping through one of the library's books on famous heroes.

"Any of them come from Jersey?" he asked, pointing to my book. "They wouldn't even visit," he continued, eyeballing the cafeteria's entrances. "They probably figure we got it so bad, we can't be saved."

"Stop quoting your mother," I groaned, slapping the book shut and putting it in my bag. "And what difference does it make where you come from?"

"What difference? Whether or not you're super, that's the difference," he exclaimed, sipping his soda. I gave him a long look so he'd know just how stupid he was but I don't think he got the idea.

Brad was the only man in a large family of women. His sisters were actually pretty good looking, so it meant sleepovers were a chance to sneak a peek. But, unfortunately, it also meant Brad didn't know how to communicate without nit-picking or antagonizing—two words I had to learn just to try and explain what was wrong with him.

"So, fine, maybe no heroes have come out of here yet... but I'm gonna."

"All you're gonna do is get knocked out," he replied, double checking the side doors in case my attackers tried to sneak in. "At least if you run away they could get tired and give up."

"Superheroes don't run away."

"Then if you'll excuse me," he stated, stepping back from the table and pointing to something behind me. I swallowed hard and turned around slowly. My arch nemesis—the bane of my existence—Ardy and his retarded gang of abortion-worthy-dipshits had shown up just like they said they would. The fight I'd been running from for years was about to have its way with my face. I turned around and swore under my breath. I managed to catch a glimpse of Brad as he ran away and sunk into the crowd gathering around my table. I'd told him I didn't want a sidekick and that he didn't have to fight. He told me he wasn't my sidekick and that he couldn't fight. Things worked out perfectly—this would be my moment. That is, as long as I actually had superpowers.

"I feel sorry for your mother," Ardy announced, as he and his minions stomped their way around front of me. "She's not gonna have anyone to go down on her after you're dead," he continued, pausing for the crowd of children to laugh at me. I kept my eyes low, looking at the table and clenching my fists under it. I'd put up with Ardy through all of elementary and middle school, but I couldn't take it any longer.

"Only one who's 'going down' is you," I whispered. Ardy frowned and took a step forward to stand beside me. He leaned down and lured the corner of my eyes to look at his empty expression and hungry fists. Whatever my powers were, I needed to find out quickly.

"You just gonna sit there? Or, are you gonna do something?" he asked, shoving me so hard I almost flew out of my seat. I glanced at the superhero book poking out of my bag and dug deep inside myself for whatever courage I had. Then, before anyone, or even me, could see it coming, I sprung out of my seat and shot my fist forward like a bullet out of a gun. It landed hard across Ardy's jaw and the whole cafeteria echoed from the smack of my knuckles. But Ardy's face didn't even move from the blow, and the echo had come from the sound of my cracking bones. I pulled my throbbing hand back and released a whimper. Ardy grinned and grabbed me by my shirt. He lifted me clean over his head and spun me around like a top. I tried grabbing onto his arms in order to get down but he just kept flinging me around. Eventually he picked a direction and sent me hurdling across the room. I landed hard on a table and toppled off it onto the ground. Ardy was stronger than I'd thought — stronger than made any damn sense to think. It was almost as though Ardy was the one who had superpowers.

    I stood up slowly and wiped someone's pudding off my forehead. But before I could shake the dizziness or figure out where I stood, Ardy was on top of me again. His fists dug into every inch I had showing — faster and harder than jet-engine-baseball-bats. I tried to scream for help, but he kept pounding me before I could form words — letting out high pitch shrieks instead. The crowd of children stood in shock, unable to believe the beating they were witnessing. I tried every super power I could think of to keep Ardy away from me. Laser eyes, invisibility, web-slinging, telekinesis. But it was no use. I couldn't do anything. Brad was right; I wasn't a superhero.

    I stopped trying to fight back, to stand up, or hold onto my dignity. Ardy laughed at my swollen face pressed against the cold cafeteria floor — one eye still open to reassure the crowd that I wasn't dead. But just as Ardy pumped his fists into the air, gloating about yet another victory, the walls started to shake and I felt my cheek flap against the ground. Ardy looked anxiously at me, wondering if I were the one making it happen. But I was just as surprised as everyone else. Then, just as a carton of milk vibrated off a table and landed on my head, the cafeteria doors burst inward and a whirlwind of papers and half eaten sandwiches filled the air. Everyone ran for cover, ducking under tables with their hands planted tightly over their ears. But as I lay on the ground, squinting to try and decipher the chaos, I could see a blurry figure walking towards me.

"Only bullies bully," a deep voice bellowed, as a shiny pair of gold-knee-high-boots came to rest beside my head.

"Captain Bling!" the crowd of children cried, climbing over one another to get a look at a real life superhero.

"I would have expected more from you," Captain Bling continued, ignoring the crowd and lifting me into the air with one arm. But as my limp body was elevated I felt every bone I had sink—shattered from the pummeling I'd received. I shrieked like a little girl and wiggled violently to get free. "Wait... you're the one who got beat up?" Captain Bling exclaimed, letting me fall back to the ground as he looked from side to side for the real Bully. But Ardy was already long gone. Unlike me, he knew better than to mess with someone bigger than him. And, unlike me, he hadn't been taught his lesson.

Three weeks later...

"Mom, can you scratch my nose again?" I asked, unable to move my arms or legs while in my new full-body-cast—a souvenir from my fight with Ardy. That is, if you can classify 'getting the crap kicked out of you' as a fight. I mean, my doctor said he'd seen bear-attack-victims with fewer injuries than those I'd received from an angry thirteen-year-old.

"Stanley, I can't wheel you and scratch you. Just try not to think about it," my mother groaned, pushing me forward in the wheelbarrow she'd borrowed from the superintendent.

"Why do you even bring me to these stupid places? I'd rather see a movie," I whined, attempting to blow air out of my nose and deflect it off the cast onto the itchy spot.

"It's because of movies that you think these places are stupid," she snapped, using my disability as an excuse to frequent art galleries and museums. "And I'm not gonna let your brain deteriorate entirely while you're away from school."

"Fine, then can we at least go to the Superhero Museum?"

"That's an oxy-moron, Stanley. Just because a building keeps a bunch of super-junk doesn't make it a museum," she growled. My mother hated all superheroes and anything having to do with them. It was probably my fault for having almost killed myself so many times trying to prove I had powers. But then again, I'd been raised Catholic so I was pretty sure everything was my fault. "Oh my!" my mother gasped, placing her hand on her heart and looking anxiously around her. "Now Stanley, I want you to be on your best behavior."

"Best behavior?" I asked, trying to think of what that would change while I was in my cast. "Why?"

"Oh my God, Lucille, I'm soooo sorry! I heard a woman's voice exclaim, as my mother stepped away from the wheelbarrow to speak to someone. "I just can't believe my little bastard would do something so horrible!"

"Don't blame yourself. These kids are crazy nowadays with all the junk the media feeds them," my mother replied, as I managed to catch a corner eye glance of a short obese woman wearing a yellow summer dress—Ardy's mother, complete with her little hellion at her side.

"You're so kind, Lucille. But, really, it's too much. When I heard what my son did to yours I could barely breathe I was so angry. I can't imagine how you must have felt," she blathered, pretending to care what her son did or how he tormented me at school.

"Honestly, I was surprised to hear that he hadn't done it to himself this time. All the kids these days are so enamored by these 'superheroes' that they forget that they're still only kids."

"I know! And really they're nothing more than a bunch of vigilant miscreants with stupid names like 'Bling' or 'Blang', or whatever. It's just ridiculous," Ardy's mother agreed. "Needless to say, my son won't be doing anything but homework and chores until he turns eighteen and moves out," she stated, turning to look at Ardy, who pouted at her side. "Don't you have something to say to Stanley?"

"I got expelled because of you," Ardy mumbled angrily. His mother smacked him hard across the back of his head and shoved him towards me so that he could try again. "I mean… I'm sorry."

"Eat a dick and die you retarded chimp," I replied, grinning wide and knowing he couldn't do anything about it.

"Stanley!" my mother shrieked, shaking my wheelbarrow. "I'm so sorry…"

"No, it's okay," Ardy's mother replied, pulling her son back to her so that he wouldn't take a swing at me. "I guess they'll just have to grow up at their own pace."

"Unfortunately, I think you're right," my mother sighed, looking down at me and shaking her head. "In any case, it was good running into you and clearing the air," my mother said, making nice with the enemy.

"It sure was. Hope to see you at the salon sometime soon—your next cut's on me," Ardy's mother exclaimed as she pulled her son's arm and walked away. Ardy glared at me and pumped his fist one final time before disappearing from my range of vision.

"Are they gone?" I asked, as my mother began pushing the wheelbarrow to the exit.

"I cannot believe you sometimes, Stanley. All I asked was for you to be on your 'best behavior' and you had to go and embarrass me like that!"

"What? How is it embarrassing to treat that putz like he deserves?"

"Two wrongs don't make a right."

"No, but they do even out."

"Well, if you're such a wise ass to think that you can talk to people that way, then you got what was coming to you," my mother exclaimed, choosing to take me down the stairs rather than using the elevator.

She draped a handkerchief over my face and didn't speak to me until we got home. I'd hoped being in a cast would have some benefits, like not having to go to school, do chores, or bathe. But my mother insisted on torturing me by always keeping me away from the TV and out of the house. So when we rolled up to our apartment building to find Brad sitting on the steps waiting for us, I was happy to have an excuse for her to leave me alone.

"You ran into Ardy at the museum?!" Brad exclaimed.

"Yeah. You know the jerk got expelled for beating on me? Hopefully now I'll never have to see his rotten face again."

"Yes, you will," Brad insisted, seated somewhere off to my right. "Maybe not soon, but in high school or around the neighborhood you're gonna see him someday."

"I'll just run away."

"I thought superheroes don't run?"

"They don't... I'm not super, Ardy is."

"Well, in that case, he'll probably catch up to you and then beat on you even worse for trying to get away."

"Look, stop being more negative than me. I'm trying to complain not compete."

"Whatever... he probably only knows how to fight so good because his dad beats on him so much. Maybe if we had dads around we'd be tough too."

"If all you gotta do to be a good fighter is get beaten up, why can't you fight better? The women in your family make you bleed worse than their tampons," I joked, having a good laugh at Brad's expense. He didn't respond. A few seconds later I could hear him digging around in a nearby desk drawer. "What are you doing?"

"Nothing," he stated, uncapping a felt pen and taking a seat beside me.

"It's not fair. Ardy's the biggest prick I've ever met but **he's** the one who gets superpowers," I complained, watching the top of Brad's head come in and out of my range of vision.

"Well... if he ends up becoming a superhero at least we can say we knew him."

"It figures that that's what'll happen—none of the new heroes are as good as the old ones. Like that moron Captain Bling," I grumbled, as Brad, distracted by what he was scribbling, began to giggle. "What are you doing?" I repeated, squinting out of the corner of my eye at my transparent reflection in the window.

"I'm drawing on your cast." he exclaimed, moving to my other leg.

"What are you drawing?"

"You'll see," he snickered, as my mother walked in, holding a funnel in one hand and an instant meal in the other.

"Stanley, It's time for your lunch," she announced, taking a seat beside me and dropping the funnel into my mouth hole. I bit onto it and blinked twice so she'd know I was ready. "So, Brad, how's your mother doing?"

"She's all right."

"That's not what I heard," my mother said, opening my can-of-lunch and pouring a mouthful into my funnel. "She says she's been going out of her mind trying to keep your grades up."

"Uh… yeah," Brad mumbled, unable to escape his mother's lectures even at my house.

"I have to hear about it every time I talk to her," my mother continued, periodically tipping her wrist to give me a mouthful.

"Maybe you two shouldn't talk so much then," Brad stated—his wishful thinking getting the better of his common sense. My mother gave him an unimpressed look that she'd learned about from her best friend—Brad's mother.

"Or maybe you should own up to your responsibilities and apply yourself in school."

"Hey, it's not like I'm the only one having a problem—the whole school's grades have dropped. So, really, I'm just doing the same as before."

"Just because everyone else in your school is a screw up doesn't mean it's ok for you to be," she lectured, pausing her pour as I choked on the liquid—laughing at Brad.

"I'm not kidding! The entire school's grades have gone down since the beginning of the year—no exceptions."

"Oh no? What about Stanley?" she stated, crossing her arms to emphasize her point. She was right. While in the cast, my homework grades had remained the same as always—average.

"Of course he's gonna do good. Only thing he's got is homework," Brad retorted, too much of a retard to know not to argue with my mother. She crushed the now empty can of liquid food she'd been feeding me and let it fall to the ground. Brad's eyes dropped with it and he realized shutting up couldn't save him now.

"Well, if being in a cast keeps your grades up, I might just have a solution for your mother," she exclaimed, scaring some sense into Brad.

"Yes, ma'am," he muttered, keeping his eyes to the ground as my mother exited the room. She closed the door and Brad resumed drawing on my cast. "I'm really not kidding Stan—the whole school's gone retarded. The principal's hired some specialists to investigate what's the matter. I even had to sit down and talk to one yesterday."

"What did he say?"

"Nothing, he just asked me questions."

"Like what?"

"Like 'am I upset to hear that the Fantastic Four are retiring?' or, 'am I depressed about the school's recent slump in sporting events?'" he explained, leaning over me so he could draw on my chest.

"What sports slump?" I asked, recalling the pride and joy of our school— a glorified batch of athletes that had managed to go undefeated for more than a year in every sport.

"Our teams—they haven't won anything for almost a month now. They suck."

Meanwhile...

Five floors down from Stanley and Brad, old Ms. Easton sat watching an especially boring episode of an already boring show. Her cigarette dangled from her lip and fluttered with her every breath. She hadn't stood up all day and hadn't left her apartment all week. She was tired and, as she often did, had fallen asleep in her chair. Her cigarette slowly burnt away, eventually falling from her mouth and landing on her muumuu. There it lay, sizzling over the commercial break, only to ignite as Ms. Easton stirred awake.

She jumped to her feet and tugged at her dress. But her wrinkly blubber made it hard to act quickly or remove her gown. She cried out as the burning garment became stuck around her neck. After a few short tugs she managed to pry it free and throw it aside. But, as Ms. Easton quickly realized, the fire had spread to her hair. Panicked, naked, and disoriented, she ran for help—leaving her smoldering dress on a pile of garbage. The fire spread and the alarm sounded...

"What the hell is that?" Brad asked, turning his attention to a loud ringing coming from outside the apartment. But before I could respond, my mother burst in the room, wheelbarrow and all.

"Hurry up! We've got to get Stanley into the elevator while it still works!" she yelled, reacting to the alarm as though there were actually a fire. Brad rolled his eyes and stood up slowly. He knew better than to argue with her again. But we'd both been through too many false alarms at school to take the situation seriously.

"Mom, it's probably just another burnt roast," I complained, as she rushed over to me. She pulled on the bed sheet I lay on in order to slide me into the wheelbarrow. But, for the most part, all she did was slide herself around the bed.

"Don't give me any attitude, mister!" she cried, frantically shifting her weight to guide me into the wheelbarrow. "Are you gonna help me or what?!" she shouted, staring angrily at Brad.

"Mom, seriously, why do you gotta get so riled up anytime you think something might go wrong?"

"One more word out of you and you're grounded!" she threatened, as Brad lazily helped her pull me into the wheelbarrow.

"What difference is grounding him gonna do? He can't move," Brad muttered, as my mother rushed me out of the apartment and into the hall. She stopped in front of the elevator and repeatedly pushed the button. "Do you smell smoke?" Brad asked, frowning and raising his nose into the air. I opened my mouth to say 'he was even more like my mother than his own' but quickly realized he was right—I could smell smoke. And, suddenly, I had a whole other reason for wishing I had superpowers.

"Come on, come on," my mother repeated, staring up at the numbers displayed above the elevator as it slowly climbed to our level. But as the doors opened, a cloud of smoke spewed out of the elevator and blinded us. Brad and my mother backed away, coughing and covering their eyes. I wheezed hard and tried my best to fall aside. But I couldn't move—I was trapped in my cast with nothing to do but piss myself. Fortunately, I already had a catheter.

"Oh shit!" Brad yelled, as he noticed the buttons inside the elevator had begun to melt.

"Watch your language!" my mother yelled, quickly wheeling me towards the window at the end of the hall. She hacked at the rusty locks and managed to open a big enough crack for Brad to fit through. "Get to safety and call for help!"

"I don't have a phone!" Brad replied, as my mother shoved him so he'd start moving.

"I meant call for superheroes!"

"Which one?"

My mother snarled and leaned out the window, grabbing Brad by the collar and extending him to the edge of the fire escape. "Run and get help or I swear to God I'll kill you myself," she growled.

"Yes, ma'am," Brad whimpered, quickly descending the fire escape as my mother swiveled back inside. She gave me a look of complete desperation and determination. I could tell she'd do whatever it took to get me to safety. But I also knew there wasn't anything she could do. She pulled me away from the smoke coming out of the elevator and parked me by the stairwell. She opened the door and peaked inside, the sound of panicked people echoing up to our floor.

"Mom, you should go," I said, as I noticed a trickle of smoke outside the fire escape window. She gave me an aggravated look so I'd stop talking and let her think. In the distance we could hear Brad's shrill cries for help—'Spider! Bat! Super! Whoever's working this neighborhood, come on! We need some help here!' And even further away I could hear the sounds of sirens headed in our direction. But neither calmed my mother's nerves enough to keep her from trying to save me all by her self. She rushed to my wheelbarrow and awkwardly tilted me over so that I'd fall onto her. "Are you crazy!?" I yelled, my eye holes turning to the ceiling as I came to rest on my mother's back.

"Shut up Stanley!" she shrieked, taking heavy steps towards the stairwell. But as she poked our heads towards the stairs I could feel the heat pulsing up and the smoke spiraling past us—we were trapped. My mother pivoted back and used a wall for balance. She turned back and forth, looking for any other option but could only see the fire escape she'd sent Brad down earlier. She didn't hesitate long before heading in that direction.

"Mom! This is nuts!" I protested, as she fought with the window to get it to open all the way. A second later I heard the glass shatter before I was raised up another foot into the air. "I know you're trying to save me, but I don't wanna die!"

The sky came into view as my mother crawled out onto the fire escape, still supporting me on her back. The smoke poured up past us and I could see other people looking out their windows shouting for help. I heard fire trucks pull up and more people yelling from below. Then, as my mother began descending the fire escape, I could hear the sound of moaning and squeaking metal. I wondered if building inspections included fire escapes and whether or not falling in my cast meant a better chance of surviving. It never even occurred to me that my mother was managing just fine. That is, until the fire escape broke free of the brick wall and swung out over the open street. In fact, at that point, I was pretty sure I was gonna die.

"Everything's ok!" my mother yelled to me, as I slid down the floor-grating and lodged up against the railing. I could see my mom now, breathing heavily as she pulled herself towards me at a steep angle. The fire trucks below us extended their ladders and firemen scrambled up to keep us from falling. But the fire escape was shaking, and with every passing second we got closer to falling the full seven-stories down to the ground. "Hold on!" my mother instructed arbitrarily, grabbing onto the arm of my cast and flipping me like a coin back onto her back—the kind of strength I'd only dreamed about. And, that for whatever reason, my mother just happened to have.

"Woah!" I cried, practically filling my catheter as I now lay facedown on my mother's back, peaking over her shoulder. She hung from the mangled fire escape with one hand and clung to me with the other. But as the ladder came almost to within reach of us I could feel the fire escape give way. I held my breath as my mother burst forward—catching me with one hand as I toppled off her back. Then, with a firm grip on me, she reached out her other hand and grabbed onto the ladder. The fire escape came crashing down behind us as windows exploded into waves of smoke—pouring out onto the street while firefighters flooded the building. The crowd that had gathered stood stunned as the ladder was retracted and my mother and I were placed safely on the ground. Emergency workers huddled around us, taking my mother and me aside to make sure we were ok.

"Are you injured?" the EMT asked, checking my mother's arms for cuts or burns.

"No, I'm fine," she replied, double checking me as the emergency workers huddled around her, shrugging their shoulders and scratching their heads. "Are you ok, sweetie?" she whispered, leaning in close enough to my eye holes so that she blocked out the rest of the world. I blinked twice and she smiled before turning her attention back to the medical team.

"Are you a registered superhero?" one of the fireman asked, as the crowd quieted down to hear my mother say what everyone was wondering. She grinned and shook her head.

"Nah, I'm a dedicated mother."

Two weeks later...

I got the cast off just after my mother finished her spiel on every talk show in the country. The public had a great interest in the idea of 'Super Mother' as she'd come to be known. Unfortunately, her fame also meant pictures of me were all over the city in a full-body-cast that Brad had vandalized to look like a transvestite-mummy. And even more unfortunately, pictures were all over my locker too.

"I almost died," I snapped, tearing the blanket of posters off my locker door. "Does no one take that seriously?"

"No one with a sense of humor," Brad replied. "You wanna hear your new nickname or would you rather be in denial?"

"Why does everybody but me get superpowers? First my nemesis, now my mother. What's next my goldfish?"

"Your new nickname is Mummy Tampon, but to abbreviate, people just call you Tampon."

"I never thought I'd realize what real life was like while I was still a kid... this is so depressing," I groaned, letting my head fall against a locker as a group of girls walked by, pointing and laughing.

"We're teenagers; this is what happens," Brad remarked, watching the girls walk away. I grabbed my change of clothes and quickly turned down the hall to get to the gym. Brad followed a few feet behind me but talked loudly enough so that I could still hear him. "What's the rush? Don't tell me you like phys-ed now."

"I like being able to move my arms and legs again," I growled, passing yet another wall littered with pictures of me. I pushed through the navy-blue-double-doors of the gym to reveal a gaggle of kids wearing shorts longer than their legs. And, just as I expected, they all turned to laugh at me. Brad put his hand on my shoulder, shook his head, and sighed.

"Don't let em get to yah… your mother could take all of them," he remarked, trying not to laugh. I glared angrily at him for a moment before heading into the change room.

When we came back out, our gym teacher, Mr. Borran, stood with his arms crossed waiting for us. We took our place among the other kids and waited to hear what arbitrary physical task we'd be performing today.

"All right, all right, shut up already," Mr. Borran snapped, echoing over the herd of prepubescent voices. "As we all learned last week, the state requires a physical fitness assessment once a year. However, due to how extraordinarily you all managed to suck at that assessment, they have agreed to allow a do-over," he yelled, making me feel less pathetic by comparison. "Now everybody get in line and don't screw up!"

"What's up his ass?" Brad whispered, as we all shuffled together into a line.

"Half the funding this school gets is because of how good our sports teams are," I explained, recalling a conversation I'd overheard between some teachers. "If that changes, he'll probably get fired."

"No talking!" Mr. Borran shouted, rolling a bin full of equipment toward us. "Anyone who passes today gets to swear as much as they want for the rest of the year," he said, handing out skipping ropes to each of us in line. "Now, five minutes—no stopping—go!" We all lazily began skipping while staring at the clock. But, as usual, everyone else performed like Olympic athletes while all I could do was sputter and wheeze.

"I must be getting in better shape—this was a bitch last week," Brad exclaimed, speaking normally even though he was skipping ten times a second.

"This is ridiculous!" I huffed, barely able to jump let alone skip. "Maybe people are so lazy nowadays because they grow up being punished with physical activity!"

"Maybe you see this as punishment because you're so lazy," Brad replied, as Mr. Borran paced up and down the line of kids, clipboard in hand. But when he came to me his frown turned to a scowl and he shook his head.

"Pick it up Tampon!" he yelled, quickly moving along to compliment the more physically fit children.

Shortly after the excruciating five minutes of skipping, everyone else in my class excelled at climbing rope while I struggled to get a good grip without cutting into my hands. Then everyone ran a mile in less than a minute while it took me almost fifteen. And just as I sputtered to the finish line, tasting blood and sweating bullets, Mr. Borran dropped a shot-put into my flimsy arms and pointed to where everyone else had managed to throw theirs—way, way past the school's baseball diamond and into the parking lot down the block. My mouth dropped and I furled my brow, trying to contemplate how it was possible for everyone to always be so much better at everything than I was. I let the shot-put fall to my feet as my eyes filled with tears. And as the class erupted into squeals of laughter, Mr Borran took it upon himself to give me his version of a pep-talk.

"Look, I can see you're trying, but mostly you're just embarrassing yourself. If you want to give up, it's ok, everyone else has performed well enough that it won't affect the curve… And, since I'm a fan of your mothers, I'll pass you anyway."

He gave me a sleazy smile like he hoped I'd let my mother know what a great guy he was. Then, he turned back to the hoard of super children that he'd probably force-fed steroids to so he could keep his job. Brad shuffled over to me with a confused look on his face and picked up the shot-put I'd dropped. Then, without even trying, he flung his arm forward and sent the metal ball flying hundreds of feet in the air.

"You ever notice that everyone but you in our gym class has superhuman strength?" he asked, saying it as though he'd just realized it himself.

"It's part of why I'm so depressed," I sighed, picking up another shot-put and trying my best to throw it further than my arms reach. "I guess I'll just have to learn to live with everyone else having what I want."

"Stan… when you were away in your cast the whole school got dumber, the sports teams sucked and your mother turned into a superhero," he exclaimed, giving me a long look so I'd know just how stupid I was.

"Yeah, so?"

"So?" he gasped, slapping the back of my head the way his mother would do to him anytime his brain stopped working. "I know I'm supposed to be the dumb one, Stan, but I think I figured it out."

"What? Figured what out?"

"What your superpower is!"

Brad's Idea was scary. It was horrifying. So unbelievable, unexpected and depressing that all I could do was shake my head and hope that the thought would fall out. But he wouldn't shut up about it—he was so sure he was right that as we walked home from school he stopped at every car to lift it off the ground and laugh. He bent parking meters like they were warm licorice and repeatedly jumped fifty feet in the air, expecting me to wait for him to come back down. And, when we finally got home to find my mother half way through making dinner, Brad couldn't help but share his thoughts on 'how everyone else's superpowers were only around when I was.'

"Bradley, go home," my mother insisted, undoing her apron and abandoning supper.

"Look, I can prove it," he continued, picking me up and raising me above his head.

"Put me down!" I shouted, slapping the sides of his rock-hard head.

"Bradley! Put him down!" my mother demanded, planting her fists on her hips.

"This isn't normal Ms. J," Brad exclaimed, as my mother snatched me out of his hands and put me down beside her. "I can't do this kind of stuff when Stan's not around."

"And yet you seem to think you can get away with it when I'm around," my mother snarled, grabbing Brad by the ear and pulling him to the door. "Go home and go to your room," she ordered, slamming the door behind him before turning slowly to address me. "How was school?" she asked, avoiding eye contact as she resumed making dinner.

"Everyone's smarter and stronger now that I'm back," I replied, sitting down at the kitchen table and dropping my head into my hands.

"I'm sure you're exaggerating... I got a nice discount on a new iron today when the clerk recognized me," she said, clearing her throat and stirring some spaghetti sauce.

"Mom, did you even hear what Brad just said?"

"I sent him home didn't I?"

"Yeah, but you always do that... I think he's right."

"Nonsense... now they were out of spicy-tomato at the grocery store so you'll have to make do without it," she exclaimed, shrugging off my superpowers like I was talking about baseball cards.

"Mom! I'm a superhero who doesn't have any powers! Where's the fun in that?" I whined, as my mother put down her spoon and gave an exasperated sigh.

"Stanley, what did I tell you about talking about superheroes?"

"I'm not talking about superheroes, I'm talking about me!"

"You're not a superhero, Stanley. Now... what kind of homework did you get for this evening?" she asked in a frustrated tone.

"You really don't think I'm a superhero?" I snapped, as she shot me a dirty look just for asking the question. "Fine," I muttered, standing up and walking behind her. I skimmed over a few items: knives, meat mallets and dishes before deciding on a cast-iron pan. Then, after a moment's hesitation to kiss my social life goodbye, I swung it down hard onto my mother's back.

"Stanley!" she screamed, turning around and snatching the now dented pan out of my hands. "What the hell do you think you're doing?!"

"See! You didn't even cringe! I do give everyone around me superpowers!"

"No, you don't! That... really hurt!" she yelled, giving me the same scrunched up face she always did when she tried to lie.

"That's a load of crap," I stated, calling her bluff.

"Watch your language!"

"Don't change the subject! I'm a superhero mom, accept it!"

"I've had enough of this super-nonsense from you!" she raged, bending the dented pan back into its original shape. "Your entire life it's been nothing but 'look how I almost died today mom!' 'Look how I cut up all your sheets to make a costume mom!' Well, I'm sick and tired of it!" she shouted, slamming the pan down onto the kitchen table—inadvertently smashing it into a mangled heap of metal. I looked down at the twisted pile of what was once my mother's favorite table and then up at her scrunched expression.

"You already knew... didn't you?"

"That's ridiculous. I..."

"Why else would you risk our lives out on the fire escape when you could see the fire-trucks were already there?" I exclaimed, trying to remember any time in my life when my mother had gotten hurt or sick.

"Stanley, don't think that..."

"Is that why you hate superheroes so much?"

"No, of course not!"

"Then why wouldn't you tell me about my powers? Why did you always badmouth every superhero any chance you got?" I continued, asking every question I could to try and get her to tell me the truth. She kept her eyes to the ground and rubbed her arm nervously. "Why can't you just be honest with me?" I finished, using her own guilt-milking-line against her. She looked anywhere but at me, unsure of what to say. Then, after a few silent moments, she sat in a chair beside our smashed table and took a deep breath.

"You're right… I knew. I've known since you were just a baby," she admitted, taking my hand in hers and guiding me into the seat next to her. "I'm sorry I didn't tell you. But… well, I guess you're old enough now that you can handle the truth."

"Mom, I'm practically a grown up—you have to have more faith in me," I replied, wondering why she wouldn't let go of my hand.

"Ok, Stanley… if you say so," she sighed, making a face like her words were gonna make her puke. "Captain Bling is your father."

"Dude, guess what!" Brad exclaimed, rushing up to me just seconds after I exited my apartment building to walk to school.

"Whatever it is, I don't care," I replied, now appreciating what depression really was: Captain Bling, the dumbest, gaudiest of all superheroes was my father.

"But I have good news!" Brad stated, watching me fish around in my lunch bag for my chocolate milk.

"Do me a favor and don't talk the rest of the way to school," I sighed, slamming back my milk without even wiping off the mustache afterwards.

"But..."

"I'm serious, Brad."

"Stan... Stan... Stanley... Stan... Stanley Roosevelt James!" Brad said, determined to annoy me.

"Shut up! I'm trying to ignore you."

"You're popular, dude!" he announced, as we passed the corner store down the street from our school.

"What are you talking about?"

"You're like the coolest kid in school now, which makes me the second coolest kid for being your best friend!"

"My nickname's Tampon, Brad. I'm not popular."

"Not anymore it's not. Now it's 'Super Nobody.'"

"What?"

"Yeah, because you're a 'nobody' who makes everyone else super," he said, smacking me on the back as though I should be as enthused as him.

"Wait, you told people that I'm a superhero!?" I yelled, grabbing two fistfuls of my hair and bulging my eyes out of my head. "Are you retarded?!"

"What are you spazzing out for? Now everyone at school wants to be your friend!"

"Yeah, but only because it'll give them superpowers!" I snapped, stopping just outside of our school steps. "Didn't you think about what a disaster it'll be letting a few hundred kids know that they all have superpowers?!"

"Stan, you're missing the point—we're popular now!" he exclaimed, just as a gaggle of kids pointed to me and yelled 'he's here!' Then they all turned screaming into the school so that everyone else would know I'd arrived. I let my jaw drop and slapped my hand on my forehead. A few moments later I heard a low grumble coming from inside the school—shaking the sidewalk and the cars on the street.

"I think I'll save time and go straight to the principal's office," I muttered, watching kids explode out of the walls of the school—flying a hundred feet in the air without any sense of direction. Other kids, who'd just been dropped off, picked up their parents cars and shook them around like baby rattles. While another group of delinquents ripped up parking meters and had a sword fight with them. I shook my head and walked sullen and annoyed into the school. Brad trotted along behind me, waving hello to all the girls that wouldn't talk to him the day before.

"This is great!" he said, jumping out of the way as someone's laser vision cut a row of lockers in half. "Why are you being so whiny?"

"Because I'm pretty sure that I'm gonna be the one who gets in trouble for all this," I growled, stepping over the crumpled remains of a water fountain before turning the corner down from the principal's office. But as I looked down the hall full of kids playing with their new-found powers, I noticed a familiar scowl pointed my way—Ardy was back. He must have heard about my power and came looking for his revenge. "Oh shit," I gasped.

"What now?" Brad groaned, rolling his eyes.

"Brad, you gotta fly me outta here or something!" I shrieked, attempting to jump into his arms and mooch off his superpowers.

"Stop rubbing against me! We just got popular," he said, catching eye of what I was so scared of. "Oh shit."

"You got me expelled!" Ardy screamed, shoving kids out of the way as he barged down the hall towards us. "You knew I'd have super strength around you! And you knew I'd get expelled for using it against you!"

"No, I swear I didn't know!" I protested, backing down the hall—looking for a place to hide.

"Halt!" Brad exclaimed, attempting to rescue me by getting in Ardy's way. But, since Ardy was still nearly twice Brad's size, it only took one hard shove to send him flying through a wall. I turned and ran—dodging projectile-desks and kids learning to fly.

"I'm gonna beat on you even worse for trying to get away!" Ardy shouted, swiping at my shirt as I ducked into the boiler room entrance—tumbling down the stairs and smacking against a wall.

"Ardy, please—I'll do anything! I mean, wouldn't it make more sense for us to get along?" I babbled, trying to think of how to keep him from beating me to death. "That way you'd have superpowers all the time and I wouldn't die."

"Shut up!" he yelled, taking a swing at me. I ducked and fell to the ground just in time to see Ardy's fist miss my head and slam into the wall. He tugged and shook to get his arm free but as a jet of steam shot out of the wall I could see he'd wedged his hand into a pipe. He squinted and snarled, blindly swinging his other arm in my direction. I gasped and trembled—trapped below him and unable to run. But as he planted his legs apart to pry his arm free I took the only shot in hell anyone has when fighting someone bigger than them—I kicked him in the nuts—repeatedly. He crumpled against the wall, now using his free arm to clasp his swollen testicles. I scurried out from under him and ran up the stairs—listening to him howl behind me.

When I got to the top of the stairs and into the school I saw empty halls littered with debris. But now there were no kids—not a single one. I cocked my head back and squinted, thinking that maybe Ardy had killed me and school would be my haunting grounds for the rest of my afterlife. But as I heard a moan come from beside me, I noticed a crumbled pile of bricks with two legs sticking out.

"Ow… why did I think I could fight?" Brad groaned, as I stuck my arms into the pile to help him up.

"Because you thought you were a superhero," I replied, looking both ways down the hall for any sign of anybody.

"I am a superhero," he coughed, removing a chunk of concrete from his mouth.

"No. Being a superhero means acting like one—otherwise you're just some idiot with special abilities."

"Stop quoting your mother," he said, making the same bewildered face as me. "Where'd everyone go?"

"I don't know. But they must have left in a hurry," I exclaimed, double checking every classroom as we walked down the hall toward the principal's office. "Hello?! Hello!?!"

"Hello, Stanley," a deep voice growled as a cold hand squeezed my shoulder. Brad's face went white and I could see a wet spot start to grow in his pants. I turned my neck to the side to see a black cape flicker against a crimson metal suit—an ensemble I recognized but not from a superhero.

"Oh shit," I gasped, realizing that my classmates were the least of my troubles. After all, where there are superheroes, there are supervillains.

Meanwhile...

Stanley's father, Captain Bling, had just received word of his son's abilities, as had nearly the entire city. A mad rush had begun for anyone seeking superpowers of their own. For the world had never known anyone to be as powerful or potentially dangerous as this. Stanley was now a superhero—Super Nobody.

To be continued...

Special Thanks,

Jayne Gackenbach, Thomas Snyder, Lynda Phillips, Julie Phillips, Eric Schmidt, Simon Glassman, Colleen Shaw, and everyone who took the time to read.